Postcards from the Gerund State

This cast of saucy and smart professors trying to navigate their roles in an academically questionable small women's college will grab your attention. The writing sparkles and sizzles. Be prepared to find yourself laughing out loud.

—Naomi Benaron,
Running the Rift and *Love Letters from a Fat Man*

An empathetic, often savagely comic portrait of the struggles of working women in what might be deemed an elite profession.
—*Kirkus Reviews*

Postcards from the Gerund State

stories

LORRAINE M. LÓPEZ

BkMk Press
University of Missouri-Kansas City
www.umkc.edu/bkmk

BkMk Press
University of Missouri-Kansas City
5101 Rockhill Road
Kansas City, MO 64110

Executive Editor: Robert Stewart
Managing Editor: Ben Furnish
Assistant Managing Editor: Cynthia Beard

Financial assistance for this project has been provided by the Missouri Arts Council,
a state agency.

BkMk Press wishes to thank Kelsey Beck, Sarah Chapman, Harmony Lassen, Max
McBride, and Henry Shi.

Quotations from the poetry of Princess Shikishi are from *String of Beads: Complete
Poems of Princess Shikishi*, translated by Hiroaki Sato, Honolulu: University of
Hawai'i Press. ©1993, School of Hawaian, Asian & Pacific Studies. Reprinted by
permission.

Library of Congress Cataloging-in-Publication Data

Names: López, Lorraine, author.
Title: Postcards from the gerund state and other stories / by Lorraine M. López.
Description: Kansas City, MO : BkMk Press/University of Missouri-Kansas City,
[2019]
Identifiers: LCCN 2019021166 | ISBN 9781943491186 (alk. paper)
Classification: LCC PS3612.O635 A6 2019 | DDC 813/.6--dc23 LC record available
at https://lccn.loc.gov/2019021166

ISBN: 978-1-943491-18-6

Contents

This one is for Kathryn Locey, Lynn Pruett, and Teresa Dovalpage: What would I do without you?

The Birnbrau Surprise

*W*e have a name for it. We even have an apt acronym, a quick way to reference our recurring bouts of bewilderment—bafflement, really—borne of the expectation that systems, especially institutions of higher learning, should work in intelligible, sensible ways. But here at Birnbrau, we learn, over and over, this need not be so. For instance, when we all started last year, we actually believed the offers we accepted and we, for one thing, expected to teach university-level students. We had no idea then that the women's college admits any female with a high school diploma who earns 700 on the SAT. We're talking combined scores here. If applicants score under 700, they will be accepted anyway, provided they write a letter to the dean, who—supported by the board of governance—has recently proposed making admission to the university "test-optional." But even now, prospective students who perform poorly on standardized tests and prove unwilling, or unable, to write letters, will still be considered viable candidates, if they drive out to the college to speak to an admissions officer. Such action, the dean says, shows initiative, and isn't this (along with grants, loans, and/or other financial resources) exactly what we are looking for in our girls?

The students themselves were among our earliest Birnbrau surprises, though now that we look back we see that we should have had inklings of such astonishments from the faculty orientation/ retreat at Amicalola Falls in August. Lucinda Aragon says she should have known after the first night when she shared a room at Amicalola

Lodge with a longtime Birnbrau professor who slept affixed to an oxygen apparatus, cloudy plastic tubes snaking to a face mask. The woman whirred, wheezed, and whooshed all night, which was fine, Lucinda says, not looking to mix it up with the infirm. The room had a balcony, but the sliding door to it was locked, half a broomstick wedged into the frame. Taped to the glass was a sign with black lettering, all capitals that read: CAUTION—RISK OF DISMEMBERMENT OR DEATH!!! Though vexed by the excessive punctuation, she couldn't blame the college for booking hazardous accommodations as she likely would have done the same to save money.

Before bed, her roommate plucked out hairpins to release what Lucinda calls "a bestial abundance" of hair, silvery tresses that reached to her hips. Next, the woman ran a hairbrush through her shaggy mane 200 times, counting each stroke aloud while Lucinda was trying to watch an episode of *Law & Order: Criminal Intent* she'd not seen before. By this time, things became less fine. Lucinda's roommate, then, gazed in the mirror, caressing her static-crackling pelt like a hooded mink cape. "Sometimes," she said, "I just get so *jealous* of my hair." *That*, Lucinda says now, is when she should have known about the Birnbrau Surprises to come.

Birnbrau is not the name of an important personage—say, some philanthropist or groundbreaking scholar. And while Birnbrau, pronounced "burn-bra," suggests women's liberation and feminist ideals, we soon learned this is misleading, even ironic, laughably so. Birnbrau, coined in the late 1800s by the founding board of directors, isn't even a real word. It's a made-up term to describe the process of converting a raw mineral into a precious metal, like gold or silver. During his plenary address at the retreat in Amicalola, old Dr. Joshua Frame, president of the university, compared this to the way heat and pressure bear down on coal, tightening carbon bonds to produce diamonds. *This is our work*, Dr. Frame said, extending a veiny claw to tug and squeeze as if to coax milk from an invisible teat.

We sat together in the chilly banquet room, staring at the stage in a solemn way. Some of us are not young. A few hoped to retire from Birnbrau. So we did not make mooing sounds; we didn't dare trade looks. And later, not a one of us rolled eyes during the ice-breaker, the Hello Bingo! game. No one quailed at the team-building activity (a tug of war in a *paved* lot?) or balked at donning blindfolds for the "trust hike," though Hailey Linder's faculty mentor led her to collide with a tulip poplar. Throughout the orientation/retreat, Jane Ellen Klamath, Kerry Fujimori, Lucinda Aragon, Devorah Grisham, and Hailey Linder—all five of us, "the newbies," as we were called, rode out these first swells—precursors to what we would come to call the "Birnbrau Surprise," to what we now refer to as BS—one after another, like brave little tugboats jouncing over waves in a choppy, yet navigable sea.

BS IS HOW we wind up teaching SPARKPLUGZ workshops to high school students, instead of the May-mester college courses we'd initially proposed. Somehow the registrar failed to open our classes for online enrollment, so when April rolled around, we had zero students signed up for figure drawing, painting, weave design, poetry and fiction workshops, while creepy Dr. Caspar had forty-one students in Neglected Agrarian Poets. When we complained about this to the registrar, a sour gasbag named Mrs. Ripley, she said, "I suppose I can see if there are SPARKPLUGZ courses available for you all," as if she were doing us a favor by enlisting us in the understaffed summer camp program, as if she had not fucked up in the first place. SPARKPLUGZ is an arts and crafts camp for high school kids, a money-maker for the college in the downtime between summer-school sessions. It's also a way for us to make twelve hundred dollars after the *Un*talented Mrs. Ripley's screw-up. We share many of the same teenaged students who plod like cattle from one of our classrooms to the next at seventy-five minute intervals from nine to five, Monday through Friday.

So here we are in late June, at the start of our second year at Birnbrau Women's College, during what should be our summer break, grabbing dewy polypropylene trays in the dining hall, eponymously called The Gag, and lining up for the salad bar. We gaze through the smudgy sneeze guard at vast bowls of raggedy greens and crocks filled with bean salads that bubble and froth, crocks mounded with mayo-slathered pasta and potatoes that emit sulfuric exhalations "like the devil's fetid breath," as Lucinda says.

"Next year," Jane tells us, salad tongs raised for emphasis. "I'm going back to the residency in Wyoming." She plops lettuce onto her plate. "I don't care what airfare costs."

We ask her if she plans to contact Tall Drink, the lean, ponytail-wearing landscape painter she'd flirted with at a community presentation we gave in Sheridan, Wyoming last year. "He's a tall drink of water," the women there would say of him. To this day, most of us don't know his name. We just call him Tall Drink, and now Jane calls him this, too.

"I *plan* to focus on my work," she says, and we know for sure Jane will hook up with Tall Drink first thing. Though she is in her fifties and the oldest of us, Jane is the looker in our group. Apart from a notch on the bridge of her nose where she once dropped a baton during a parade, her facial structure is a marvel of symmetry: her cheekbones high and sharp, her brow smooth and well-shaped, her aquamarine eyes wide and limpid, yet shrewd, shrewd, shrewd. Long ago, Jane was a national champion figure skater, and she still sports one hot and banging bod. Tall Drink will no doubt pick her up from the airport in Sheridan.

We inch along behind a slow-moving glacier of a girl with a large woven bag dangling from one arm. When she reaches the aluminum cylinder of cherry tomatoes, the girl pauses to cast surreptitious looks port and starboard, not bothering to glance aft at our puzzled faces. She withdraws the container from its nest of ice chips, opens her bag, and upends it. Tomatoes tumble like rubber balls into the maw of her purse. Then she thrusts the container back in its icy socket.

A dining-hall worker, an exhausted-looking Filipina, emerges from the inner kitchen, and Kerry calls out in her high, fluty voice, "Excuse me, but we need *more* tomatoes."

The tired woman glances at the salad bar. "No way," she says, "not again." She removes her white apron, as if chasing a cherry-tomato thief is not something one does in an apron, and rushes off in pursuit of the girl. Another cafeteria worker appears, bearing a tub of slimy mushroom caps to set in place of the tomatoes, but mushrooms are not tomatoes, and we all know better than to eat mushrooms at The Gag. We avoid the three Ms: mushrooms, mayonnaise, and meats, as well as most dairy products. Eggs are risky, too. Even ice from the rarely cleaned ice maker has given a few of us the runs. So far, we've had no bad experiences with lettuce or cherry tomatoes or fruits with peels. Packaged yogurt is also safe, if we check sell-by dates. Once, Hailey almost ate a yogurt older than Lucinda's granddaughter.

We load our salad plates with wilted lettuce and dig through the ice chips for yogurts that have only just expired. We eat at The Gag because the new president of the college encourages us to mingle with students during meals and because the dining hall offers deep faculty discounts. Sure, we get sick once in a while. Last semester, an exchange student from Egypt was hospitalized with E. coli. But even if we risk bouts of vomiting and diarrhea, even if we hazard paralysis or death, we save money by eating at The Gag, and that's important because our salaries are very low. Also, we lose weight this way.

During lunch in the crowded and cacophonic dining hall, teenaged boys—summer campers—at a table near ours spray chocolate milk at one another through their straws, and Jane says, "*Please*, boys, you don't want to do that." They pause to consider this and assess Jane's authority, before nodding at her in a forceful way. Yes, in fact, they *do* want to blow chocolate milk out of their straws. They resume this activity until Lucinda stands, face flushed, her black hair flying, to say, "Knock that crap off!" And they submerge straws in waxy cartons, their adolescent eyes shiny with wariness and resentment.

Hailey aims her spork at the boys. "Better they spit milk at each other than drink it."

"I don't mind if they blow bad milk all over this place. I only wish they wouldn't throw paint in the studio." Kerry fingers her silver-blond hair, picking acrylic chips from it. "Paint's expensive." She says she encourages students to create pixelated images or patterns from dots, when they'd rather flick paint at their canvases and decide what this looks like after the fact. "It takes them less than five minutes to finish a piece, and it takes the workshop half an hour to figure out what it is. Then I spend over an hour cleaning up."

Devorah cocks her head, squints. "Didn't Jackson Pollock fling paint?"

"He *dribbled* it," Kerry says, "in an exacting way."

"W HAT'S WITH THAT bearded boy?" Jane says as we head back toward the Center for Creative Arts where all the SPARKPLUGZ classes are held.

"The one who smokes his pen?" Dev asks, as if there were more than one teenager with a beard among the campers. This kid is larger than most his age, but still it's curious that a sixteen-year-old has grown such a long and dense beard. *Hormones?* He tends to sit at the back of studios or classrooms, propping his feet on an empty chair and puffing in a nonchalant way on his pen.

"I've seen that kid," Lucinda says. The bearded boy has opted for poetry with Dev, instead of fiction workshop with her. "Smokes a Bic ballpoint."

"Why smoke a *pen?*" Kerry squints against the sun's glare, her freckled forehead crimping like dotted silk.

Hailey shrugs. "Sometimes a pen is just a pen, right?"

"I can't engage him at all," Jane says. "Most kids want to learn just enough to draw the Avengers or Spiderman. He couldn't care less about comic book graphics."

"Well, I give him credit for that." The summer camp kids, Hailey says, need to grow into their imaginations. In weaving workshop, they make placemats with merchandise logos or their initials on them. A few weave abstract words into these: Love, Peace, Joy, and so on. One girl wove the word "mange" into her loosely strung and fraying placemats. Hailey was impressed until the girl said these were for her Italian grandmother.

Lucinda changes the subject back to the bearded boy, asking about him, and we tell her what we know—which is not much, apart from how he acts, or fails to act, in our classes. And as if conjured by gossip, the very boy appears behind a short hedge near the auditorium. He's bent forward, cradling his stomach and squawking with laughter.

Devorah jerks her chin at him. "Speak of the devil."

We must approach him since the auditorium is smack on the pathway to Creative Arts. If it were not, we would have pretended not to see him and turned in another direction. He's the kind of boy that people pretend not to see, and they feel okay about this.

"Hello, Charles," Jane says.

With a plump hand, he wipes the mirth from his face, stands upright, and draws a ballpoint from behind his ear to his mouth. As he sucks on the pen, his gaze travels to Hailey, who's told us what he said of her port-wine nevus—a purplish splotch shaped like a map of some unknown continent with peninsulas running to her chin and headlands skimming her left cheek. The birthmark, he's observed, makes her look as if she's been smacked with a berry pie.

We draw close enough to peer over the short hedge and glimpse the object of his amusement. A few of us gasp, and one grows dizzy. She has to look away. At Charles's feet, a hemorrhaging chipmunk twitches and quakes, seizing with convulsions. No doubt ravaged by one of the feral cats that roam the campus, the poor creature—its stubby tail no more than a bloody gout—writhes toward the hedge.

"You think this is funny?" Kerry says.

Charles puffs on his ballpoint and exhales to create an imaginary smoke ring that he penetrates with an index finger. Then he points his pen at the chipmunk. "Dumb thing doesn't know how stupid it looks."

We trade glances, wondering if we should put an end to its suffering and *how*, when a gray tabby pounces out to bear the chipmunk off like a limp gym sock.

We gape at Charles who continues smoking the Bic ballpoint. "*What?*" he says. "They're just rodents."

We ARE COLLEGE professors. We are women between the ages of thirty-two and fifty-five: Two are in their early thirties, one in her late forties, and two in their fifties. Three of us have children, and two have grandchildren. Four have Master of Fine Arts degrees, two have doctoral degrees in addition to these, and one has a Master of Arts degree and a Ph.D. One among us, as mentioned, was a figure-skating champion as well as a somewhat less accomplished baton-twirler in high school. Another is a pointillist painter who was awarded an NEA Fellowship, her work now displayed in fine arts galleries in Atlanta and Charleston. She was married for twenty years to a man she couldn't love, no matter how she tried, a man who nonetheless broke her heart when he left her for a woman who—ostensibly—could love him. Her adult children are creative and responsible, one a poet and the other a visual artist and teacher like her mother. Still, twenty years is a long time to go without love and dairy products (her ex-husband is lactose intolerant). *We do what we can*, she says these days, and *somehow we do what we can't*, meaning she now thinks she can love her former husband.

Another in our group has composed a short-story collection that contains a narrative about us, but only one of us has read the manuscript, and she's hurt by the omission of her birthmark. An oversight, or an erasure? Her brother, a therapist, tells her to imagine placing nagging questions like these in a box, sealing it, and putting it away, but this doesn't always work, and she can't stop thinking about the birthmark and wondering *why* it is absent from the story.

We are all friends, and most of us have many female friends outside of our group. Friends we know well and trust. One is in love with such a friend. It is a deep, deep secret, though at least two of us know about this. She rarely talks about the friend she loves, and that was our first clue. Plus, we can see how she feels about this friend when the two women are together. The one who is in love with her friend has a mother who is a pain in the neck and a mean bitch. We can never say this, even when the one who has a bitch for a mother is not around, because the word is highly charged and offensive to another one of us. So when we are together, we say this mother is *quite a character*. We say she is *really something*, meaning most of us can't stand her, meaning she is a complete bitch. Two of us would like to see her slapped, and we have discussed this privately.

We have all had other women help us with our children, with our careers, with our personal struggles, but one of us has a female mentor who is pure poison, a woman who makes her feel ungrateful no matter what she does to reciprocate. The mentor is a diva, we all agree, distinctly lacking in diva accomplishment. Her greatest talent: the ability to make others feel beholden and undeserving. This, too, we cannot discuss openly. Since the one who has the toxic mentor is also the one who cannot bear the word "bitch," we say the woman is *really something* and *quite the character*. Sometimes we say *bless her heart*, and the two of us who are Southerners know this means that we find her clueless and contemptible, while the non-Southerners take it to mean that we might push this mentor off a cliff if no one were looking.

While most of us agree that hell exists, we don't believe in God. Even so, all but one of us consider ourselves to be spiritual. A few of us have meditated and burned sage, and one has tried chanting. The one who is not spiritual claims to be agnostic. She would be an atheist, she says, if she had more time. Though agnostic, she believes in the devil. In fact, she's shared his bed for years, and she hopes with all her heart there is a hell to house him.

We have all worked for wages since we were about sixteen years old. Only one of us took off six years to raise children. Two others worked in addition to raising children, and one held two jobs (full and part-time) while a wife and mother, and then three jobs when she became a single parent. Among us, three have been married and three have been divorced. None has ever received alimony, and one, since she earned more than her ex-husband while they were married, was sued for spousal support, but the judge, a woman, ruled in her favor. One of us has been married and divorced multiple times. She thinks we don't know this, but when she drinks, she talks about her marriages, the divorces, and then she forgets and goes back to thinking that nobody knows about her marital history. We have all gotten traffic and parking tickets, but only one has ever been arrested—for writing a bad check. Coincidentally, or not, this is the one who has been married and divorced multiple times. She also believes no one knows this about her, but we all do because she talks about her arrest, too, when drinking.

Most of us have been hit on at work by a supervisor, and some of us have lost jobs after rejecting such advances. Three of us have been stalked, and all of us have been threatened by men. All but one of us have been molested when we were young girls, mostly by cousins and uncles, but once this involved a stepfather. The one who has a mean bitch for a mother was never interfered with as a child. Two or more of us have been raped. One of the two believes she was not raped, even though this happened night after night for years. But because her rapist was her husband, a sex-addict, and a man she could not love, she denies being assaulted. The other was raped by a stranger in a Kia. The first new car she ever owned. She tells how she returned it to the dealership at a loss the next week. Though she stayed up all that night to file a report and then went to a hospital for the rape kit, though she took the bus to the police station for several line-ups, her rapist was never caught. Another two of us might also have been raped, if we count drinking enough to blackout, waking up with men whose names we don't know, and discovering the sticky evidence of sex, even in places we would not expect to find it.

Another one of us has been battered by her now ex-husband, and she knows it, and she talks about it all the time. She tells of trips to emergency rooms, a fractured cheekbone, a deviated septum, contusions mottling her arms and thighs. She describes losing consciousness once when her larynx was nearly crushed. She insists such experience changes a person, as if to suggest domestic violence makes a victim stronger, kinder, and more tolerant. She tells how glad she is that she never harmed her abuser in a physical way, but by the way she says this, we can tell she would like to harm him in every possible way. In fact, she comforts herself at night by imagining how she might torture her former husband. Fantasizing about his rent flesh and agonized shrieks makes for sweet, sweet lullabies. Yes, she would like to beat him unconscious with a claw hammer and revive him with a panful of icy water in the face, before wrenching off his fingernails, flaying his skin—layer after bloody layer—and then dousing him with gasoline. She will sing "Happy Birthday" when she strikes the match. However, she lacks the means and opportunity for this. Plus, she does not want to be arrested again.

Three of us have had abortions, and of the two who have not undergone the procedure, one is the most vocal advocate of reproductive rights among us. While she'd like us to think she's had to terminate an unwanted pregnancy, we know otherwise. We just do.

So, of course, we were put out when old Dr. Joshua Frame, the air-milker, retired, and despite the many well-qualified women that applied for his position—including Muriel Cheek, the dean of students, who had essentially done the job for doddery Dr. Frame over the past decade—the ancient white men who form the Board of Trust selected Dr. Robin Cormorant, a man much less qualified than the women candidates, as his replacement. New to the college, we were dumbfounded by this early Birnbrau Surprise. When Dr. Cormorant addressed faculty and students at our fall convocation, he said, "Good speeches should be like miniskirts, short enough to attract attention but long enough to cover the essentials." Despite this, he delivered a mega maxiskirt of a speech, managing to offend us more than his tasteless comparative for sheer duration. Bless his fucking heart.

HANK, THE TWENTY-SOMETHING director of SPARKPLUGZ, looks to be about twelve. He's so freakishly handsome that he behaves as if he's gifting us with his presence. Though fit and trim, Hank uses a geriatric scooter to get about the highly walkable campus. During the staff meeting two days before the campers arrived, he offered to house faculty in dorms during the camp, so as to save us the daily commute, and when Lucinda said she was fine driving back and forth each day, he explained that this will cost her half her stipend, since it turns out we are also being paid for supervising the campers overnight for the duration of camp—yet another Birnbrau surprise.

The next day, we packed linens, blankets, pillows, alarm clocks, clothing, toiletries, books, and teaching materials before moving into the dormitories we now share with our young charges. We were warned not to bring food to avoid "attracting more vermin," but straightaway, we piled into Kerry's minivan to drive to Walmart for rice cakes, granola, trail mix, PowerBars, crackers, cookies, fruit, and gallon jugs of filtered water. Jane brought a mini fridge from her home studio to install in Lucinda's room, a suite, where we keep perishables. We signed pledges before receiving keys to our rooms, promising to preserve the campus as an alcohol- and tobacco-free environment, and hours later, we set up a full bar in Lucinda's suite.

None of us smokes though.

We're assigned to various rooms in the largest dormitory on campus. Prior to this, we had never set foot in the building, so the first day, we gazed about, murmuring, "Okay, I get it." And: "*Now,* I see." As we explored common areas and units, we undersood why so many residential students appear shell-shocked as they shuffle about campus, some in rumpled pajamas like asylum patients, and why the exchange students—even those from countries that oppress women, countries where stoning women for flirting is not frowned upon—are desperate to return home after the first semester.

Residential students are warehoused in small rooms like prison cells with dank and slimy cinderblock walls and ever-gritty linoleum floors. The splotched industrial-pile carpet in the common area calls to mind AstroTurf and animal sacrifice. The bathrooms are chilly and bare. Though windowless, the corridors creak and whistle with drafts. Students say the campus is haunted, and when we stand in the hallway, we think, well, that makes sense. The mattresses on metal frames are damp and alarmingly stained, as if obtained through some crime-scene discount. Kerry borrowed a basketball pump from the gym to inflate an air mattress she bought at Walmart, and Dev sleeps upright in a vinyl chair that she wet-wiped and blow-dried. Hailey layered her bed with blankets to sleep in a down-filled sleeping bag atop it. Jane has bought hammocks with frames—two for one at Home Depot—for her and Lucinda to assemble in their rooms.

Kerry, Dev, and Jane are the lucky ones, assigned to the floors designated for girls. Lucinda and Hailey are on the boys' floor. "You don't want to know," Lucinda says when we visit her room for drinks, "about the bathroom on this floor," and then she describes it for us.

The mildewed hand towels. The ever-slick toilet seat. The skid marks also on the toilet seat. The piss-slippery floor near the toilet. The mold-peppered shower curtain. The moss-bearded tiles. The lack of toilet paper, no matter how many times she replaces the bare cardboard tube with a fresh roll. The greasy gray scrim circling the rusted tub. The sodden bath mat. The gargantuan cockroach carapace—fat and waxy as a date—upended in the center of the floor, its appendages rigid as rebar. "No one steps on it," Lucinda says. "No one kicks it out of the way."

"It's actually a water bug," Hailey tells us. "It's too big to be a cockroach, unless it's one of those imports from Madagascar that people keep as pets. We all walk around the thing."

"Why don't you sweep it up? I brought a broom you can use." Dev doesn't like suggesting this. She will throw the broom away once it's been used for that.

Hailey shrugs, and Lucinda says, "We can't move it now. I'm conducting a study." She shows us a pastel-pink Post-it Note titled "Days of Dead Cockroach." Under this, there are four vertical pencil marks diagonally slashed by a fifth.

On the Fourth of July, we have a daylong cocktail hour that begins as soon as the campers board buses for a field trip to the lake that will culminate in a fireworks display. College-student volunteers are chaperoning the trip, since Birnbrau Women's College has declared this a "faculty furlough day," and our checks will be adjusted to reflect this. (Hello, again, Birnbrau Surprise!) In the empty dormitory, we complain and gossip over drinks and snacks until the sun goes down, and Jane rises to flip on the fluorescent lighting overhead.

Devorah's disgusted with the rhymed doggerel produced by the campers in her poetry workshop. "Why do they think that every poem has to sound like a nursery rhyme or a limerick? And why do their rhymes have to be so simplistic and predictable? If I never again see *love* rhymed with *above* or *dove* . . ."

"How about *shove?*" says Lucinda, who teaches fiction workshop. She claims her students don't get that characters have to want something. It's the first rule of story. The kids in her workshop can't make clear what it is their characters want. Instead they create sad characters that think about sadness, or else their characters are insane, drunk, or on drugs, and they, too, reflect a lot—albeit involving crazy and/or intoxicated thoughts—without doing much.

"What about us?" Jane says. "Would anyone be able to say what it is we want?"

Hailey shakes her head. "We're actually not characters."

Lucinda lifts an eyebrow, a dubious look on her face.

"I think I know what we want," Kerry says.

"Remember this must be a longing, not just a practical need, like for money or more comfortable shoes. *Oof.*" Lucinda kicks off sandals that pinch her toes. "Longing, in story, is something that the characters believe they need in order to preserve their sense of who they are, and it's something that they can never attain, or if they attain this, it will forever change who they are. It's paradoxical, you see."

"Wow." Hailey considers her own conflicted desires, and the birthmark.

Kerry nods. "I know what this is." She dreamed the previous night of Leon Russell, the aging rock star with penetrating blue eyes, a recurring and lustful dream. As his snowy hirsute face hovered over hers, a runnel of perspiration trailed down his pore-pitted nose to dangle at its tip—a perfect opalescent globe—before splashing on her forehead. An icy plop woke her to discover that condensation from the air conditioner was dripping from the ceiling.

We look at Kerry, ready to hear her discuss love, the impossibility of achieving this, but the overhead light flickers and a howling gust whooshes through the corridor. Though most of us are used to this by now, Dev flinches. She worries that when her mother dies, she will find a way to return as a phantasm, to continue making her disapproval known in one way or another. Perhaps she will return as a woodpecker, like the one that drills just above her dorm window, rousing her each morning with a sharp headache.

A GHOST NAMED AGNES drifts about the campus, mainly spooking students, though Frank Means, who teaches ceramics workshops, claims to have seen her image wavering once before the low-fire kiln. Agnes was a student at Birnbrau in the mid-1900s. Some say she was enrolled before World War II, and others are convinced she attended the college after the war. Most agree that this was before the Korean War, back when basement swimming pools were in vogue, the kind that were installed under movable flooring. At Birnbrau, there was such a pool below the main auditorium, which used to be a gymnasium and a dance floor. Pull a lever and the polished boards would retract to reveal a sparkling turquoise rectangle, an Olympic-sized pool that the university was proud to house and gladder still to rent out for meets.

It's the same old story, we say, the usual kind of thing. Agnes, a bashful, plain-looking freshman, was seduced by one of her professors, a family man with a wife and passel of kids. Some say he taught classics, but others insist that he taught philosophy, the latter unable to resist the easy irony of imagining Agnes as a student in his ethics course. When we retell the story, we make him a professor of our least favorite subjects. Devorah insists he taught math, and Lucinda swears he was a professor of religious studies. Hailey believes he taught *his*tory. Jane says he imparted more than a few hands-on lessons in biology, specifically human reproduction.

"Service learning," puts in Kerry.

"It was a practi-*cum*," Lucinda says.

We snicker and snort, and if we did not know us, if we were in the haunted hallway somehow listening to ourselves, if we were Agnes cupping a ghostly ear to the door, we might think we were wicked crones. Though we cackle, we flush with shame over laughing at poor Agnes, who—as the story goes—became pregnant before the end of her first semester. Some say she revealed her condition to the professor, who had promised from the start to leave his wife and passel of kids for the sweetly shy Agnes.

Others contend that she could not bring herself to tell him of her shame. Those who maintain she confided in the professor also say that she was rebuffed by him. If she let *him*, he'd reasoned, she must have let others. How could he be sure this was his doing? Some claim he blamed her for trying to entrap him. They say the professor told Agnes that if this came to light, he would call her a liar, and his word would stand against hers. Who did she think people would believe? After all, he was a well-respected educator and church deacon (according to Lucinda), and Agnes was no more than an immature and emotional girl (this from Jane) from Atlanta (Dev says), who didn't love him (Kerry, here), because if she did, she would never have put her mentor (adds Hailey) in this compromising position. The ingrate.

Whether she told the professor or not and however he reacted if he did learn about the product of their secret love, the outcome was tragic for Agnes, who—as the legend has it—either hanged herself from the diving board of the empty pool (drained for maintenance) or plunged headlong from it to pulp her brain against its concrete base. After winter break, a custodian supposedly discovered the gymnasium/dance floor parted and the girl's lifeless body either: (A) dangling from the high dive or (B) sprawled in a sticky puddle at the deep end. As a consequence, the pool was filled with cement, the flooring permanently affixed over this, though some say it was closed because the flooring never worked properly and upkeep proved costly.

Dean Muriel Cheek, who was a student at Birnbrau back in the day, denies there was a pool under the auditorium. She keeps blueprints in her office to show "investigative reporters" from *The Birnbrau Outlook* who turn up each October to do a Halloween story on Poor Agnes, the Ghost of Birnbrau Women's College. Muriel Cheek also invites these reporters to peruse the full set of yearbooks in the library. The only two people named Agnes in these were faculty members: a typing instructor and a home economics professor, both well past child-bearing years when they taught at Birnbrau. But a good many students and a few faculty members, including Devorah, are African Americans from Atlanta. Black people from Atlanta, Dev says, are known for being conspiracy theorists, if not conspiracy buffs, especially after the child murders. Most Black Atlantans at Birnbrau think this is a cover-up. "Come on," Dev says. "You expect us to believe that in over fifty or so years, only two people at the college were named Agnes?"

"If she died in December," says Hailey, who—though neither Black, nor from Atlanta—moderates the yearbook, "she wouldn't have been around for class pictures in the spring."

Though it has been hot and humid as dog breath all day, another howling current sweeps through the corridor, rattling the door this time. The power surges before cutting out. Silence pulses in the dark. Then scuffling sounds in the hallway. Someone's approaching the entry to Lucinda's suite. We stare at the base of the door, straining for a splintered glow, a flicker of shadow. A fist hammers the door, and we jump.

"Who's there?" calls Kerry, as if she expects a reply: *Open up. It's me, Agnes.*

Lucinda lurches to yank the door wide. But the threshold is vacant. Lights flash on. Since she's up, Lucinda asks who wants another drink. We all do. While she pours these, Devorah tells about April Madison, an undergraduate who claims to have woken one morning to find Agnes, a burnt rope around her spectral neck, sitting at the foot of her bed. "It'll be all right, honey," Agnes said. "You and the baby, you're going to be just fine." This, Dev says, was before April even bought an early pregnancy test.

Jane holds up two fingers. "Okay, so we have at least a couple levels of hearsay."

"April Madison is far from a reliable narrator," Lucinda says.

Kerry shoots Dev a puzzled look. "Why on earth was the rope *burnt?*"

Dev shrugs, and Hailey stands to stretch. She wanders to the window. "Oh, ho," Hailey says, looking out. "The little skunk."

Lucinda steps over to join her. "The *big* skunk, you mean."

"From here, he looks little," Hailey says. "And call me Nancy Drew because I've just solved the Mystery of the Invisible Door-knocker."

"And possibly the Mystery of the Power Outage, too." With a flutter of fingers, Lucinda beckons the rest of us to the window.

"*Charles,*" Jane says. "He must have given chaperones the slip."

"Moves fast for a bearded boy," observes Dev.

Kerry peers at Charles below. "Wonder how he got the wind to howl in the hallway."

"Well," Hailey says, "that might have been Agnes."

In the last days of camp, we slap together the arts journal, a collection of student work that we had no idea we had to compile until the SPARKPLUGZ director puttered up to us at the beginning of the second week to ask how the lit mag was coming along. Now, with digital cameras borrowed from the yearbook office, we snap photos of artwork to arrange on pages of the journal that the campers call *SuperSPARX,* for its comic-book inspired theme. This works so well with artwork produced in Jane's classes that we suspect she's behind the idea. The rest of us must quickly assign projects to do with comic-book superheroes in one way or another.

"At least," Lucinda says, in defense of Jane, "superheroes have longings. They want things. They don't just sit around feeling sad or thinking drunken and/or insane thoughts."

On Thursday evening, the penultimate night of camp, we assemble a full draft to send as a PDF to the printer, so the journal will be bound and ready to distribute before campers are collected by their parents on Saturday. Around eleven, we realize that we will have to stay up all night to fit student work in the allotted pages. Our publication criteria: Each camper must have at least one piece in the journal, though we strive to include two—creative writing and visual art—from as many as we can—and each course must have an equal number of pieces. This is not easy. In fact, we compare the process to a GRE analytic problem, the kind for which test-takers must make a chart.

Though Devorah has offered, we do not chart the submissions. Lucinda tells Jane privately that it is kind of controlling to suggest this. She resents that Dev has assigned superhero haikus and can fit her requisite number of pieces in just a few pages. The shortest stories by Lucinda's students each take more than half a page, single spaced and in ten-point font. Hailey's put out with Jane for pushing the comic book theme. The most her students could manage was to paint words like BIFF, BAM, and POW on hastily woven coasters. The best Kerry could do was encourage her students to name their random paint spatters for super-villains, like "Wicked Freckle Cloud" and "Dr. Deathly Germ Sneeze."

After midnight, Kerry snaps at Hailey for bending an artwork she hasn't yet photographed, creating a blanched crease in "Mr. Evil Vapor."

"It's fine," Jane says. "It looks like lightning. Couldn't you just call the thing, 'Mr. Evil Lightning Vapor'? I think that's actually edgier."

"Oh, I couldn't do *that*," Kerry says, "not without asking the boy."

"Maybe he's still up. I can ask him." Hailey rises for the door. "Who painted it?"

"Charles."

Hailey sinks back into her seat.

Lucinda shuffles through loose-leaf pages. "Don't we have something else by him?"

We look at one another, shaking heads. How is it, we wonder, that he created only one piece in two weeks of camp? And this is a painting, Kerry says, that resulted when Charles overturned a pot of India ink with his elbow.

"'Mr. Evil Lightning Vapor' it is, then." Lucinda hands Kerry the digital camera to photograph the piece before more harm can come to it.

The flash stings our eyes.

WE PICK UP boxes packed with bound copies of the journal from the printer after our last classes on Friday. We store these in the closet of Lucinda's suite, before a final cocktail hour to celebrate . . . *What?* Going home, we suppose, to write, paint, draw, weave, and lament that so little time remains before the new semester starts. Lucinda mixes drinks, pours wine, and hands Hailey a beer. Reluctant to take a boxcutter to the cartons to see for ourselves, we speculate instead on how the journal turned out.

"*Super*heroes," says Hailey, thinking of those last-minute coasters.

"That wasn't an easy theme for my group at all," Kerry tell us, and not for the first time.

Lucinda hands Kerry Chardonnay in a Solo cup. "It's done now."

"Think of it," Dev says. "If we were superheroes, what powers would we have?"

"I'd want brute strength." Lucinda flexes a bony arm. "I'd be scrawny, but fierce, able to bend steel, like Superman. I'd lift cars off babies, beat up thugs—that kind of thing."

"Do many babies get trapped under cars?" says Kerry.

"I guess I'd mainly beat up thugs." Lucinda gazes into the distance, as if putting a particular name at the top of a list of these.

"Would you want to fly, too," Dev asks, "like Superman?"

"Not really." Heights make Lucinda queasy.

Jane smiles, strokes her chin. "*I'd* want to be invisible. I could go wherever I want, do whatever I please, and no one would ever know what I was up to."

"*Hmm . . .*" Hailey drains her beer bottle and reaches for another.

"I'd want to time-travel," Kerry tells us. "Is there a superhero who time travels?"

We shrug, unsure what superhero that might be, and Lucinda says, "Superman can rotate the earth in a different direction to reverse things, can't he?"

Kerry sips her wine, wincing at the Chardonnay's tartness. "I don't want to do *that*. I just want to go back in time by myself."

"Why?" Jane suspects that Kerry has no intention of smothering Hitler in his crib or even investing in Microsoft. No, instead, Kerry would go back to the early years of her marriage, taking with her the ability to love an unlovable man.

Kerry flushes. "Oh, I don't know. Just to do things differently."

"*I'd* want to fly." Dev pictures herself shooting skyward, knifing through a dense froth of clouds, up and up to the frigid summit of the troposphere and into the stratosphere, where temperature inversion occurs, and she will soar toward deep blue warmth just before reaching the mesosphere. She opens her eyes, troubled to find us nodding at this. "What about you?" Dev nudges Hailey's gym shoe with her foot. "What superpower would you want?"

Thinking again of her birthmark, Hailey shrugs.

Footsteps pound the corridor, and the door bangs open. The bearded boy stands in the threshold, his eyes hollow. "Did you see her?"

Dev and Jane rise to block bottles on the dresser. Hailey hides her beer bottle behind her, and mouth open, Kerry gapes at him. "What are you doing here?" Lucinda says.

"She says her name is Agnes," he tells us, his voice high and strained. "I loved her once, years and years ago, and now she says she can take me places I've never seen."

Dev narrows eyes at him. "What does she look like?"

"She's wearing a white dress," Charles says.

We trade looks.

"And she has this rope around her neck, a burnt rope."

"Bravo!" Jane applauds, and Lucinda joins her, as does Kerry after a bit.

"Well done," Dev says, now beating her palms together.

"You should have signed up for theatre camp," Lucinda tells him.

"You're a good little spy, too," Jane says.

The boy bends at the waist—a deep bow, one hand rotating to issue a final flourish.

"Who *are* you?" Before he can answer, Hailey lunges to kick the door shut.

During the first meeting with the campers in the main auditorium that some say is built over the swimming pool where Agnes took her life, the director of SPARKPLUGZ stood onstage, asking teenagers and faculty who'd attended the camp before to please stand. We remained in our seats, along with a handful of first-time campers, including the bearded boy. "Take a look around," Hank said. "These are SPARKPLUGZ survivors, and we are so, so proud of them." But he didn't say why.

Weeks later, on that last Saturday, we hunker on the steps outside the Center for Creative Arts squinting in the sunlight. The shorter campers are posed in front, faculty and taller kids in back for a group photo—all of us now SPARKPLUGZ survivors, wearing crimson camp T-shirts, the cost of which will be deducted from our stipends. This, we hope, will be the last Birnbrau Surprise of the summer, and we can gear up for a fresh batch in the fall.

When we see the picture online days later, Lucinda's eyes will be closed in it as if she is asleep and enjoying a sweet, sweet dream, and Jane's shrewd expression will be obscured by the dark-lensed aviators that she will claim she forgot to remove. Hailey, standing too far to the right, will be bisected, only half of her face captured in the shot. The birthmark again excluded. In a shadow, only Dev's teeth glow, like the Cheshire cat's vestigial grin. And Kerry's image, somehow double-exposed, appears like a hologram, ghostly as an image of Agnes, as if she is already leaving us to travel back in time, to satisfy that unattainable longing. Each of us will examine faces, one by one, and though we remember exactly where he stood and how he puffed on his pen when the photographer urged us to smile, we will not find the bearded boy in that photo. There will be no trace of him at all.

Passionate Delicacy

Lucinda Aragon swallowed a small yawn and glanced at the clock. She perched at a desk in the back of the room, her pencil poised over the grading sheet while Kayla Martin, a freckle-faced girl with a nose like a snout, stood before the dry-erase board demonstrating for the dozen girls in the class how to wrap a gift. Lucinda gazed at the ceiling. Of all the topics, in an entire world filled with topics, *this* was what the girl had chosen—gift wrapping. No doubt literal-minded Kayla had fixated on the *present* component of "presentation." Her lisping voice was amplified, clear despite her braces and the occasional spittle that sprayed from these. Her dirty-blond ponytail quivered and her hazel eyes shone with fervor, as though she were rededicating her life to Jesus, instead of taping green and red holly paper to a shoebox.

"You take this little old thing off the bottom of the bow." Kayla pulled the waxy square from the adhesive tag. "See, like this, and stick it on just wherever you want." Beaming, she held up the wrapped box for all to see. The class clapped appreciatively, though, surely, most had been wrapping gifts for years.

Lucinda gave Kayla a high-average mark for delivery and an average score for organization but subtracted points for content. Limited comprehension, after all, had landed the girl in this remedial class that Birnbrau Women's College euphemistically called *Language Enrichment Laboratory!* (Yes, always the exclamation point, which made Lucinda feel she ought to shout when saying it.) This was a course designed to prepare students with low SAT scores to meet minimum written and oral proficiency requirements before entering Freshman English. As she tallied the score, Lucinda recalled an essay in which Kayla compared a female character in a short story to Eve, who had been tempted "by satin," and she erased the minus sign beside the *C* grade.

On this first day of extemporaneous oral presentations, the class had already endured a stream-of-consciousness rant dealing with zombies that Lucinda had to cut short by clapping when the speaker finally paused to draw breath, and after that, a speech on feng shui that consisted of the student reading haltingly from a magazine article on the subject. In this context, Lucinda considered Kayla's presentation to be the best so far, as she stepped to the front of the classroom to lead the post-speech discussion.

At Birnbrau, most professors kept the wall-length windows shut that fall, the venetian blinds slanted to avert the sun's glare toward the ceiling, and the air conditioning cranked to a constant throaty rumble. Autumn afternoons in Turley, Georgia, had not been much cooler than summer that year, even as late as mid-November. Tornado weather, colleagues had told Lucinda, when she moved to Georgia from California, her natural disaster experience limited to earthquakes, which were not precipitated by protracted heat and humidity.

"Any comments for Kayla?" Lucinda now asked the class.

"I thought it was good," said Katie, another porcine-faced girl with freckles who so closely resembled Kayla that Lucinda had asked them the first day of class if they were sisters, somehow offending both girls. Even so, they always sat together, near another girl named Kelly, who, though slighter, shared their hair color and complexion, along with the upturned nose. When the three wore their sorority baseball caps, Lucinda struggled to tell them apart.

"I liked that she *actually* wrapped the gift," Kelly said. "She really showed *how.*"

"Nice speech," said Penny Dominguez, no mistaking her for Kayla, Katie, or Kelly. Captain of the soccer team, Penny was a sun-bronzed girl with a mass of coarse black hair knotted into a scrunchie that matched her gray sweatpants.

Meredith Knell, a car accident victim with brain injuries, lifted a palsied hand. "I have one question." Her voice quavered, her speech as garbled as that of the profoundly deaf. She would be the next and last presenter that day. "What's in the box?"

"Nothing." Kayla shook the demonstration gift soundlessly. "It's empty."

Exactly, thought Lucinda, but she said, "Show of hands, please. How many of you knew how to wrap a gift before hearing Kayla's speech?"

Every hand, but Merry Knell's, shot up. "I can't wrap . . . anything." She flashed a grin, exposing a good bit of gum and longish teeth that gleamed against her scar-mottled face. Merry Knell could barely hold a pencil. She had to be helped to her classes by her roommate, Nadezhda, an art major from Romania who was placed in the remedial class because Birnbrau offered no ESOL instruction.

"Keep your hands up," Lucinda said, "and look around." Eleven of the twelve students held hands in the air. "What does this suggest about relevance?"

A few blank looks met her gaze, but most of the girls glanced down, suddenly transfixed by their desktops.

She rephrased: "How useful is this speech for an audience that knows how to wrap gifts?"

"Not so useful, I guess," Penny said. "But, damn, at least, I understood the girl—none of that living dead or *fun-sway* stuff. I still don't know what all that's about."

Lucinda nodded. "Good point. The speech was clear. But did we *need* to hear it?"

Kayla's face crimsoned. She blinked several times.

"An exceptionally clear speech." Lucinda initiated another swift burst of applause. "High points for clarity. But let's remember relevance." She checked the wall clock—fifteen minutes of class remaining. "Merry Knell, you're up next. Would you like to address us from your desk?"

"I'll go up front." She rose shakily from her seat. Nadezhda, her thick dark braid swinging, rushed to her roommate's side to guide her to the podium, which Merry Knell grasped like a walker, her sparse hair spilling into her boiled-looking face like the fringe of a pale shawl.

"Hello, everybody," she said in her mangled way. "I'm Merry Knell." She leaned to one side, freeing a hand to signal Nadezhda, who again bolted up front with a rolled poster.

"This is me now." Merry Knell pointed to herself as Nadezhda unfurled the poster: an enlarged photograph of a curly-haired cheerleader doing the splits on a football field. "That was me before my accident." With a quivering hand, she gestured at the poster Nadezhda displayed. Someone—possibly one of the K-girls—drew a sharp breath, and Merry Knell said, "Yeah, I know. I was a lot different. Okay, so here's my speech."

Nadezhda rolled up the poster and returned to her seat.

"Right after I graduated from high school, I was in my car with some friends over by the Rock. You guys know the Rock?"

Several students nodded. Even Lucinda, who lived in Athens, had seen the Rock, an elephantine boulder with an odd shape that loomed near the park entrance. Something of a Turley landmark, the Rock was so familiar that no one, except Lucinda, seemed to notice its pronounced resemblance to the human pudendum. Decades ago pranksters painted it chalky pink, atop which others later scrawled sentimental graffiti—flowers, cupids, and curlicue-scripted names enclosed in plump hearts skewered by arrows.

"We were stopped at the red light. You guys know that light there by the Rock? We were stopped there, when this other car pulls up in the next lane, and this real good friend of mine, Brady, reaches over to honk. Turns out, he knows the guys in the next car, so he asks if he can drive, and I was, like, 'fine,' and I hopped out of the car. I ran around to the other side, got in, slammed the door shut, and honest to God, you guys, that's the last thing I remember."

The girls seated in front sat still, their necks elongated and heads inclined in rapt postures. Lucinda hadn't yet lifted her pencil. Over several weeks, she'd grown so accustomed to Merry Knell's distorted speech that Lucinda could make out most of this. Now the intensity of her focus rendered the girl's words crystalline, even irresistible in the way a hypnotist's suggestions compel entry into twilight sleep.

"They say," Merry Knell continued, "I was in a coma for three months. Three whole months! When I woke up, my mom and my brother were there. They told me it was a head-on collision. You know where the two westbound lanes go into one? Brady must have swung into the oncoming lane to pass those guys and crashed into this minivan. At first, I couldn't talk because my brain wasn't working too good yet. My mom said no one died, and that was lucky. Days later, I still couldn't get words out, but I was, like, wondering about my dad, like, where was he. Why didn't he come to see me? Turns out, he booked." She lowered her eyes.

Booked? Lucinda glanced about, but no one else seemed puzzled by this.

"Just like that, he moved out, divorced my mom. Turns out, he couldn't take it: the accident, the coma, all that." Merry Knell shook her head. "Plus he had this girlfriend none of us even knew about . . ."

"I stayed in the hospital a super long time—months and months. Had all kinds of therapy. I had great therapists and nurses and real good doctors. At first, they said I couldn't walk anymore." Merry Knell flashed a toothy grin. "And, hey, look at me now. I got better. But when the hospital let me out, I couldn't do anything by myself. I'd stay alone in bed all day until my brother got home from high school, and he had to carry me to the tub and clean up all the poop and pee and wash the sheets."

Some of the girls tittered. A few glanced back at Lucinda to gauge her reaction to the scatological references. Lucinda ignored them, fixing her gaze on the podium, as she imagined Merry Knell's long lonely days spent swaddled in befouled bedclothes while she waited for her teenaged brother's ministrations.

"He didn't ever complain or say anything bad to me. When my mom got home, she'd put this zinc cream on my bedsores and fix up my hair. My brother . . ." Merry Knell cleared her throat. "He didn't know how to fix hair, but he was a really good brother."

Katie traded a look with Kelly, who shrugged.

"Little by little, I got better and better. I still have accidents and sometimes I just kind of go blank, sort of pass out, you know. Nadezhda helps me at school. She helps me put my clothes on and get cleaned up. Thanks, Nadezhda."

Heads swiveled to behold the Romanian exchange student, whose sallow face remained impassive below a thick curtain of bangs.

"I was going to go to the University of Georgia. I even got accepted. I wanted to be an animal doctor, but with the brain thing, I couldn't go there. I still can't remember stuff or talk too good. So here I am. Now, I want to be a physical therapist and help out people with problems like mine. And that's it. That's my speech. Do you have any questions?"

Penny's arm shot up. "Hey, what happened to the dude who crashed your car?"

"Brady." Merry Knell licked her lips and smiled. "He goes to Notre Dame. We stay in touch, except he doesn't call or text me because he's a *guy*, you know. So I call him, but he's always busy. We're still super good friends, and he's *totally* hot. You'd really like him."

"What happened to your brother?" Katie asked. "You said he *was* a good brother."

Merry Knell's smile dissolved. "He *was*."

"What happened to him?"

"He took my grandpa's gun and shot himself." Merry Knell took a deep breath and exhaled slowly. "He's waiting for us now, for Mom and me. He's waiting for us in heaven."

The entire room whooshed silent.

"Hey, don't be sad," Merry Knell said. "I love this school. I love my life and my friends and my teachers, like Professor Aragon here." She nodded at Lucinda in a jaunty way. "I had a bad accident, so now here I am. And I'm really glad to be here."

The evaluation sheet before her still blank, Lucinda sprang from her seat as Nadezhda helped Merry Knell back to her desk. "Comments?" she said.

Some girls wore pinched expressions on their faces. But hands rushed over heads.

"Simeko." Lucinda called on a diminutive black girl, one of the best students in the group. "What's your opinion?"

"Why, that speech deserves an *A* plus, plus, plus."

"I don't give *A* plus, plus, pluses." That was the exclusive province of Lucinda's idiotic colleague Dr. Caspar, a vapid elfin man who dispensed superlative grades as indiscriminately as he'd hand out candy canes to children waiting to see Santa Claus. She shook her head to release an image of him wearing a leaf-green leotard and slippers that curled at the toes, while randomly passing out peppermint sticks at the mall. "There are no such things."

"Well," Simeko said, "it was just the best speech I ever heard in my entire life."

The others murmured assent, prompting Lucinda to ask, "What made that speech work so well? Why did it have such an impact on us?"

"It made me feel all emotional," Penny said, "like I wanted to cry or something." *Emotion?* Surely, this was something new for Penny, who copied the back of a book jacket for the introductory paragraph of her last essay and then coolly called Lucinda "a racist against our own people," when she'd summoned the girl to her office to compare the two passages word for word and ask what Penny had to say for herself.

"What's the term for that?" Lucinda said. "When words move us emotionally?"

Simeko curled her upper lip in distaste, as though she'd been handed a scalpel to dissect a kitten in order to find out what made it adorable. "It's that pathos thing, isn't it?"

"That's right." Before the tower clock chimed, Lucinda launched into a quick review of the rhetorical triangle, winding up with an appreciation for the efficacy of pathos in Merry Knell's speech, which all agreed was going to be tough to top.

JUST MINUTES AFTER the last bell, Lucinda nosed her small car out of the parking lot and toward Jefferson Davis Boulevard before the rush of departing students, hoping to beat them and the traffic generated by the nearby cluster of poultry plants. Though Birnbrau's brochures boasted that the campus was "nestled in the foothills of the Blue Ridge Mountains," one of Lucinda's students more aptly described the location as "nestled in the fowl (sic) wing-pit of a plucked fryer," referring to the brothy stench that emanated from the aluminum cylinders clustered like massive missiles in the heart of Turley. Due to the poultry plants, the town itself was undergoing a metamorphosis. Young immigrant laborers from Central America replaced aging white residents who moved farther north and upwardly mobile African Americans who relocated to the suburbs of Atlanta. Meat-and-three Southern restaurants, Ace hardware stores, and roadhouses were being supplanted by taquerias, ferreterías, and cantinas. Independent taxi companies had mushroomed—se habla español stenciled on their doors—to meet the demand for transporting workers from their homes to the plants and home again. At four, these cabs would throng the boulevard, along with cars driven by commuting students and poultry trucks.

Late afternoons, refrigerated eighteen-wheelers bearing iced carcasses to vendors labored along the narrow highway Lucinda took to her home in Athens. She dreaded nothing like being stuck behind a chicken truck, especially on the way home, though morning trucks, with their live cargo emitting horizontal funnel clouds of fluff and effluvia, were far nastier things. Afternoons, the plodding semis stalled Lucinda unbearably as she rushed to the daycare in Athens to pick up the baby, who was not really even her baby. Fourteen-month-old Dulce was her daughter Anita's child, but Anita could no more collect Dulce from daycare than she could care for her on her own, though she stayed home all day. At the time, Anita wasn't capable of much more than watching television talk shows where people, goaded by

the host, flung accusations, curses, and sometimes even chairs, at one
another. Since giving birth, being fired from her job at a fast food
restaurant, and losing her boyfriend—the restaurant manager and
the baby's father—to his wife and young son, Lucinda's only child
had sunk into a post-partum depression that had lasted over a year.

Before Dulce was born, Anita had nattered on and on, almost in
a fever. Diego, the boyfriend, would leave his family, she'd said. They'd
take a two-bedroom apartment in the complex right across the street
from Cluckers; they'd work different shifts and never need daycare;
they would name the baby Diego, Jr. (even though Diego's toddler
already had this name); and after the divorce was final, they'd (somehow)
get married in the Catholic Church, have a huge reception (chicken
nuggets catered by the restaurant) and invite all their coworkers and
friends, even Diego's wife and son would attend (although this struck
Lucinda as especially doubtful) because really there's no reason for
hard feelings. Anita had priced reception hall rentals and visited party
decoration stores. She asked Lucinda to give her away since her father,
busy with his second wife and their young children, declined, saying
he didn't approve of her marrying a man who already had a wife and
child. While tempted to point out a bitter irony here, Lucinda didn't
have the heart to as much as snort when she heard this.

When the baby was born and Diego stopped taking her calls (and
Lucinda's live-in boyfriend moved out), Anita gave up her wedding
plans, her excited speeches. In fact, she said less and less until these
days, she rarely spoke, except in unilateral conversations with the
television, mostly during commercials. "*Right*," she'd say, "those breath
mints will make him want to kiss you forever and ever." Or: "You
can't use the word *suffer* when you're talking about a freaking head
cold." Just after Dulce was born, Lucinda would drive Anita to sessions
at the mental health center downtown, but when she asked her
daughter if these helped, Anita just shrugged. After a few months,
she refused to go.

Lucinda's grandbaby was born the previous year in September.
Despite teaching fulltime, she would get up in the night with the
infant, change her diaper, and wake Anita for breastfeeding. Lucinda

crammed her desk and bookshelves into her bedroom and turned her study into a nursery for Dulce. The baby was much like Anita—wavy black hair, rosebud lips, and honey-colored eyes, tilted like a cat's—but raising Dulce proved somehow *easier* for Lucinda, or maybe she was better at things this time around, more patient, less anxious. She'd glance at Anita on the couch in her wilted, sour-smelling pajamas, staring, as if in a trance, at those angry people on television, and then Lucinda would turn back to the baby, who'd reward her with a wet, gummy grin, and she would wonder how she'd gotten this second chance, when she did not deserve it, when she was not yet finished with her first chance.

Whatever the reason, Lucinda was determined not to squander it. Though far from satisfied with Dulce's daycare, a factory-like arrangement of rooms containing cribs, playpens, and miniaturized tables and chairs, Lucinda had to concede that it was the best she could afford. She reminded herself of this as she entered the office leading to the gleaming white hive of box-like playrooms, abuzz with fluorescent tube lighting and reeking of pine cleanser and salty foods. The platinum-blond director glanced up when Lucinda reached for the sign-out clipboard. "Hey, Granny," Miss Missy said. The woman wore leopard-print leggings and teetered on absurdly high lamé stilettos.

Lucinda gave a perfunctory smile. "How are you?"

"Busy." Miss Missy widened her mascara-smudged eyes for emphasis. "Real busy and tired. God, I'm tired." There was something in her face that called to mind the K-girls. With her faded freckles and swooped-up nose, the daycare center director could be their mother or their superannuated and tarted-up *granny*.

"Well, you don't show it," Lucinda lied. "Love the shoes."

As she made her way down the hall to Dulce's room, Lucinda peeked in the windows of various classrooms, a wall-mounted television flickering in each. All of the aides and workers looked familiar to her, though they were rarely the same people. There was "real crazy turnover" in the daycare business, Miss Missy often complained. These women reminded Lucinda of her students, or rather, they suggested future glimpses of her students. The loud woman changing diapers in the infant nursery could be Simeko, some twenty years later. The muscular Latina talking on her cell phone and cupping her ear against the crying toddlers in her care would be Penny, still trying to get away with not doing her work. And the anonymous hair-netted ladies she spied in the kitchen could be any of the others. She could easily picture her students—older and duller—toiling here in the near future, all but Nadezhda and Merry Knell. She didn't see anyone like Merry Knell.

Dulce's small face bloomed at the sight of Lucinda. She dropped the toy telephone she'd been holding with a clang and bustled through the knot of noisy toddlers in her playroom toward Lucinda with her arms outstretched, her eyes moist, and her smile almost too broad for her plump cheeks. "Nana! Nana! Nana!" she cried. Lucinda, who rarely generated any discernible reaction by her appearance—except dismay in her students when she showed up to administer exams—was thrilled by her granddaughter's glee. Though these reunions repeated daily from Monday to Friday, Dulce's exhilaration at the sight of Lucinda never waned, though the desperate look in her eyes had dimmed.

The first time she'd left the baby at the daycare, Dulce, just three months, howled as if Lucinda had chucked her down a flight of stairs. And Lucinda blubbered all the way to the county line. After a few weeks, Dulce no longer bawled when dropped off at daycare, though she hardly seemed pleased about it, and Lucinda's tears remained clotted in her chest, rising to her throat only as she meandered behind a lumbering refrigerated truck on her way to claim the baby from the place, too chicken herself to swerve into the oncoming lane and pass the thing, even when the broken yellow line on her side of the highway allowed this.

At home, Lucinda fed Dulce mashed sweet potatoes, turnip greens, and flaky bits of trout for dinner. She now held a forkful aloft, saying, "Fish, fish. Does Dulce want fish?" The kitchen nook smelled of smoke, as Lucinda had left the burner under the pan on too long after removing the fillets. The setting sun blazed through the bay window, imbuing the room with a gauzy ocherous glow.

Dulce nodded, banging her heels on the highchair. "Fitz," she said. "Fitz, fitz." She opened her mouth and waggled her pointy pink tongue. Though Dulce was old enough to feed herself finger foods, Lucinda used mealtimes as opportunities to teach her granddaughter new words. These emerged for Dulce like teeth, the prominent ones surfacing first: the nouns—*Nana* (for Lucinda), *Doolee* (for herself), and *cack* (for the cat), then the verbs *go*, *gimme*, *eat*, and the prepositions *up*, *down*, *out-shide*. Lucinda expected the adjectives to arrive next, picturing assorted aunts and uncles appearing at the door with suitcases to join the immediate family. These would be followed by the adverbs, the late-arriving cousins—all welcome on special occasions, but some more superfluous than others. Lucinda considered a lesson on this family tree for her students, who padded their sentences with so many modifiers that they often lost track of their nouns and verbs.

After Dulce finished eating, Lucinda tried to get her to say *mama* by repeating the word and pointing into the living room, where Anita sat watching a countdown of the top one hundred sexiest celebrities. But Dulce had little sense of the importance of that word or why she might need it. "Mama, mama, mama," Lucinda said, when an unfamiliar sound, or lack of sound, emanated from the living room. Her daughter had switched off the TV and stood in the doorway facing them. Her lips moved, and words spilled out. Anita was speaking. To her!

"What?" Lucinda said. "What did you say?"

"I *said* I should get child support from that asshole."

"That's right." Lucinda had wanted to suggest this for months now.

"I *said* I should get a court order for a paternity test."

"You're absolutely right."

"Then we could afford to put Dulce in a better place, maybe even a preschool."

"I bet we could."

Anita folded up her blanket and thrust it in the hall closet. "And I *said* that maybe you should adopt Dulce." Anita glanced at Dulce, who was poking orange bits of potato into her mouth, and then back to Lucinda, her tilted eyes clear, unblinking. "We both know I'm not taking such good care of her. You should adopt her."

Lucinda nodded—her heart tight with fear that her daughter would snatch back her words.

"Good," Anita said, "then that's settled."

During Lucinda's next trip to campus, the car's air conditioner wheezed in a warning way. The unending summer weather had no doubt strained the thing, so she shut it off and rolled down the windows. When chicken fuzz swirled into her car, Lucinda blew it away from her face as best she could, trying not to think of the birds in the truck ahead, though she could see they were packed so tightly in their cages that they could not change position or even stand upright. Their curdy droppings oozed through the mesh, plopping onto the backs of the hapless birds below.

Lucinda's early classes passed quickly and without much incident, except that Leota Firth accused her of assigning her a low paper grade because of being racist toward white people. This tempted Lucinda to suggest she compare notes with Penny Dominguez. In no time, it seemed, she again settled, with her evaluation sheets, at the back of Language Enrichment Laboratory! Katie, this time, stepped up front, bearing a bulky object enshrouded in a black garbage sack. This she unveiled and plunked atop the podium. It was a flesh-colored plastic shell, shaped something like half of a torso, with grimy straps dangling from its sides.

"I'm Katie, as you all know," she said, "and this here is my back brace. I have a birth defect—curvature of the spine, also called scoliosis. My spine is crooked, kind of shaped like an *S*, so I have to wear this brace at night, and I used to have to wear the thing all day, too. I don't have anybody to help me with it." She sent a sharp look in Nadezhda's direction. Then she told how she'd endured her curved spine and her back brace. How her doctor accused her of not wearing it when she was supposed to, though really she had worn it *every day*, and how her parents were always checking up on her, lifting her pajama top to see if she had it on, and how because of this she couldn't have a normal life. Her eyes brimmed, and she wiped her nose with her wrist. Merry Knell had given her the courage to talk about her suffering, and she hoped everyone learned something *relevant* from her speech, like she'd learned from Merry Knell's.

Kelly and Kayla led the applause that followed this presentation. They stomped their feet, and one of the two emitted a piercing whistle. Again, Lucinda stepped up front to lead the debriefing. No one had much to say. Her provoking questions failed to counter her students' reluctance to criticize a girl who had shared something as intimate as a plastic back brace with grubby straps.

Simeko Tyler, next up, approached the podium bearing a slate-colored jeweler's watch case. "My name is Simeko." She opened the box, tilting it to display its contents: a milky ball, the size of a jawbreaker, nested on a burgundy cushion. "This here is my grandmomma's eye."

A few girls gasped.

Simeko lifted the ball out of the box and rotated it for all to see the dark pupil. "It's a fake eye, you see. An actual eye would dry up. But this thing is made out of porcelain, I think. Grandmomma got it put in after she lost her eye in a fight with my granddaddy, except he wasn't my *real* granddaddy after all, and he got *very* pissed off when he found out about *that*. The neighbors called the sheriff's deputies. They clapped his ass in jail. An ambulance came for Grandmomma, and she was gone a long, long time. When she came back, she had this fake eye."

Penny Dominguez raised her hand. "Doesn't she need it? That eye?"

"She's dead, dummy," Simeko said. "She left me this eye in her will, said I should always keep it and know she's watching on me every minute, every day." Tough little Simeko's voice broke, and she squeezed out a few shiny tears. "I am the granddaughter of a dead one-eyed woman, who is always watching on me."

This opened a harrowing speech on domestic violence: husband and then second husband against grandmother, boyfriends against mother, Simeko's ex-fiancé's drunken attempt to extinguish a cigarette on her cheek. "I smacked that shit-grin off his face and jammed his nose with my elbow, and I am never talking to him no more. 'Cause my grandmomma's watching on me." She held the eye aloft and strobed the class with its ceramic gaze. "And she's watching on you, too."

After Simeko's speech, Lucinda almost suspended the oral presentations to shift the focus to the much less disturbing topic of subject-verb agreement. But Lee Radcliff wandered into the classroom, reeking of cigarette smoke and beer. She'd missed the previous week of class, and Lucinda had been wondering when Lee would ever turn up again. It'd be helpful, she thought, to have a speech grade for the girl, whose email address began with "barwench" and who was repeating Language Enrichment Laboratory! for the third time. Besides, she told herself, it's best to catch students like Lee by surprise. Last semester, the girl had latched on to Lucinda's instruction to make the speeches memorable and brought in a drinking glass containing a goldfish. During her speech, Lee had plucked the fish out by its tail, popped it into her mouth, and swallowed it whole, causing Alexis Shearer, a dance major (and vegan) seated in the front row, to tumble from her desk in a faint. Lucinda had no idea what Lee's speech had been about, but that goldfish was unforgettable. "Are you ready to give your presentation, Lee?" Lucinda asked before the girl could cradle her head in her arms and commence snoring.

"Sure!" Lee ambled up front to report on the previous evening's episode of *Law & Order: Special Victims Unit*. The change of topic provided relief, and last night, Lucinda had fallen asleep on the recliner before the television drama ended, so she was glad to find out what had happened. This emboldened her to continue with the speeches. She called on Penny Dominguez, who popped her saliva-webbed retainer from her mouth and confessed herself of the agonies concomitant with a protuberant overbite.

When Lucinda returned home after collecting the baby from daycare, she found her daughter, fully dressed for once—even wearing blue eye shadow, lip gloss, and Lucinda's tri-amber earrings—but slumped on the couch, holding a pack of frozen peas and diced carrots to the left side of her face. The television was turned off; the dusty green-gray screen gaped, vacant as a hollow socket.

"What's going on?" Lucinda asked.

Anita lifted the frozen pack revealing an angry splotch. "She hit me."

"Who hit you?" Lucinda shifted her hip to turn the baby away from the sight. Dulce squirmed, trying to see.

"That bitch, that's who, Diego's wife." She rotated the peas and carrots and reapplied them to her cheekbone.

"Down!" Dulce cried, wriggling, and Lucinda had to set her on her own feet before she lost her grip and dropped her. Dulce tottered toward her mother, eyes wide and mouth open.

"How did she get into the house?" Lucinda imagined the enraged woman squeezing in through the bathroom window that was kept open to prevent mildew.

Anita shook her head. "She didn't come here. I went over to Cluckers to ask Diego to provide DNA for the paternity test, like Legal Aid told me to. I called up a paralegal over there, see, and he said I had to *ask* Diego first, said I could only get a court order if he refuses to cooperate."

"Honey, I could have gone over there, or we could have phoned him."

"Well, *I* called a cab, and *I* went, and there she was, big as life. She works there now—*assistant manager*," Anita said with bitterness. Before her pregnancy, Diego had promised her that position. "She took one look at me and climbed over the counter and wham! She knocked me down." Anita shook her head, her chin wobbling. "I didn't get to ask about the test."

Dulce stood at Anita's knees, staring at her mother's face in a solemn way.

"He's such a chicken-shit, Mama. He didn't even stop her. He just hid in the back office. The cashier had to pull her off me, and I ran out of there. Guess that makes me a chicken-shit too." She sucked in a ragged breath.

"No, sweetie, you did the right thing by leaving," Lucinda told her. "Let me see your face." Anita flinched as Lucinda fingered the chilly, swollen flesh. Redness welled on her damp cheek like a wine stain, but the bone seemed intact. "I can take you to Athens Regional."

"Nothing's broken. It's just going to be a bruise. All's they'll do is to give me another cold pack and charge like two hundred dollars for it."

"We should call the police," Lucinda said. "That's assault. I bet witnesses will—"

"*Mom*," Anita said, "just forget it, will you? Calling the police won't do any good. If you call, I won't talk to them. Just let it go." Holding the peas and carrots to her cheek, she buried her face in her hands. "I don't get it," she said, her voice muffled behind her fingers. "First Dad and then Diego—how come nobody loves me?"

"That's not true." Lucinda sat beside her daughter, pulled her close, and stroked her hot quaking back. Dulce's fat-padded hands, like plush pink starfish, reached up, and she touched Anita's hair, petted it. "Mama," she said. "Mama, Mama, Mama."

THOUGH ANITA REFUSED to change her mind about calling the police, she did phone Legal Aid after breakfast Monday morning. As Lucinda wiped oatmeal from Dulce's sticky cheeks, she overheard her daughter giggling at something the paralegal said on the telephone. "He has a really cute voice," she told her mother after hanging up.

"But what did he say?"

Dulce bobbed and weaved, ducking the damp washcloth. "No, Nana, *no.*"

"They're drawing up a court order. He'll be served this week, and he has to comply or be held in contempt of the order."

"*They're* serving him, right?" Lucinda marveled at how quickly Anita had picked up this officious discourse. Her daughter had gone from playing an elective mute in some existentialist drama to sounding like the assistant DA on *Law & Order* in less than four days.

"Yeah, they'll send a messenger out with the papers." She nodded, the bruise on her cheek now an amber-rimmed blotch the color of eggplant. "Wonder what all you have to do to become a paralegal," she said, rubbing her chin.

Lucinda shrugged and unfastened the tray to free Dulce from her highchair. "Did you get a chance to ask about the other thing?"

"What other thing?"

"You know," Lucinda said. "The adoption."

"Oh, I forgot all about that."

As Lucinda drove to campus that day, behind yet another rig loaded with doomed chickens, she decided to give a speech herself before continuing with the oral presentations in Language Enrichment Laboratory! She planned to ask the class: Is this what you think public speaking is? Griping about back braces and retainers? Charting family histories of injury and abuse? Showing how to cover an empty box with decorative paper and ribbon? Is this how women speak? To say "he's such a fine guy," and "he has a really cute voice"? Is this what it amounts to? When we finally step up to the front and seize the podium, is *this* all we have to say?

That afternoon, Nadezhda was scheduled to speak, and Lucinda dreaded hearing the atrocities she'd likely report from her home country. Nadezhda's parents no doubt endured Nicolae Ceaușescu's infamous reign. Perhaps the girl would limit herself to discussion of the food and fuel shortages. But she could easily veer into the outlawing of contraception and the rash of bloody "home" abortions that followed. From there, Nadezhda might segue to the unwanted babies flooding orphanages, the epidemic of failure-to-thrive infants, and the warehousing of diseased and deformed children. Then she'd likely bring up "Systematization," Ceausecu's plan for razing the villages in a psychotic attempt to modernize the country. And what was that Lucinda had recently seen on television about the shooting of dogs for sport in the streets of Bucharest? She remembered the photo of a greyhound bitch with a gaping hole clear through her muzzle where some gun-bearing monster had blasted the poor creature. Perhaps, this, too, would come up during Nadezhda's speech, and Lucinda cringed at the thought.

The car's air conditioner cleared its throat decisively and coughed before shutting down with a sigh. Lucinda rolled down the window, her lips clamped to avoid catching tufts of down in her mouth, as she continued planning the short speech she would give.

But only half a dozen students arrived for Language Enrichment Laboratory! that afternoon. There had been rumors of an impending tornado warning at lunch, but nothing official yet. In an email, Dean Cheek exhorted everyone to continue with classes until they knew for certain which way the weather would turn. The sky had yellowed, grown metallic, the air pressurized, as Lucinda imagined the atmosphere to be inside a balloon inflated almost to the point of popping. She phoned the daycare center, and Miss Missy boasted that the facility and the staff were "tornado ready," whatever that meant. Lucinda also called home. A busy signal pulsed in her ear. She pictured Anita tying up the line with the cute-voiced paralegal, but more likely, her daughter had failed to cradle the receiver properly that morning.

With so few present, Lucinda wavered about giving her talk. She would only have to do it again when the other half of the class turned up. And Nadezhda was decked out in her native costume: bulky white leggings under thick shoes with rawhide strips that criss-crossed to her calves, a pleated red skirt, an embroidered cotton blouse, and a muslin shawl that trailed in back to the hem of her skirt. She beamed so when Lucinda complimented her blouse that there was no way she could curtail the girl's speech, which would doubtless be about her home country. Nadezhda had even brought a slide projector, which she set up on a desk near Lucinda's in back.

As Lucinda headed to her seat, Merry Knell caught her elbow. She willed herself not to shrink from the girl's touch. "Me and Nadezhda are going to Athens today," Merry Knell told her. "My mom's driving us out to see Widespread Panic."

"Widespread Panic?" For a moment, Lucinda thought they'd planned to witness helter-skelter reactions to the storm before she remembered the successful hometown band that returned to Athens regularly to perform free concerts.

"It's my favorite band," Merry Knell told her. "Maybe we'll see you there."

Lucinda nodded, though surely the outdoor concert would be canceled. The eager look on Merry Knell's face prevented her from saying this. The girl released her arm, and Lucinda continued to her desk where she brought out her grading sheets and called Nadezhda to the front for her presentation.

"My name is Nadezhda," the Romanian student said, as she stood before the podium, remote control in hand. "I am speaking to you today about my country, yes? And these are the traditional clothes we wear in Romania. So I'm speaking about my country, yes? But also about art. These things I care about. My country is my home and very beautiful, but for a long time was troubled. Is the inspiration for many artists, yes? Please, Penny, shut off the light."

The room darkened, and Nadezhda clicked an image onto the screen. An oil painting: a gray background with an intricate and elegant twist of silver in the foreground, a delicate flowing thing as lovely as a crystal stream. "Do you know of Hedda Sterne? This is her work" Nadezhda said, without waiting for an answer. "It is not titled, but they call it *USA*, like this country, yes?" She clicked on another slide—a pastel and oil rendering of a denuded tree, also spare and exquisite. "And this one is called, 'Tree.'" Nadezhda went on to explain Hedda Sterne was born in Romania, but migrated, and still lives, here in this country.

Then Nadezhda projected a photograph from the early 1950s— one with which Lucinda was familiar—of famous artists, including Rothko and Pollock. The group consists of about fifteen men, who are arrayed in chairs or standing before two tall windows, and towering over the men—standing on a stool, no doubt—is the sole woman in the group, a girlish figure in a bulky belted dress with unruly hair that flips up above her ears, creating a shadow behind her that looks as if it is cast by a spy, an interloper in hat and trench coat. When she'd first seen the photo, Lucinda wondered who the only woman in it was.

"This is Hedda Sterne," Nadezhda said. "It is so funny. Many believed she disappeared after that picture, but she continued to paint. And she is still alive. She is the last of the Irascibles." Nadezhda smiled. "The last of these grumpy men, she is a woman, yes?"

Lucinda leaned forward, squinting at the projected image. Her flesh pimpled as if chilled, though the classroom was so warm that she debated turning up the air conditioning before deciding against this, as the motor would drown out Nadezhda's deep but low voice.

"Hedda Sterne's retrospective is called 'Uninterrupted Flux.' Is almost a hundred pieces of her work from galleries and museums all over this country, yes? The reason it is called this is that Hedda believes she was never famous like Jackson Pollock or Willem de Kooning because her art is not about identity, not about *her* identity. She says . . ." Nadezhda reached for an index card tucked into her waistband and read from it: "'I am only one small speck, hardly an atom, in the uninterrupted flux of the world around me.'"

Nadezhda replaced the card and clicked on another slide of a painting: an effusion of color—spilling out like a tumble of bright veils, the image as overtly sensual as the previous paintings were elegantly austere. Harem swirls in shades of aubergine, fuchsia, apricot, and cobalt densely muscled, as if molded by unseen gusts, but feminized by sinuous curves and seductive labial folds, layers within layers, both a deepening and a blossoming of hue and shade. Lucinda craned her neck, squinting to see it better, to see it more, while suppressing the urge to rush up and touch the projection screen, to run her fingers over the image it displayed.

"This is my painting," Nadezhda said. "I came to America to follow in the foot marks of Hedda Sterne. As you see, my painting is about me, about my identity, yes? To me, art is the expression of what is inside a person, but with passionate delicacy. So I am not like Hedda. Though her art, it encourages me, gives me hope that if I get angry enough, maybe one day I too might become irascible." She gave a wink. "My country, Romania, is my home and where I am from, yes? This art shows where I am going. So my speech, like my art, it is to express what is inside me. Thank you." She bowed and ducked back to her desk.

Lucinda's mouth had hung open during most of Nadezhda's speech. Her eyes burned from not blinking. Her fingers buzzed, and her legs tingled as she strode to the front of the classroom. The girls seated before her seemed stunned, their faces frozen with wonder.

Before they could collect themselves to beat hands together, the public address system squawked, and Dean Cheek announced the path of the tornado had shifted, moving east in the direction of Turley toward Athens. Commuters were advised to vacate the premises, while dorm-dwellers were directed to the vast underground gymnasium before the storm hit in the next few hours. Students rushed out of the classroom, and Lucinda hurried to catch up with Nadezhda, to tell her how her presentation had *hammered* her. By the time she'd collected her papers and headed out, Nadezhda had vanished into the elevator with Merry Knell.

In the parking lot, Lucinda unlocked her car and scooted in. She could be at the daycare in half an hour, if she didn't get stuck behind a semi. This early, the streets were fairly clear, but soon they'd congest with drivers anxious to outrace the tornado. She'd made good time to the highway, when an eighteen-wheeler, exiting from the processing plant, plunged in front of her, braking to a crawl just before the county line. First opportunity, Lucinda would swoop past those martyred chickens. The double yellow line gave way to a broken one on her side of the highway. Lucinda held her breath and punched on the gas.

ACCORDING TO THE weather broadcast she heard on the radio, the tornado's path diverged again, veering sharply south. Athens remained as sunny and clear as it was when Lucinda left it that morning. Despite the band's name, the concert promoters had not quailed, and she hit traffic near downtown, where people were arriving early to get good seats. Other than this, the city was undisturbed, and would remain undisturbed by the storm. Surely, this was something to celebrate, so when Lucinda returned home after collecting Dulce, she convinced Anita, again dressed and wearing make-up after meeting with the paralegal, to go out to dinner.

They headed for Zoorrific, another fast food chicken restaurant—a chain competitive with Cluckers—where they advertised chicken nuggets and tater tots shaped like animals. Though it was only early November, the restaurant was already decorated for Christmas. A stiff artificial tree stood in one corner with an array of gifts displayed on its skirt. As she waited to order, Lucinda thought of Kayla, suspecting the wrapped boxes to be empty. Many young families filled the restaurant. Several children stared at the mock presents, but Dulce showed no interest in these. Once in her highchair, she and Anita scribbled on the kid's menu with crayons.

When Lucinda returned to the table with their food, Anita pointed out a help-wanted sign on a nearby wall: *Assistant Manager Needed.*

"You interested?" Lucinda asked her daughter.

The restaurant door yawned wide and in walked Merry Knell, supported on one side by Nadezhda and on the other, by her mother. Mrs. Knell was a droopy-eyed woman with ashy gray hair that Lucinda had met during Parents' Weekend.

"I am *done* with chicken." Anita unwrapped Dulce's nuggets and arranged them atop her tray. "Right now, I'm leaning more toward the legal profession. Think I could be a lawyer?"

"Absolutely," Lucinda said. "Of course, you could be a lawyer." She glanced again at Nadezhda, hoping to catch her eye. But Merry Knell instead claimed Lucinda's gaze. The damaged girl pushed away from her mother and roommate to take one choppy step after another, on her own, bypassing the holiday tree and decorative gifts, as she staggered toward the counter, so she could ask for what she wanted.

Peach State Surety

*D*evorah Grisham knew the bail bondsman, knew him from somewhere. Even across the Ingles parking lot, she recognized his Creamsicle-orange T-shirt, its imprint of the winged Rich Uncle Pennybags flying out of a birdcage familiar to her, apart from the Monopoly game. Dev also recognized his walk, an oddly deliberate shuffle-step, as he approached. Face obscured by a baseball cap's bill and sunglasses, this fellow appeared to be in his late forties. Though she'd never have admitted it to Karla, sometimes white people, especially middle-aged men, looked alike to Dev. She reached for the envelope of banknotes in her purse. The get-out-of-jail-free card image on the bondsman's T-shirt was misleading, cruelly so, as the envelope held more than a month's salary. Dev glanced up again. Yes, she knew that T-shirt and the swinging gait. Glimpsing the leather-holstered sidearm, Dev drew a sharp breath.

This was something new.

When he reached Dev, standing beside her car, the bondsman whipped off his shades, revealing brown eyes and eyebrows arched like rooftops in astonishment. "Professor Grisham?" He gestured at the scarf wound around her head. "I didn't recognize you at first, with your hair done up like that."

No time for the flatiron that morning, she'd wrapped her head in paisley silk. "Good morning, Harlan," Dev said, glad that he couldn't discern the heat in her face. Harlan was a student in the poetry workshop she taught at the public library on Wednesday nights.

Though she'd moved here nearly two years ago and had grown accustomed to running into students at stores and gas stations, Dev still couldn't get over how small Turley was by comparison to Atlanta, how stifling and inescapable it often felt to her. She indicated his T-shirt. "So you—"

Harlan swept a hand over his chest. "I been with Peach State Surety going on ten years now. I often wear this, so I figure folks know. Course, some might take me for a client." He scratched his bristly chin. "Hadn't featured that."

"So then you're . . . *handling* it?" Dev trained her eyes on his sweat-glazed face and off the pistol. More than disliking guns, she abhorred and dreaded them in a phobic way. She'd close her eyes when firearms appeared in TV programs or movies and turn away from gun show billboards along the highways. Hoplophobia—she'd looked it up online—was the neologism for this "irrational" aversion. Now that she stood in the presence of an actual gun, Dev suppressed the urge to slam into her car and speed away from the thing.

Harlan cocked his head. "Say what?"

"My mother's bail?" Dev said. "You're, um, doing the, the—"

"Oh, my gravy!" Harlan backpedaled, eyes agog. "That's *your* mother? The grand-theft-auto lady?"

Dev nodded. Uncountable pinpricks of humiliation jabbed her all at once, the way a sleeping limb tingles, except this sensation spread throughout her body, intensifying the hoplophobia instead of distracting her from it. "She hasn't actually appeared before a judge on those charges. She hasn't yet been found—"

"But your name is Grisham, and hers is . . ."

"Nolan," Dev said. "She remarried and goes by my stepfather's name."

"I see." A sympathetic frown crimped Harlan's chin. "So *that's* the why of you being here. Well, that *is* a bad business, and I'm sorry for your troubles. I got to go back to the truck for my clipboard. I didn't take you for my client, Professor. I figured I'd run into you on a lark, and I was fixing to ask your thoughts."

Dev's mind blanked. "Thoughts?"

"On my sonnet." He grinned with shy pride. "Now, the what-you-call-it, the rhyme scheme is surely Shakespearean, but the innards are all the way Petrarchan. I like to mix things up a bit, experiment with form and content and such." Harlan's face tightened with anticipation.

Though it was just April, the sun beat down on the blacktop, and mist from the previous night's rain squiggled up like lazy wraiths. The ticklish smell of fresh-mown grass mingled with car exhaust, and Dev stifled a sneeze. She hadn't yet opened the folder of sonnets by students in the poetry workshop, planning to read these—as was her custom—over a hamburger and fries just before the class met. Still, Dev felt safe in saying, "It's very original. No one but you could have written it."

Harlan whooshed with relief. "I wasn't sure about the meter or where the accent hits with certain words. I mean, the lines *seem* to work, if you say them a certain way, and then again, they also sound strange." With that, he discussed his doubts about the title and mentioned some difficulty with the final couplet.

Dev, a smile staling on her face, averted her eyes from his sidearm, as though it were a suppurating goiter. Barely a word registered for her. *Men!* Of course, he would turn this into a chance to talk about his own work. Harlan's voice inflected, signaling a question, and Dev forced herself to focus. "Beg your pardon?"

"I said, idea-wise, it's kind of like my haiku. You remember my haiku?"

She nodded, though she could not recall his haiku. Waves of mortification and anxiety continued to build, engulfing her so that the word itself—hi-coo, high coup?—detached from meaning to seem more peculiar than discussing a sonnet she had not read with a bail bondsman.

Dev's sandaled feet expanded with the heat, the leather straps now digging into the swollen flesh. Under the tight scarf, her head pounded. Perspiration damped her temples and trickled between her breasts. She pictured her mother at home, arranging her green cleaning supplies and blithely preparing for "Cinderella Saturday," their weekly

tradition of daylong housework followed by dinner at the Seafood
Shack and a movie, as if the sixty-year-old former librarian were not
out on bond for car theft, as if her only child, a poet and professor
at Birnbrau Women's College, were not making payment to the
bondsman Dev's uncle had engaged to put up the full bail amount,
a bondsman who now wondered if he might have done better with
the Petrarchan form.

"Maybe I'm resisting the Petrarchan just to *be* contrary," he said,
"and I ain't serving the poem." Harlan had been attentive when Dev
remarked in workshop that poets serve only one master: the poem.
Others around the table also perked up with those words, and Dev
grew uncomfortably aware of being the only nonwhite person in the
room. Her family had descended from slaves just as surely as the
adult learners were the product of those who—if they were not slave
owners—tried to hold on to slavery and then to Jim Crow for all
they were worth. In fact, Karla, a Brill County native, mentioned
that the Ku Klux Klan rallies were held in Turley as recently as 1992.
Whatever their various private and shared histories, the idea of serving
a master provided an apt metaphor, one that the group grasped with
terrible acuity.

Dev now assured Harlan that most poets experience doubts about
their work. "We don't so much finish poems," she told him, "as release
them into the universe." She extended her arms, palms upturned to
demonstrate this, as if poems were winged creatures—like Uncle
Pennybags on Harlan's shirt—that she was setting free. Harlan nodded,
but his expression remained dubious, and after making a few more
rueful observations about his sonnet, he at last lumbered back to his
truck for the necessary paperwork. Dev peered after him—*that deceitful
shirt, the obscene gun!*—bitter juices roiling in her stomach.

BAD POETRY, BAD chicken, or both? Devorah led the sonnet workshop
that Wednesday night in the conference room of the Turley Public
Library, sitting at the head of the glossy oval table and burping
surreptitiously to alleviate some serious reflux. She'd pounded down
chicken nuggets and onion rings, instead of her usual burger and

fries, with a Diet Coke at the Collegiate Grill while she read the folder of poems. She discovered that she'd been right in her assessment of Harlan's piece: No one else could have written it. Who'd want to? The inconclusive final couplet read, "Her legs are long so she is lean and tall/while I am short and thick and kind of bald." He had titled the sonnet, "What Hope Have I?" What hope indeed?

The group inspired Dev to supplement the list she'd started at the beginning of the academic year. *Rules for Student Poets*, she called the series of strategies for preventing some of the more excruciating moments in workshop. By December, she had a dozen tenets, beginning with Rule No. 1 that encouraged heeding spellcheck, and then Rule No. 2 that banished a series of abstract and general words, including *love* and *truth*, all forms of *beauty*. On the last day of the fall semester, when students brought in favorite poems to share, Dev added what she thought would be the last—*Rule No. 12: No poems by dying boys*. With the community workshop, though, the list expanded, and after reading Harlan's sonnet, Dev made a mental note to insert *hope* in to the list of forbidden abstractions.

Still, Harlan was not the worst student poet in the lot. That distinction belonged to Sharla Turnbull Greene, a middle-aged woman whom Dev privately renamed Sharla T. Orange. From her outsized mane of curls to the tanning-bed tint of her skin, the woman was the color of a dull tangerine. Sharla had introduced herself the first night of workshop, saying that she hoped the class would help her write lyrics for Gretchen Wilson, her favorite country music star. Every poem Sharla wrote portrayed a perfidious man laid low by an avenging woman. How she managed this in a haiku still amazed Dev. *Blade glints in my hand/Liar's blood pools 'neath my feet/Cheating gets you kilt.* "Kilt?" Dev had said. "You really want to use *kilt*?" And Sharla, an educated professional who wore tailored pantsuits and toted a leather briefcase, insisted the word was "true to the poem's persona," even after Harlan had pointed out that it made him think of "bagpipes and such."

Though a scant three lines, Sharla's haiku begat two new rules: *Rule No. 13: Haikus should focus on the natural world and not on vengeance for betrayal. Rule No. 14: Avoid dialectic misspelling.* The latter of these Dev dubbed "the kilt rule" for short. On top of this, Sharla tended to contextualize her commentary in temporal relationship to her divorce—BD and AD, as Dev came to think of this. "Before my divorce," Sharla would often say in prelude to some naïve belief. Or she'd begin with, "After my divorce," to share an insight that had arisen for her like a phoenix from the ashes of her marriage.

Sharla also had the habit of invoking the royal "we," to align herself with Dev in a way that suggested they co-taught the course. To open that night's discussion of Tillie Cogswell's sappy sonnet about a terminally ill boy, a poem that triggered appreciative moans from Chrissie and Rae Lynn, a pair of octogenarian sisters, Sharla shot Dev a conspiratorial look, before saying, "We could do with much less sentimentality in this poem."

Dev gasped, then coughed to mask this. What if Tillie were writing about a personal tragedy? (Still, the poem triggered Rule No. 22 or 23—she was losing count, though maybe she could amend the earlier rule. *Rule No. 12: No poems* by *or about dying boys.*) Though she had explained about persona and urged students not to conflate the speaker in the poem with the poet, most wrote about personal experiences. In the fall semester, April Madison, a junior in Dev's poetry workshop at the women's college, had written a graphic poem about rape. (*Rule No. 7: No poems that are gratuitously violent or sexual.*) When it was critiqued for being "over the top," she'd burst into tears and fled the classroom. Dev had followed her to the restroom. There, she learned April had been attacked in the stockroom of the discount department store where she'd worked—her two-year-old daughter, Faith, the product of that assault.

Now, Tillie's soft-featured face folded, her glasses clouding in the bifocal area. She was a great-grandmother, she'd announced on the first day. Tillie then told of winning a poetry prize in high school and how she'd dreamed since then of being a poet. "A dream deferred," she'd said, with a glance at Dev to see if she caught the allusion, "for more than half a century." Tillie printed her poems in a calligraphic font on scented pink stationery, a sheet of which now rattled in her puffy, liver-spotted hands.

"There's much to appreciate in this sonnet," Dev said, mainly to comfort Tillie, but also to contradict and distance herself from Sharla. She belched softly, easing the fiery pressure in her esophagus, and wracked her brain for something, *anything* to say in praise of the piece.

Harlan, again wearing his Uncle Pennybags T-shirt, came to the rescue. "Hey, aren't we supposed to summarize and say what's working in the poem before the critique?"

"That's right." Dev turned to Josh Knochenmus, a twenty-five-year-old foreman at the chicken processing plant. "Will you summarize the poem for us, Josh?"

"Basically, the speaker of the poem is sad about a kid's death." Josh dipped his head, mullet bobbing to punctuate his statement. With intricate tattoo sleeves crawling up both arms and in a Black Death T-shirt, Josh had introduced himself the first night as a "hardcore Wallace Stevens fan." Of all the student poets in workshop, Josh was most promising for his succinctness, and his curiously erotic poems about eviscerating poultry.

"Thanks, Josh." Dev's heartburn morphed into cramping, a sensation much like a coat hanger rearranging itself in her stomach. "What's working here?"

Chrissie Johnson raised her hand. "The little boy seems sweet."

Her sister Rae Lynn nodded.

With difficulty, Dev approached the dry-erase board. The last time she was observed in the classroom by Dr. Caspar, he'd said she "failed to interact with visuals," so she now made an effort to do more of this in all her classes. With a pungent blue marker, Dev printed EMOTION on the board, and BOY. "What else?" She remained facing the board while she grimaced. Surely, this was the worst gas of her life. "What can we say about the form of this poem? What about its rhyme scheme and meter?" Dev forced herself to turn to the group, an apparition of startled faces ringing the ebony table like Ezra Pound's "petals on a wet black bough."

Dev tried again. "What about the imagery? What images do you perceive?"

"Basically," Josh said, "we have the boy."

This generated discussion of the boy, his blanket and stuffed bear, the bedding. Clearly, the group confused imagery with concrete nouns. Instead of correcting this, Dev capped the marker and sat down, leaning forward to accommodate stomach spasms. After students lauded images in the poem—that is, after they pointed out its nouns— and praised the writing in more ways than Dev thought possible, critique ensued.

Sharla, who'd remained silent while others complimented Tillie's sonnet, issued the first salvo. "Isn't this poem a little trite," she said, "somewhat maudlin for our tastes?"

Only minutes remained before the mid-workshop break. Encouraged by this, Dev hazarded a quick rebuke. "*We* must remember criticism lacking specificity also lacks objectivity. It's as useless as praise that is too general and vague."

Despite her artificial tan, Sharla flushed to the inky roots of her citric hair. She was an attractive woman, oddly fixated on darkening her complexion. This reminded Dev of how her cousins would abrade their skin with scouring pads to exfoliate the effects of the summer sun before school started in August. "You want specifics? I'll give you specifics, line by line, word by word." Sharla held Tillie's poem aloft. "Let's start with the title, 'An Angel Rises.'"

"Please!" A white-hot shaft of pain lanced Dev's side. She winced, and the adult-learners gaped at her. When the paroxysm passed, she said, "The more we can trust that feedback is informed and encouraging, the more the workshop will benefit our writing."

Tillie cut Sharla a look that was the great-grandmotherly equivalent of *nyaah, nyaah.*

Sharla pulled her briefcase onto her lap and snapped it open. She swept her notes and pen off the tabletop into it. "I can see that you're not interested in what I have to say."

"It's not that," Dev said. "I just don't understand why you have to be so judgmental."

Sharla snorted. "That's what I do." She rose from her seat and stalked out. Unlike her experience with April Madison, Dev had no desire to trail after her. If the door's hinges were not stiff with rust, the woman surely would have banged it shut.

"I DON'T KNOW why you can't give a person a proper greeting," her mother said through the closed door to Dev's room.

"My stomach hurts, Mother. I had to get to the bathroom." After relieving herself, Dev had chugged Pepto-Bismol from the bottle in the medicine chest. The chalky aftertaste still coated her tongue as she stretched out on her bed, waiting for the antacid to take effect. She focused on the branded kerchief given to her by Hailey Linder, a colleague in the art department. A dust-catcher, her mother had called the gesso-stiffened square with the letters BWC (for Birnbrau Women's College) burned into it. The kerchief *had* collected a fine fur of grit, and though she struggled against her compulsion for cleaning, Dev suctioned the fabric with a mini-vac and framed it months ago. She stared now at its glass frame—her bed, lamp, and nightstand reflected as if it were a portal to another room, where another Dev sprawled under a halogen glow, wearing an expression on her face that seemed to ask: *And now what?*

"Shall I bring you some ginger ale or a cup of tea?"

"I'll be okay," Dev said. "I just need to rest."

"I can fix you some toast or heat up a can of chicken soup. There's half a banana. I saved it for you, knowing I couldn't get to the store, now that I'm not *allowed* to drive . . ."

Dev peered at the door as if she could behold her mother, standing on the other side of it: arms crossed, chin set, horn-rimmed glasses magnifying her small, accusatory eyes. Dev had attended the middle school where her mother had worked as the librarian. One afternoon, she'd been sent to the office by a teacher to retrieve fieldtrip forms. The school secretary led her to the stockroom for these, and through the open door, Dev overheard voices from the vice-principal's office. "You better return that to the library before Bitch-pants fines the living daylights out of you," the vice-principal said, and a man—*the principal?*—chuckled in response. Flustered, the secretary had nudged the door shut.

Bitch-pants, Dev now mouthed. Next week they would meet with the lawyer, a doctor's appointment followed that, and then the upcoming court date. *What on earth were you thinking?* If asked, her mother would say, "I had to teach them a lesson." That was the why, as Harlan would say, of Martha Copley Grisham Nolan's commission of irksome to criminal acts. When she listed teachers at the school who'd violated copyright law by showing DVDs to their classes in a letter to the FBI (copied to the school board), she had done so "to teach them a lesson," though the FBI never acted on the information, and she'd been the only faculty member whose contract was not renewed the next year by the district. When she drove around Atlanta distributing Dev's stepfather's belongings among various Salvation Army and Goodwill drop-off locations, this, too, was "to teach him a lesson," after he'd vanished over a Memorial Day weekend. Again, Dev's mother was cut loose, set adrift with no income to keep their house when he moved in with another woman, which was the why of his three-day disappearance.

Devorah willingly offered her home to her mother. Martha had sacrificed mightily to raise her after being widowed when Dev was an infant. She'd not remarried until Dev left home for college. Dev's mother had kept her daughter from the quagmires—teen pregnancy, drug addiction, violence, crime—into which many classmates, friends, and even cousins had plummeted. Martha worked full-time, while earning a master-of-library-science degree. She'd given up a lot, poor Bitch-pants, and Dev, who had never before seen her mother this vulnerable, though no less proud, was eager to help her. "*Temporarily*," Dev had promised Karla, encouraging her to take a rafting guide job in North Carolina last summer. "Just until she finds work and a place of her own." But that had been ten months ago.

". . . and we have some turkey kielbasa and noodles in the freezer," Martha said, wrapping up her inventory of the refrigerator's contents.

"I *said* I'm not hungry." Dev raised her voice to be heard, but in the silence that ensued, she worried that her mother had taken offense at her tone and might now be considering ways to teach *her* a lesson, so she added, "Thanks, anyway."

"By the way, you had a phone call from that white girl, that Karla."

"Karla called?" Dev froze, holding her breath. "What did she say?"

"She asked to speak to Dev, and I said, 'Do you mean Devorah?' If I had wanted you to be called 'Dev,' surely I would have written that on your birth certificate. 'Dev' sounds like a nickname for Satan. I told her so, and I could *feel* that girl's eyes rolling, even over the phone."

"What did she say? Did she ask me to call back?"

"She wanted to know how you were doing. And I told her *we* are doing just fine, thank you very much. She said something about taking a trip to the Pacific coast."

"*When*, Mother?" Dev sat upright. "Did she say when?"

"She did not, and I did not ask. I am not your personal assistant, Devorah. It ought to be enough that I keep this place clean and prepare meals, even if I'm not working now. I will thank you to keep that in mind. And please remember to turn off the light when you finish in the bathroom. Leaving lights on is an egregious waste of nonrenewable energy." With this, Martha retreated from the door, floorboards creaking in her wake.

Dev sank back into her bed, closed her eyes and pulled a pillow over her head.

"You're not who I thought you were," Karla had said the last time Dev saw her at Common Grounds, a coffee shop near Birnbrau campus. Karla returned her key and phone, and Dev handed her a box containing a silk blouse, an African violet, and a book of Christina Rossetti's poems, gifts from Dev that Karla had left behind. When Dev asked what she meant, Karla shook her head, as if such a question proved her point. Dev still didn't understand. Had *she* changed or had Karla misperceived her? ("You keep saying you're bi," Karla told her another time, "when you're more of a gold-star than I am. Why not *own* it?") Dev considered this, thinking of Karla in a way that was like running her tongue over a sore spot in her mouth, a tender chasm where a healthy tooth had been yanked. Dev reached for her cell phone. She hardly used it, rarely turned it on, so as not to have to take her mother's calls, and this was no doubt why Karla tried to reach her on the landline.

No texts, no messages. After she moved out, Karla got a new phone, and she told Dev it would be easier for her if they didn't talk for a while, so Dev hadn't asked for the number, thinking she could always reach her by email. But now, Karla had called *her*. Her new number would appear on the landline log. Dev set her phone down and rolled out of bed.

Her mother sat on the sofa in the darkened living room, awash with bluish light from the television like a moonlit monument, a bespectacled statue commemorating indignation. She wore an ivory shirt with beige slacks, a get-up more suitable for checking out books to patrons than watching a PBS documentary about climate change. Martha alternated natural science programs with dramas on *BET*, often claiming she had no interest in "white people's so-called problems." Dev sometimes wondered if her mother would be more outraged at her for being in love with a woman or for being in love with a white person.

Martha now patted the cushion beside her. "Come watch this with me."

Dev shook her head and slipped past her for the telephone. Timpani beats replaced the documentary narrator's gloomy voice, drawing her gaze to an image of polar bears onscreen.

Her mother's obsidian eyes narrowed. "It's enough to make you sick."

Back in her room, Dev scrolled the phone's screen for the number. She dialed it. The phone rang and rang until Karla's familiar voice chirped in the recorded message, promising to return calls "as soon as I can." Dev opened the laptop on her desk and tapped out a quick missive. The swift reply zinged her like static shock. But it was an automated message: *I will be traveling with limited access to email over the next few months . . .* Had Karla already left for the Pacific Crest Trail? She'd talked about it often, the three-month hiking trip she had planned since reading a best-selling memoir on the trek, saying she hoped to trace the author's path, though she'd surely not undertake such a journey alone. Who would go with her on that hike?

Dev shut the laptop and flopped back on her bed. The meringue-like peaks and swirls in the stucco ceiling wavered, shape-shifting like clouds. In one corner, a huddle of fluffy hens appeared, and Dev thought of Josh. The flock quivered, dissolving into clumps of clotted cream. "Concupiscent curds," said Dev, quoting Josh's favorite poem. To the left of these, she made out an arctic beast, a solitary she-wolf—head tipped back and howling.

Her mother knocked on the door to her room. "How are you feeling now?"

The lupine image flickered, effacing into miniature stalactites of blanched plaster.

"I'm better, thanks."

"Remember to turn off the lights and unplug your lamp before you go to sleep."

"I won't forget," Dev said.

Floorboards moaning, her mother's soft footfalls receded.

DURING OFFICE HOURS the next Wednesday, Dev penciled the ten-letter word for a faint constellation near Apus and Mensa—C-H-A-M-A-E-L-E-O-N—in the newspaper's crossword puzzle. She glanced up before reading the next clue. Tiffany Saunders, after ascending the corrugated aluminum stairs to Dev's office without making a sound, manifested in the hallway like a spectral figure. Tiffany, a willowy girl who had been outspoken in Dev's seminar on women poets last semester, now hung back, her long brown hair curtaining her face.

"Hi, come in," Dev said. "Take a seat." She set the newspaper on her desk. "Have you given more thought to the independent study?" Weeks earlier, Tiffany had asked Dev about conducting a tutorial with her in the fall.

"Sort of." Tiffany sank into the chair facing Dev's desk. She scanned the office: the framed diplomas, the wall calendar with its dismal image of a rainy street and a caption that read: *April is the cruelest month*, the bookshelves holding slim volumes of poetry along with thick anthologies and writing manuals. A shelf of tchotchkes caught her eye. On it, Dev had arranged five rubber ducks ordered from a novelty distributor. The ducks were likenesses of some of her favorite poets: Shakespeare, Dickinson, Poe, Whitman, and Eliot. Though Dev had sent for the company's latest "duck-simile," the Rita-Dove duck hadn't yet arrived.

"Nice ducks," Tiffany said.

Dev nodded, smiling in an encouraging way.

"Actually, I'm not here about the independent study." The girl gazed at her lap. She wore raggedy blue jeans and a white eyelet blouse. Her bony fingers worried threads fringing a hole that showed her left knee. "I've been thinking, since our seminar, I mean. I've been thinking about starting up a newspaper on campus with some friends."

"Something like *The Birnbrau Outlook*?" Devorah refused to refer to the paper by its unfortunate initials, though the periodical, moderated by Dr. Caspar and staffed by a buffoonish band of honor students, was such an extravaganza of factual and typographical error that it might as well emit an offending smell. A recent article on the "treat of nuclear war" entailed interviewing townspeople, including two retirees "sitting on a wench" in the local park.

"Not really." Tiffany shook her head, her chestnut hair swaying. "It would be different than that."

"How so?"

"The *B.O.* leaves out a lot." The girl stared at Dev, her gray eyes wide and unblinking.

"What do you mean?"

"In *The Outlook*, and in the college, there's zero recognition of people like us. Maybe you've noticed that it's very . . . *straight* around here." Her next words rushed out. "So I've looked into this, and turns out we need a moderator, someone on faculty to help us register as a campus organization and get start-up funding."

Heat flooded Dev's face. Last year, a new hire, a tennis coach, had asked about partner benefits for her live-in girlfriend when she met with the director of human resources to complete her paperwork. As a consequence, she'd been denied a contract. "Regrettably," Dean Muriel Cheek had said at the next faculty assembly, "we must continue our search for this position." The spurned coach blogged about her dismissal, but since she'd not signed on as faculty, this had been her only recourse. No way could Dev, now paying her mother's legal fees, afford to lose her job! "I *can't*," she said. "It would be a lot to take on, and right now, I'm swamped. I'm teaching a poetry workshop at the library, and I have other commitments."

Tiffany glanced at the desktop, the *Atlanta Journal Constitution* on it folded to display the crossword puzzle that Dev had begun.

"Maybe this is something you should do through the Women's Center," Dev offered. "I can speak to Professor Linder—she directs the Center—I'll ask her for you, if you'd like."

"But I thought . . ." Tiffany shook her head. "Never mind. Sorry. I should go." She stood, stepped toward the door.

"Tiffany, wait," Dev said. "What about the independent study in the fall?"

The girl turned back, a baffled look on her face. Then she spun away, hair flaring like a cape. Gym shoes soon bounced down the steps like a wildly flung ball.

Dev rested her elbows on her desk and cradled her forehead in her hands, her stomach again clenching.

"You okay?" Lucinda Aragon, whose office was next to hers, stood in the doorway. Holding a wicker basket and wearing a fleece vest and white turtleneck with wheat-colored slacks, she looked like an earless Easter bunny.

"I think I'm developing an ulcer," Dev said.

"And I was just going to offer you a peach." Lucinda tilted the basket for Dev to behold the fuzzy orbs nested in it. "They're hothouse this early in the season, though I got them at a roadside stand. Have one."

Dev selected a blush-colored fruit. Its bittersweet fragrance perfumed her fingertips.

"Give it to your mother, if you can't stomach it." Lucinda jerked her chin at the T.S. Eliot duck, with its round spectacles and severely parted hair. "Do I *dare* to eat a peach?" she said, mimicking the poet's stagey voice. She lifted one from the basket and bit into it. "I do," she said, with her mouth full. "And it's really good. It doesn't taste hot-house at all."

Dev rotated the fruit in her hand. Contoured like a plump cheek, its skin was taut, velutinous as the bare arms described by Eliot in the same poem. She pressed the firm flesh, releasing another nectar-scented emanation.

"Now the question is . . ." Lucinda dipped her head, regarding Dev over the rims of her glasses. "Do *you* dare to eat a peach?"

Dev gave a weak smile and set it atop the newspaper on her desk.

"What I really came to ask is if you've ever written a statement of teaching philosophy." Lucinda bit into the peach again. An amber rivulet of juice trailed down her chin.

Dev shook her head. "I don't think so. Why? Are you applying for something?"

Heels pinged like hooves on the aluminum stairs, and Lucinda stepped to the threshold. Then she turned to Dev to say, "Someone here to see you." And she scampered off, bearing her basket of peaches.

Sharla Greene—looking especially orange, as if she'd just emerged from a tanning bed—bustled into the office. She plopped into the seat Tiffany had vacated. "I hope you don't mind my barging in like this." She set her briefcase on her lap, snapped it open, and pulled out a sheet of paper to hand Dev. Her sonnet, of course, a piece titled, "The End of George." "So," Sharla said, "we never got to discuss my work on Wednesday night, and I'd like your feedback on it."

Dev summoned tremendous tact in critiquing the poem, which did not work for her on any level. The meter was off, the rhyme cruelly overworked and then tortured, the language clichéd, the diction bumpier than a camel ride across the Sahara, but worst of all, the content was beyond predictable: a betrayed woman—*surprise!*—avenges herself by dispatching the eponymous George with a cast-iron skillet. To top it all off, the sonnet's last line was purloined from Shakespeare, though attributed to George. His epiphanic dying words: "Hell hath no fury like a woman scorned!"

"It seems to me," Dev told Sharla at the end of her assessment, "that you are writing the same poem over and over, and I don't understand why you want to do this."

Sharla gave a thin smile. "I might have expected that kind of reaction." She replaced the poem in her briefcase. "Before my divorce, I'd have been devastated by such discouragement." She bit her lower lip, suppressing sentiment for that tender pre-divorce self. "Now, I know my strengths and resources, and I see that these can be threatening, especially to younger women."

Dev drew back, confused.

"Someday you'll understand the world and how it works. Right now, honey, you have no idea . . ." Sharla rummaged in her briefcase before withdrawing a photocopied image that she slid across the desktop. In it, a toddler in white robes and wearing the KKK's pointy cap reached for a black state trooper's clear plastic shield. "That was taken half a mile from here."

Dev's face grew hot and salty; her ears throbbed. "Why are you showing me this?"

"The child in the picture, that's Josh from workshop, the poulterer whose poems you so admire." Sharla pointed at the name in the caption. "Still think he's a wunderkind?"

Dev, transfixed by the image before her, nevertheless nodded. She traced the little boy's peaked hat with an index finger. A look of amazement on his face, the toddler in the photo reached for his own reflection in the trooper's glossy shield, and the black officer gazed down at him with a bemused expression. There was a poem—something ineffable and transformative, something lyrical, even incantatory— here. Dev considered Dr. Caspar's criticism of her teaching. This was as powerful a visual as she'd ever handled. "Can I keep it?"

Sharla shrugged. "That's just a copy I brought to prove my point." She snapped her briefcase shut and rose. "I bet you've never even been to a Gretchen Wilson concert. You're a lot like I once was. Before my divorce, I had no idea who I was or what I was dealing with." She gave Dev a pitying look. "I know what you need."

Dev looked up from the photo, half-expecting Sharla to suggest that she find someone unsuitable to marry in order to benefit from the enlightenment that comes of divorce.

"You need to make up your mind who you are before you tell other people how to express themselves." Sharla turned and strode out of the office, her heels ping-ping-pinging on the steps as she descended them.

THAT NIGHT DURING workshop, which Sharla did not attend, Dev asked Josh to stay a few minutes after the others left, saying she had something for him. When the conference room emptied, Josh stood before his seat, his folder and notepad stacked before him on the table. Dev reached into her carryall to produce the picture Sharla had given her. She placed it atop his notepad.

"What's that?" he said.

"It's yours. Someone gave it to me, but really it belongs to you."

Josh wiped his hands on his Black Death T-shirt before reaching for the photocopy. He seemed to have an endless supply of such shirts—all in black, of course—but with an array of designs from various concerts by the group that Dev, after investigating online, discovered was the first all-African-American heavy metal band. This one featured an orange graphic of a rat with a long hairless tale, and below the rat, appeared the words: *Black Death, European Tour 1347-1351* in a gothic font.

Josh lifted the paper, drawing it near to study the image.

"It's you." Dev indicated the caption. "There's your name."

Under his whiskery chin, his Adam's apple bulged, but his eyes remained steady and unblinking, focused on the image. He shook his head. "That's *not* me."

"Isn't it?" Dev squinted at Josh, willing him to recognize himself as he once was and to marvel, as she did now, at the changes wrought over time, how he—a "hardcore Wallace Stevens fan," an aficionado of an all-black hard rock group, a poet poulterer—had expanded beyond his narrow, blinkered beginnings. He had to see that he was an artist, and like any artist, his first dazzling creation had been the self.

Blushing, Josh denied connection to the little boy, but he kept the copy. He placed it in his folder with care before turning away from Dev and shuffling with deliberate ease out of the room. The poem in that image, it was his poem.

In the Brill County Courthouse, Dev waited with Abby Doaks, her mother's lawyer, while Martha visited the restroom. Though she wore tailored suits and toted a costly briefcase like Sharla, Abby had the pouter-pigeon bosom of a Depression-era farmwife. Her face was wind burned, her auburn hair dull, and her voice as hoarse as if she spent her downtime leading pep rallies at Turley High. "The doctor faxed me her medical records," Abby rasped. "But they're not helpful. Martha's in tip-top shape, no signs of early-onset or extreme anything."

Except vitriol, thought Dev. Days ago, at the clinic, the doctor, a man about Dev's age, had made the mistake of asking, "So, have we been through menopause?"

"I can only speak for myself," Dev's mother began, yanking up her bitch-pants with lightning speed, "but I would say that if this is an experience *we* have shared, then you must submit yourself as a specimen to the scientific community . . ." Oh, she had gone on and on, while Dev, who'd accompanied her for the intake, stared off into the middle distance as if too preoccupied by daydreaming to take in her mother's rant. Later, the doctor, in private consultation with Dev, had suggested psychiatric evaluation, but like Dev, he lacked the temerity to tell Martha this himself or even jot it in her records.

"Let's just hope I can get it knocked down to joyriding," Abby now said. "This judge has a reputation for fairness, especially with first offenders."

Martha rounded the corner, patting her charcoal helmet of hair in place. She wore a tan-colored twinset with brown pants, and she'd just applied a fresh coat of coral lipstick. "Now I am prepared to address the court."

Abby squinted at her. "*What?*"

"I am ready to take the stand, to explain my side of things."

"That is a very bad idea," Abby said. "You need to let me—"

"Remember that you work for me." Bitch-pants issued a cool smile.

Actually, Dev was paying the legal fees, but she shrugged at the lawyer in a helpless way.

Abby gazed from Martha to Dev and back to Martha again. "You're acting against the advice of counsel. I strongly urge you to reconsider."

"I will speak in court," Dev's mother said. "And that is final."

Abby shook her head, glanced at her watch. "We'd better go in."

The courtroom was much less daunting than Dev expected after watching a fair number of legal dramas on television. Large windows imbued the space with natural light that shone on the well-polished wooden benches. The state flag—the revised, non-Confederate version—was mounted behind the judge's bench, along with Old Glory. A few people milled about, including a uniformed bailiff, a densely muscled man with a holstered nightstick and another dreadful gun, the second Dev had recently seen.

Abby ushered Dev and her mother to one of two tables facing the judge's bench. Their case was scheduled first that morning. A harassed-looking man in a rumpled gray suit greeted Abby in a jocular way before taking a seat at the other table. More people entered the courtroom, filling the benches behind them, including the arresting officer and the couple—a black man and white woman, both wearing flip-flops, cargo shorts, and camouflage printed T-shirts—whose truck Dev's mother had stolen. ("Has he no pride?" Martha had asked, prefacing a screed against black men who took up with white women.) Now the couple sat with the cop, chatting as if they'd become friends. Since the incident, the downstairs neighbors had printed flyers to look like wanted posters, using the booking photo no doubt obtained from the chummy policeman. They'd distributed these in tenant mailboxes and under wiper blades of cars in the building's parking lot.

After a few minutes, the bailiff spoke in a rapid falsetto, releasing a barely intelligible stream of words. "*All-rise-the-courtroom-of-Judge-Estrogen-will-now-come-to-order.*" Funny name, thought Dev. A door to the right of the judge's bench flew open, and out stepped a robed figure with a gingery mane framing an over-tanned face. Dev's scalp tightened. She squeezed her eyes shut to dispel this especially powerful visual, one that nonetheless persisted when she looked again. No trick of mind or eye—the woman now behind the tall desk was Sharla Turnbull Greene. Not Estrogen, but *S. T. Greene.* The courtroom procedures commenced without Dev taking in a word. She gaped at Sharla until her eyes burned, and then she blinked and fixed her gaze on Abby, who had begun speaking. Sharla neither returned Dev's gaze nor evinced a flicker of recognition.

"If it pleases your honor," Abby now said, "we would like to have the charge of grand theft reduced to joyriding, since my client attempted to return the vehicle to its owners."

"*Joyriding?*" Sharla eyed Dev's mother, doubt stamped on her titian face.

Martha stood. "Your honor, I would like to address the court."

"By all means," Sharla said, adopting the same bemused look that the trooper wore in the photocopied image. At last, she made eye contact with Dev. And winked. Martha stepped into the witness box and was sworn in. Though Dev longed to rush forward, to offer herself in place of her mother for punishment, she sat as still as if she'd been injected with a paralyzing drug.

Abby established Martha's identity before asking about the events leading up to "the incident."

Martha Copley Grisham Nolan spoke in a deceptively rational tone as she told how she noticed the neighbors' empty truck idling when she set out for her daily walk. She said she returned after several minutes to find the truck still unoccupied and parked with the engine running. Dev's mother explained that this creates greenhouse gasses that harm the environment and endanger public health. "Children are most vulnerable to this because they breathe faster than adults and inhale more air per pound of body weight." She nodded in a thoughtful way. "This wasn't the first time they'd left that truck idling."

Abby said, "Did you ever speak to your neighbors about the problem?"

"Many times. The last time I'd mentioned this, they were profane with me."

Sharla cleared her throat to speak from the bench. "What happened when you returned to the truck after your walk?"

"The driver's side door was left unlocked, so I opened it to turn off the engine. Then I had the idea to drive the truck and park it somewhere else just to make them aware—"

"To make them aware?" repeated Sharla.

"To teach them a lesson," Martha said. "I thought they might remember better if—"

"You're a teacher, *too*?" Sharla's tone sharpened, and Dev winced.

"No, your honor, I am a former media specialist."

"So you entered the truck?" Abby said.

Martha admitted driving it around the block before remembering that she needed some groceries. Since she was near Ingles, she picked up a few things for dinner, and when she returned home, she found a squad car was parked where the truck had been. "It was also unattended." Martha sent a pointed look at the officer behind Dev. "With the engine running."

Abby concluded by asking about the neighbors' retaliatory prank with the faux wanted posters. Then, the man in the rumpled suit posed a few interrogatories, but these were halfhearted, as though he were saving energy for prosecuting more heinous crimes. Finally, Sharla spoke. "I've heard enough. You can step down, ma'am."

Martha returned to the table to sit between Abby and Dev, who grew dizzy imagining the penalties Sharla could impose to get even with Dev for dashing her hopes of becoming a lyricist for Gretchen Wilson—a staggering fine and prison, for sure, maybe years, instead of months. She fixed her gaze on the tabletop to steady herself.

"If the prosecution has no objection," Sharla said, "I hereby reduce charges from grand theft to joyriding as stipulated by the defense."

The prosecuting attorney glanced up to say, "No objection, your Honor."

"Mrs. Nolan, I am placing you under six months of probation."

Dev's heart surged. She raised her eyes to gape at Sharla, at Judge Green, for that was who the woman was to Dev now. Her mother wasn't going to prison! Then it plunged: Bitch-pants wouldn't be going *anywhere.*

"You are not an environmental officer," Judge Greene continued, "and if you were, you would cite such a violation rather than commandeer the vehicle."

Martha looked down in a contrite way.

"You must learn the limits of your authority. In view of that, I am ordering psychiatric evaluation and counseling for the duration of your probationary period. Finally, I *recommend*, though I cannot order this, that you relocate during your probation to prevent further conflicts with your neighbors." She turned to Abby. "Make sure your client understands these terms."

"I will, your Honor."

"To your neighbors," Judge Greene said, addressing the gallery, "I quote Sir Winston Churchill who said, 'Nothing is more costly, nothing more sterile, than vengeance.' In other words, you cannot get ahead while you are getting even, and you must think about the future and the impact of your behavior on our environment."

The judge banged her gavel, startling Dev nearly as much as she had with her words.

JUST BEFORE NOON, Dev strolled with her mother toward DiColo's Restaurant and Piano Bar for lunch. She had left her car in the courthouse parking lot since it was sunny and bright, the crisp kind of day that bedazzles windshields of parked cars and sparkles on mica-flecked sidewalks, imbuing images with sharp definition. Dev stepped over cracks in the pavement, the way she would as a little girl.

Martha issued a sidelong glance. "I don't know what we're celebrating."

"You could have gone to jail. She let you off easy."

"Joyriding! There was no *joy*," her mother said. "The judge insinuated that I'm insane, but she's the one who's insane if she thinks I'm moving out of our apartment."

But Dev had phoned her uncle while her mother completed paperwork with Abby. Good brother that he was, Uncle Kyle agreed to have Martha stay with him. As Dev drew breath to tell her mother this, Bitch-pants squinted at her, her forehead pinched and shiny. She looked cranky as a spoiled child teetering toward a tantrum. It could wait. In DiColo's, Dev would order iced tea for Martha and Chardonnay for herself. Even if it wrecked her stomach, the wine would infuse her with something close to courage. Her mother called the raised voices of others while eating in public, "bad dinner theater," saying they set her teeth on edge. Martha would listen with civility, even if she seethed within, while Dev laid out her plans over lunch.

They passed Saul's Clothing, Next Chapter Books, Frames You-Nique, and then an outdoor café. Beside an empty table holding the remains of a meal stood a baby stroller. The baby in it gurgled, playing with her pink toes. Martha pointed at the café's plate-glass window, through which Dev could see a plump girl chatting with the counterperson. "Can you imagine leaving an infant like that?" Martha said. "Someone ought to teach her a lesson."

Dev lunged for the door and swung it wide. "Excuse me," she called into the dim cafe. "There's a baby alone out here."

"*Kaylee*—I completely forgot!" The girl flew to the stroller, sputtering apologies and self-recrimination. She lifted the baby to buss her cheeks, and then she thanked Dev for summoning her. "I thought I'd be just a second, but it's no excuse."

Smiling, Dev retreated to take her mother's arm.

Bitch-pants jerked free. "It's too hot for that."

"Mother, please, we're nearly there." She again hooked Martha's elbow and steered her in the direction of DiColo's Restaurant and Piano Bar. As she hurried her mother along, Dev averted her eyes from the green plaque at the center of the Square, an historic marker with gilt lettering legible from the sidewalk along the perimeter, a few yards away. By this time, Dev knew what it said without reading the inscription. Its familiar message now threatened her newfound resolve, so in the superstitious way she'd avoided cracks in the pavement, Dev clenched her eyes shut. She would not look, she did not look—nope, still not looking—yet there it was all the same: *Turley, Georgia: The Chicken Capital of the Peach State.*

Careful Interventions

*I*n the auditorium, Jane Ellen Klamath gazed with tenderness over the sea of black tasseled caps. Martin Schumer, dean of humanities at Birnbrau Women's College, stood center stage at the podium to address faculty and students assembled for the first convocation in August, his soft tenor cracking as he touted faculty achievements over the past year. There were not many of these, though Lucinda Aragon, an English professor and Jane's closest friend at Birnbrau, had her manuscript—a first book—accepted for publication. Perspiration glazing his forehead, Dean Schumer drew this announcement out, with much to say about the challenges of creative production while teaching full-time. Despite its pallor, his was a cherub's face fronting a smallish head atop a long-armed, thickset body. Jane glanced at Lucinda, seated beside her. Instead of humbly staring into her lap, as Jane would have done, Lucinda squinted at Martin, her profile sharpened by a dubious, even accusatory expression. She gave a curt nod—suspicions confirmed—when the poor man mispronounced her name and then stammered out her book's tricky title.

Jane, at first glance, loved the dean, every tic and bumble—from the knuckle-popping to the compulsive blinking of his pebbly eyes. Of course, Dean Schumer, in his forties, was a decade too young for her and quite likely gay—he was much too pleasant to be straight— though he was, in fact, married to a torpedo-shaped woman, who was both a neurosurgeon and certified hot-yoga instructor. Sweet Martin more or less raised their triplets on his own. He would set his cellphone out at meetings, in case his teenaged sons or daughter should summon him. It buzzed often with their calls, whereupon he would snatch it up and excuse himself from whatever proceedings were underway, returning only to draw swift conclusion to these. No way would Jane dare to display her phone during a meeting. She didn't even turn it on while she was on campus, so distressing were the calls from her adult sons.

Jane's eyes moistened now with fondness as Dean Schumer spilled his notes on the stage. She winced when he bumped his head on the lectern after stooping to collect these, and she swiveled in her seat to cast sharp looks at those who snickered at this. Applause erupted as Dean Schumer shambled off stage, and the president of the college, a silver-haired man with a permanent smirk on his tanned face, strode to the podium. In a loud and sarcastic voice, Robin Cormorant thanked Dean Schumer, and then he leaned over the lectern, leering at the audience. Though it was well past the scheduled time for dismissal, Dr. Cormorant rubbed his hands together like a torturer ready to select a few favorite instruments. "Now, if you'll open your program to the schedule of events . . ."

How Cormorant loved assemblies! He insisted faculty don full regalia for these, and his favorites were outdoor graduations. He relished nothing more than forcing professors into heavy camphor-fumed robes and roasting them under the blazing Georgia sun. During this drawn-out convocation, Jane had sketched a series of trees on her program. As she scanned the list of upcoming assemblies—*another* convocation in spring?—she affixed a noose to a gnarled oak in the margin. Using the rhinestone-studded pen Jane had given her in celebration of the forthcoming book, Lucinda jotted lists on her program. One headed by "soy milk" was likely a grocery list, another a to-do list, and the third—*rusted tambourine, gingham apron, dead mice*— must have been story ideas. Jane caught her friend's eye and winked. Lucinda jerked her chin at the stage, opened her mouth to insert an index finger, and mimed gagging.

Devorah Grisham, a poet who taught composition and literature, tittered at Lucinda's side. While Dev, one of the few black faculty members, could afford to laugh openly, the most Jane would hazard was a brief grin, masked by her raised program. Lucinda much enjoyed mocking others behind their backs, and she'd grown bolder after finding a publisher for her manuscript and scoring a campus interview for a tenure-track position at a research university. The book was a collection of stories that Jane would not read out of affection for her friend. Lucinda based one story on the time they'd spent together with a few other colleagues at a Wyoming artists' residency years ago. Though names were changed, Hailey Linder—a textile artist in fine arts who *had* read the manuscript—told Jane that people were not well disguised in it, intimating that the character based on Jane came across as something of a Machiavellian manipulator. No, it was better for their friendship—Jane smiled again at Lucinda—if she never read the thing.

Lucinda's wiry black hair escaped from its thick braid, forming an inky nimbus under her tasseled cap. As the president droned on, with no sign of stopping, she wore a disbelieving look of revulsion on her face. One glimpse of her wild hair, those flashing eyes and flaming cheeks, that mobile mouth spraying spittle when she was worked up, which was most of the time, and the head of the search committee would slap Lucinda's dossier shut and cry, "Next!" Excitable and strange-looking women like Lucinda were not viable candidates for prestigious universities that offered tenure, which was why they wound up—among the hopeless multitude gathered here—at Birnbrau Women's College, everlastingly adjuncted by yearly contracts.

After half an hour more, Cormorant, reluctant to release his captives, issued protracted closing remarks, and at last, he dismissed the assembly. Relieved applause burst from the audience. A few brazen students whistled and hooted. Jane clapped with vigor, but Lucinda made a show of drawing her hands together and apart without touching palms to one another. Dev, again, chuckled, as she tapped three fingers against the heel of one hand. The women rose from their seats, chairs scraping and voices buzzing about them.

"Help me round up Tiffany Saunders, will you?" Lucinda searched the audience, a predatory look on her face. "I thought I saw her on the left side, in back."

"Sniffing Tiff or the other one, the LUG?" Jane said, using the acronym for lesbians-until-graduation.

"Sniffing Tiff is Tiffany *Marquart*, the girl who's allergic to everything, and Tiffany Saunders isn't a LUG. She's a true lesbian—or, I should say, a lesbian-for-life," Lucinda said.

"How do you know?" Jane said as they made their way to the aisle. But the women were stalled by a professor of ancient civilizations, a fuzzy-eared hobgoblin who stood patting his robe as if to find keys and blocking the entire row.

"How does anyone know anything? Gossip, of course. Someone must've told me."

"I think she *is* a lesbian-for-life." Dev nodded. "I mean, I've heard that, too."

"Whatever the duration of her lesbianism," Lucinda said, "she's signed up for a tutorial with me this semester, and she still hasn't come by with the paperwork for it."

"What? You need gym shoes? *Again*?" Jane often joked that conducting an independent study earned just enough to purchase a pair of Adidas, excluding tax. But as soon as her words escaped, Jane regretted them. Lucinda's on-and-off boyfriend had just moved out for the third or fourth time, and despite the small advance on her book, she now struggled to pay rent on her own, while supporting her grown daughter and granddaughter. No wonder Lucinda was anxious about the independent study—she needed the pittance it paid.

At last they reached the aisle, and Lucinda snorted. "Oh, I can always use gym shoes, not to mention groceries and gas for my car."

"Ladies." Randy Birch, a lanky biology professor, shuffled toward them. If not for his black robes and headpiece, Randy resembled a workman who'd just emerged from the crawlspace of a house. His face was gritty, reddish dust powdered his sparse eyebrows and lashes. Bleach-spattered blue jeans and mud-crusted boots showed under his regalia. He paused to address Lucinda. "Buenas noches," he said in an accent that was painful even to Jane's ears.

Lucinda made a performance of looking at her watch and then lifting her gaze, degree by degree, before fixing it on Randy's face. Though just half past three, Randy—and even Jane knew this much—had wished Lucinda a good night. Poor Lucinda, the sole Latina on faculty, often had to endure excruciating attempts by colleagues to demonstrate their embrace of cultural diversity through butchery of the language that she had only acquired in college.

"¿Como estoy?" Randy said.

With palms upturned, Lucinda shrugged. "I have no idea."

Randy grinned. "Come on, now. I know you speak Spanish."

"*That's* the problem," Lucinda told him.

He squawked with laugher, and Dev and Jane joined in as if Lucinda had delivered an effective punchline. Randy, then, shuffled off, calling "hasta la vida" over his shoulder.

"Didn't he just ask you how *he* was?" Dev squinted after Randy, cocking her head.

Lucinda nodded. "I should have said 'idiotic.'"

"The nerve of him." Jane gestured with her program at his denim-clad calves, as he ambled to the exit. "Why, we'd get yanked into Muriel Cheek's office if we ever *dared* to—"

"Oh, I know," Dev said. "Men can get away with anything—jeans, sweatpants, flip-flops—as long as they have that tie."

"For solidarity," Jane said, "they ought to wear uncomfortable clothing to campus. They should suffer alongside us, like comrades."

"That reminds me," Dev said. "Are you coming to the poetry reading next week?"

Jane pretended not to hear this.

"Last semester," Lucinda began, also ignoring Dev's question, "I saw Frank Means coming out of his freshman seminar wearing biking shorts, sandals with socks, and—of course—the tie." She repeated her gag-me motions, and Jane hoped this wouldn't become one of Lucinda's pet gestures. These were contagious for Jane, who had adopted Lucinda's habit of flashing the bird last semester. After the corrupt Dr. Caspar had pressured Jane to change a grade for one of his honors students, a blond dufus who couldn't even *trace* a recognizable image, Jane had followed him out of her office and flipped middle fingers of both hands, popping a double-bird behind his back. She had not expected Caspar to whip about and catch her in the act. Despite the stunned look on his face and the shame furnace-blasting her cheeks, both colleagues—dispatched by confusion to a territory beyond protocol—behaved as if Jane had waved farewell. "Goodbye, then," she'd said. Dr. Caspar fluttered fingers at her, but his short legs managed extraordinarily long strides, and he'd loped away like a man pursued.

"The reading's only an hour," Dev said. "I'll take you to dinner with the poet before it."

Lucinda's tongue skimmed her upper lip. "Dinner and drinks?"

"Well . . . *dinner*, for sure." Dev's brow creased. "*Maybe* they'll reimburse drinks . . ."

But they all knew the women's college, founded as a Baptist institution, would never cover as much as near-beer. Jane relented in the face of Dev's discomfiture. "I'll go if you do," she told Lucinda, "and *I'll* buy our drinks. What do you say?"

"I *guess*," Lucinda said, as if consenting to donate bone marrow to someone she disliked.

"*There*, there she is." Jane pointed at a girl-shaped blur in the background. "Wasn't that Tiffany Saunders? She took one look at you and dashed for the door."

"What the hell? Is she scared of me?" Lucinda's florid face wadded like a fist. "Why on earth would anyone be afraid of me?"

"I really couldn't say." Jane looked to Dev for a second opinion, but the poet had darted past the crowd for the exit. With much flapping of malodorous robes, the covey of professors that had been plodding along with her and Lucinda now scattered like pheasants flushed from the briars. Within seconds, President Cormorant's sardonic voice boomed out. "¡Hola, profesora Aragon! Una momentito por favor."

JANE HAD CHOSEN her small cottage off Highway 60 for its closeness to the lake and for the natural light that poured through its many windows. The house itself was just a one-bedroom dwelling constructed as a vacation getaway. It was a fifty-minute drive from the Birnbrau campus and somewhat difficult for visitors to find, but Jane considered that an advantage. As it had no room for a studio, Jane, with the help of friends, had converted the garage into a bonus room, a space where she could paint and sketch, as well as access even more sunlight when she raised the garage door. For Jane, the garage/studio was the heart of her home, though she enjoyed the cottage's small airy rooms, the compact tidiness of these. They were well kept because she spent most of her time in the converted garage. She'd even placed a futon near her easel, so she could nap or sleep through the night when she painted more complicated pieces. Though she was a plein-air artist, after an initial sketch or quick watercolor, Jane developed details in her landscapes inside her garage.

On the highway toward home, Jane visualized the landscape that she had sketched from the shore over the weekend. That morning, she'd undercoated the foreground—the water—in white, and while the undercoat was still damp, she had blended in azure from the base up to capture the reflection of the sky at the bottom, preserving pure white in the distance. By evening, Jane would fill in the reflected treetops, the sky and clouds in the water. She envisioned the controlled brush strokes that would portray the lake's depth and movement. Nothing challenged her skills more than rendering water—her specialty—with its rippling skin of infinite folds and pleats, its multitude of lights and shadows, its sheen and spectrum of colors, the inverted forms it mirrored. Jane would have to work in a focused way to complete the painting before the semester started in earnest. By late September, she would have to give up her own artwork or suffer the frustration of half-started projects. "Abandon all hope," Jane murmured as she pushed the new semester from her thoughts.

Her cellphone on the passenger's seat trilled, pulsing with phosphorescent green flashes. She glanced at it and tightened her grip on the steering wheel. Earlier it displayed two missed calls. She knew who these would be from. *Tall Drink of Water*, Lucinda called him, mimicking the Wyoming women who referred to him this way.

She'd met him a few years ago while on a faculty retreat near Sheridan, and Jane had contacted him when she returned to the artists' residency earlier in the summer. They'd spent much of July together, riding out on horseback from his ranch to paint and picnic on the range. Her last week in Wyoming, Jane had packed her bags and left the residency to stay at his place. Now that she'd returned to Georgia, he called and called.

Tall Drink, only two years older than Jane, eschewed email and texting, saying he liked hearing her voice. Since he wouldn't Skype with her, Jane suspected he was more of a technophobe than a romantic. No matter his preferred mode of communication, Jane knew what he wanted. But fifty-five-year-old women do not abandon teaching positions with benefits, even if untenured. Water-scape artists living near lakes have no business moving to the dry and dusty plains. Mothers of difficult sons within driving distance don't just run off with boyfriends. If he wanted, Tall Drink could come to Georgia to be with her, and though she hadn't dared to ask him, Jane wished with her whole heart that he would.

Her teenaged Toyota now vibrated in a disturbing way, juddering like a superjet about to penetrate the sound barrier. To counter this, she flipped on the radio. Steppenwolf blasted through the speakers. Jane turned the volume up and shouted along with the gravelly vocalist: *We were born, born to be wild!* Just as the song ended, Jane reached her street. There, in the yard at the corner of the block, stood Dennis Formosa wearing gym shorts and holding pruning shears. When Jane tooted her horn and waved, he set his clippers on the lawn and hurried into his house as if he'd forgotten something. Dennis had been so alarmed by her gift of a lariat to thank him for picking her up from the airport after her first trip to Wyoming that now—years later—he still fled for cover whenever she drew near, as if Jane had signaled with the gift a desire to lasso him. Ridiculous man! Though Jane hoped to remarry, she had no desire to squander her future on someone as timorous as Dennis. The rope had shown him for what he was, and the last time she'd flown to Wyoming, Lucinda had driven her to and from the airport.

Jane pulled into her driveway, and with a glance at the drawn curtains, she sucked in a sharp breath, holding it—one, two, three, four—and then releasing it in a slow and measured stream as if to cool a cup of tea. She turned off her car, chunked open the door, and slid out into the sweltering late afternoon, a lacey scrim of gnats haloing her head. Jane swiped at these with her purse. She inhaled deeply again and smiled in a determined way before pushing open the front door—left unlocked, of course. Jane stepped into living room. "Wallace?" she called. "*Wallace?*"

The cottage stood silent, cool and dark. Jane sniffed musky traces of sweat and body odor, the sour smell of unwashed clothing. Had he run off from the halfway house in Atlanta and hitchhiked here, or had he been discharged and delivered by the state transport system? Weekly infractions had deferred her younger son's release for months, leaving Jane with no idea when to expect him. She set her keys and purse on the kitchen counter, but on second thought, Jane snatched these up again. She would have to keep things in her bedroom now, locked in the floor safe under her bed. The door to her garage/studio—usually ajar—was shut, likely latched from inside. Wallace was no doubt snoring on the futon near the easel that held her painting of the lake, the blanched and azure undercoat awaiting the peculiar grace of upended treetops, the delicate drowning of clouds and sky.

A WEEK LATER, AT DiColo's, Jane grew muddled by encountering April Madison, a student of two semesters ago, near the dimly lit piano bar. April sallied forth, wearing a black pencil skirt and burgundy blazer with a nametag affixed to the lapel. "Professor Klamath, how great to see you!"

"April?" Jane said. "I thought you—"

"I'm better now." April grinned, baring smallish teeth. Hers was a Pre-Raphaelite face—wide hazel eyes, plush ruby lips, rosy cheeks framed by lustrous red-gold hair—combined with a Rubenesque body, though even Rubens might have been daunted by the amplitude of April's form. "Much, *much* better now." The girl stooped to whisper something in Jane's ear that sounded like, "I'm just one urine test away from getting faith back."

Jane struggled to make sense of this. "Good news?"

"My parents have Faith now. If I test clean next month, I can regain custody."

"Wonderful!" Jane smiled. While she knew April had a daughter, Jane had forgotten the child's name, and she'd no idea that April had forfeited custody. But, as if she starred in a reality-TV show, April Madison expected others to be well versed in her life's events.

April beamed. "I guess you'll be joining Dr. Grisham. She's already here with Narciso."

"Narciso?"

April gave Jane a pitying look. "Narciso *Navarette*, the visiting poet."

Jane pictured the flyers made by Dev's student assistant, Kayla, a girl whose ineptitude distinguished her even at Birnbrau. She'd posted canary-yellow sheets about campus that read *Pottery Reading/N. Navarette*, along with the time and date. Jane had been too distracted by the typo to wonder much about the poet's first name. Still, she'd meant to look him up on the internet beforehand, but she'd been pulled into a disciplinary hearing that afternoon, as a substitute for Dean Muriel Cheek, who'd had a migraine.

"Follow me." April led Jane into the depths of the crowded and noisy restaurant. After a few steps, the girl paused, turning to say, "Professor Grisham's the greatest, isn't she?"

Succulent aromas—roasted garlic, grilled meats, yeasty rolls, tart vinaigrettes—filled Jane's nostrils. She glanced at the steamy plates set before diners. "She's very nice," Jane said, eyeing pan-seared scallops atop a bed of spinach on one candlelit table.

"She really saved me, you know." April indicated a table in the far corner of the restaurant where Devorah sat with a man whose tweed-jacketed back was turned to Jane. "In fact, I consider Dr. Grisham to be my spiritual mother."

"You *do*?" But wasn't there some bad business about the girl's obsession with Sylvia Plath in the aftermath of Dev's seminar on women poets last fall? April had read and reread the poems, memorizing their lines to recite these randomly throughout the day. Jane had once overheard April muttering "You do not do, you do not do / Any more, black shoe . . . ," as the girl coiled frozen yogurt into a cone in the Birnbrau dining hall. And didn't she try to have her name changed at one point—to Sylvia Plath Madison? Though perhaps Jane had imagined this.

April nodded. "I've got to get back up front, but enjoy your meal." The girl pivoted away. "Oh, and, Professor Klamath, don't order the oysters," she called over her shoulder. "They smell a little off to me." Utensils clattered on china at a nearby table.

Devorah waved Jane over. "This is Narciso Navarette." She stood to make the introduction, but the poet remained seated, nodding his leonine head in acknowledgement. He looked to be in his mid-fifties like Jane, and also like Jane, he dyed his shaggy hair to cover the gray. From where she stood above him, white roots glistered like hoarfrost where his dark hair was parted. Though symmetrical and strong-featured, the poet's face wore an aggrieved expression, a visage Hieronymus Bosch might have captured for an eighth deadly sin: Vexation.

"Pleased to meet you," Jane lied. She slid into the bench seat alongside Dev, likewise facing their guest. "Are you enjoying your visit to Georgia?"

Narciso regarded her with hooded eyes. "I *live* in Georgia." Like April, the poet clearly expected his biographical information to be common knowledge.

"Narciso is part of the *Georgia* Poetry Circuit," Dev said, "a consortium of in-state poets who travel around giving readings and craft talks."

"Then how are you enjoying our campus?"

The poet shrugged. He glanced at his empty glass. "Where's the waiter?"

Before Dev could answer, Lucinda bustled over, wearing skinny jeans in a bilious shade of green, along with an orange sweater—an outfit that made her look like a Dr. Seuss character, wide-bottomed with spindly Grinch legs and long flat feet. Lucinda plopped into the vacant chair beside the poet, and before Dev could perform introductions, Lucinda said, "When did April Madison start hostessing here? I thought she worked at the library."

"She did, but . . ." Almost imperceptibly, Dev tilted her head toward their guest.

"Oh, I know she had that breakdown or whatever, that day she stripped off her clothes."

The poet turned to regard Lucinda with interest, though she took no notice of this.

"They *do* keep the library too warm in winter," Jane said. "It's a waste of energy." One afternoon in December, April had stalked about the stacks, shedding her sweater, jeans, and undershirt, shouting lines to "Lady Lazarus"—*I eat men like air!*—as she shelved books in her bra and panties until campus security officers arrived to blanket and escort her from the building.

"Wasn't she supposed to go back to work at the library after rehab?" Lucinda said. "That's what the librarians told me."

"Those librarians never keep their word." How many times had they promised to procure Vasari's *Lives of the Artists* for Jane through interlibrary loan without ever doing this?

Dev cleared her throat. "Lucinda, I'd like to—"

"Hold on." Lucinda put up a hand. "This was supposed to have come from Cormorant himself. He's the one who promised she'd be reinstated in her classes *and* her work-study job."

"*Robin Cormorant*," Jane said. "How can you trust a *man*—"

The poet aimed his gaze in her direction.

Flustered, Jane cleared her throat. "How can you trust *anyone* with two bird names?"

After this, Dev managed to introduce the poet. Lest Lucinda repeat Jane's error in assuming he was from out of state, Dev explained his connection to the Georgia Poetry Circuit.

At this, Lucinda's face grew incandescent. "Is the circuit just for poets?"

"It's called the Georgia *Poetry* Circuit," Narciso said.

"Why isn't there something like that for fiction writers?"

"Because they have . . . ," the poet said, "*everything else.*" Then he instructed Dev to order another scotch for him and rose to lumber toward the men's room.

"What a flaming asshole," Lucinda said.

Dev picked up a menu to scan as if this might speed things along.

"Am I wrong?" Lucinda looked to Jane, who opened her mouth, plunged a finger in, and faked a dry heave: the gag-me gesture already part of her repertoire.

April Madison appeared at her side. "You didn't have the oysters, did you?"

Jane dropped her hand to her lap, shook her head. "We haven't even ordered yet."

"I'll send your server over." Then April leaned in. "By the way, that's eighty-dollar scotch he's drinking. I thought you should know."

"Cut him off," Lucinda cried. "Cut him off at once."

Dev clutched the table's edge, as if she might otherwise faint, and Jane said, "Eighty dollars a bottle or eighty dollars a glass?"

"A glass."

"Why, he's drinking up the entire stipend for my independent study." Lucinda turned to Jane. "I know you said you'd get drinks, but you are *not* paying for that."

Jane dropped her gaze to the table, the votive candle flickering on it. A knot of tallow sizzled before bursting on its wick, and she thought—irrelevantly, irreverently—of Joan of Arc.

"I'll have the server tell him we ran out of the pricey stuff," April said. "You can use my discount for the first drink, and it will only be, like, sixty-five dollars. Can you cover that?"

A doomed look on her face, Dev nodded. Determined to share the cost with Dev, Jane would slip her some cash when Lucinda was not looking. A poet, of all people, should know what it means to be undercompensated and ill-treated. April promised to expedite the meal so they could get to the auditorium on time for the reading. Then she bustled away from the table.

"That girl just thinks the world of you," Jane said, hoping to lift Dev's spirits.

"He's going to be furious." Dev stared out, transfixed by the candle on the tabletop. Its guttering glow sparkled in her obsidian eyes, giving her the look of a prophetess. "I know it. He is going to be pissed off, and he looks like a tantrum-thrower, doesn't he?"

"I'll deal with him," Lucinda said, and Dev glanced up in alarm.

"April says you *saved* her," Jane continued. "In fact, she calls you her spiritual mother."

"I didn't help her at all. I was the one who introduced her to Sylvia Plath in the first place. I encouraged her to submit that paper for the Plath conference, where she fell in with those druggies. Now, her therapist won't let her read Plath anymore, or Emily Dickinson. He wants her to read *Longfellow*." Dev's eyes widened with incredulity. "Can you believe that?"

Lucinda shot Dev a let's-be-frank look. "Ever consider spiritual birth control?"

ONE FRIDAY, WEEKS later, Jane's older son Jeremy and his wife, a large brunette with all the charm of an aphasic, deposited their sons—a nine-month-old and a three-year-old—with Jane, in order to participate in some therapeutic couples weekend. Wallace had been staying with her for over a month by then. Her younger son's hair had thinned on top. Like his brother, he'd put on weight and looked a decade older than his thirty years, yet Wallace had a girlfriend now, Alyssa, whom he met at weekly sessions he called "group." Alyssa, a blonde with stringy hair and ruddy weals like angry subdural worms on both wrists, could be Jane's daughter-in-law's twin insofar as charisma went. Alyssa now spent most of her time at the cottage, sitting on the futon, looking blank and saying nothing. No way would Jane subject her grandsons much to those two.

So she took the boys to the lake each day. In the mornings, Jane lugged the baby in a backpack, along with diaper bag, blankets, and picnic lunches, plodding along the trail like an overburdened mule. She towed her older grandson by the hand as they trudged the lake's perimeter. They stopped often to examine shiny stones and flowering plants, to glimpse turtles and fish skimming the water's undulating surface, and to gape at iridescent dragonflies hovering over the sun-spangled water like jeweled hatpins magically suspended in midair. When they picnicked on the shore, Jane gazed at the boys, straining to remember her sons at their ages. Instead, she kept picturing her grandsons as grown men—large, bald, grim grotesques of their sweet-voiced, clear-eyed child selves.

On Sunday, Jane stayed out at the lake with her grandsons until dusk. Jeremy and his wife, tense and unsmiling, collected their sons at eight without thanking Jane and—*worse!*—without embracing their children. Alyssa returned to wherever she stayed when not at the cottage. Exhausted, begrimed, and sticky with perspiration after a humid day at the lake, Jane looked forward to nothing more than a bath and an early bedtime. She'd brew a cup of chamomile to sip while reading Vasari's *Lives of the Artists*, which she wound up ordering for herself online. But it turned out that Wallace had asked Alyssa to leave, so he could speak to Jane alone.

He blocked the doorway to the bathroom before Jane could draw her bath. "I've got some good news for you, Mom," he said, a rare smile lighting his thick face.

"What is it?" In a dizzying moment of hope, Jane imagined he'd found a job.

"Alyssa's pregnant! You're going to be a grandma again."

If Wallace did not understand why Jane flew to her bedroom and locked the door, why she leaned against it, the knob pressing into her back as he jiggled it and tried to push it open, well, that was too bad. Choked by disbelief and anger, she couldn't point out that neither Wallace nor Alyssa were employed and that, as a consequence of this, they had no medical insurance, or to observe that they had nowhere—apart from the cottage—to house a newborn. Jane could not utter a syllable without risking a breakdown like April Madison's in the Birnbrau Library, with rent clothing and mad-woman squalls. *You do not do, you do not do!*

What on earth would *she do* with a bipolar grandbaby?

When Wallace finished ranting the usual rants—that she was selfish, that she cared more for her art than her sons, that she never supported him in anything, that their father left them because of her and who could blame him for it—he muttered something about going for a walk to clear his head. His footfalls receded, the front door slammed shut, and Jane slunk to the floor and crawled to her bed to reach the lock-box underneath it. She reeled her purse from this and dug in that for her cellphone. Jane tapped in the Wyoming area code and now-familiar number. At the rumbling sound of his voice, something gave in her like a faulty sluicegate banging open in a storm, and Jane—a professional educator; a plein-air artist; a mother of adult, if disappointing, sons; a dependable grandmother; and an indisputably mature woman who had not wept in a copious way since her now ex-husband told her he no longer loved her, over two decades ago—blubbered into the phone, convulsing with hot, snotty tears like a child.

Tall Drink asked a few questions that Jane—heaving and hyperventilating—couldn't make out to answer. Then he listened to her sob, but in a few minutes, he hung up.

AFTER HER LAST class the next day, Jane headed from the Fine Arts Center toward the Godwin Humanities Building, where she had a committee meeting scheduled for 3:10. On her way, she stopped at the campus post office to dispose of whatever mail had accumulated in her cubby-hole over the past week. There, she found Devorah, leaning against the bank of post office boxes and staring at a cream-colored envelope and embossed card that she held in both hands. Was she imagining this or were Dev's dark eyes damp, her voice huskier than usual when she greeted Jane?

"Unexpected news?" Jane pointed at the card in Dev's hand.

Dev cleared her throat. "A wedding invitation—you remember my friend Karla?"

Jane recalled the pixie-faced young woman who'd roomed with Dev when she started teaching at Birnbrau, before Dev's mother moved in with her. "How nice." Jane wondered if Dev might be upset about not getting asked to be a bridesmaid. "You must be thrilled for her."

"Yes, thrilled." Dev pulled a tissue from her blazer pocket, honked into it. "I heard your son's staying with you," she said. "How's that going?"

"Great!" Jane keyed open her box and yanked out a stack of ads, flyers, and catalogues to thrust into a nearby recycling bin. Wallace and Alyssa had not spoken to her that morning, ignoring her cheerful overtures along with the pancake breakfast she'd prepared for them, yet now Jane grinned with such force that she could glimpse her cheeks bunching beneath her eyes. Dev said she was glad to hear this and edged away, heading for the door. Jane relocked her mailbox, continued on toward her meeting.

Onion grass sprouted freely on campus, and sniffing this caused Jane to crave a burger as she strolled toward the Godwin Center. Once there she would convene with Lucinda, Frank Means, Dean Schumer, the odious Dr. Caspar, and Hailey Linder in textiles. Hailey, a petite blonde, had a face with the exquisite simplicity of a Vermeer subject. The birthmark shading Hailey's cheek somehow inflected, rather than detracted from her loveliness. Altogether they formed the search committee to replace Kerry Fujimori, a painter who resigned when her parents passed away, leaving an inheritance that allowed Kerry to devote her time to art. The lucky dog, thought Jane as she entered the meeting room and took a seat across from Lucinda and Hailey. Though Jane anticipated hearing all about the certain fiasco that was Lucinda's campus interview last week, she searched her friend's face for traces of despair, as a preview to what would no doubt prove to be a sad, if predictable tale.

But Lucinda was in her usual mood of gleeful outrage as she scanned the agenda before her. "Fucking Frank Means," she said. "How'd that schlemiel get on this committee?"

Jane shrugged, and Hailey said, "To me, it's weird that he hasn't met with us from the start." While Lucinda, in English, served on the committee due to Jane's careful interventions, Frank Means, a ceramicist in fine arts, actually *belonged* on it. But the potter's laziness was exceptional, even world-class, and Jane had no doubt he had schemed his way out of the obligation until this point, taking it on now only to avoid some more demanding commitment.

"With him onboard, we'll accomplish exactly bupkis," Lucinda said. Outside the first-floor conference room, an engine growled in the adjacent parking lot, the recognizable mind-scraping roar of Frank's absurd super-truck. "Here he comes now—big stupid car, big stupid voice, big stupid hair. Can there be any doubt that the man's schlong is really quite schlort?"

Hailey laughed, and Jane issued a subdued smile. The Yiddish was a troubling sign that Lucinda had reconciled with her boyfriend, a Jewish accountant years younger than she. Lucinda had at one time planned to convert to Judaism in order to marry him. But grandmothers typically did not wed professional men in their early forties with no detectable defects. Jane's gaze traveled from the yellowed buttons on Lucinda's pilly beige sweater up her scrawny neck to her livid, sharp-boned face. "Fucking Frank Means," Lucinda said again.

"How did it go?" Jane whispered to her after Hailey excused herself to retrieve the cellphone she'd left in her office. "The campus visit?"

Lucinda's coffee-bean eyes grew round and vacant, her expression that of a cartoon character staggering about after getting conked on the head. "You won't believe this, but I got the job. They called on Friday with an offer."

"That soon?" Jane *didn't* believe it. She squinted at Lucinda for sharper focus. Surely, her friend was mistaken or deluded, the balance of her mind undone by disappointment.

"I was the *only* candidate they brought in. The fiction writer, this old guy, died last spring. They couldn't wait to conduct a full search next semester, so it was like I was competing with myself." Lucinda laughed. "And I almost defeated me, if you can believe that."

Jane nodded. Now, *that* she could believe.

"Of course, I asked for more money when the chair called with the offer."

"You *did*?" Jane was astonished that Lucinda had the presence of mind—the gall, really—for this, when she should have been blindsided by joy, overcome and incoherent with gratitude, eager to kiss the collective feet of all members of that search committee.

"They'll get back to me on the money," Lucinda said, "but they can't very well rescind the offer just because I asked for more. Can they?"

Jane shook her head. In Lucinda's case, they might be tempted, though they'd probably do no such thing. "Congratulations," she said, feeling as if she'd just stepped off a whirligig. Jane thought of the unfinished painting in her studio, certain she would never finish it now. Was this vertiginous and hollow sensation jealousy? Was it grief that her friend would be leaving? Was it disappointment in herself? Perhaps an amalgamation of all three, along with heavy dollops of other foul and dark emotions blended in her like the mixing of too many colors to produce a revolting purplish brown.

Like a swashbuckler, Frank Means burst into the meeting room, his poufy hair glistening in a way that suggested hairspray. He was again wearing bike shorts and a polo shirt onto which he'd clipped a bowtie. Martin Schumer and Dr. Caspar then arrived together. When Hailey returned, wagging her cellphone in triumph, Martin opened the meeting. Glancing at the faces ringing the conference table, Jane teetered at the precipice of precognition—a dizzying flash of déjà vu. Excepting Kerry Fujimori's replacement by Frank Means, this group comprised the same committee she met with last academic year. After narrowing the search to three candidates and just before scheduling campus visits, funding for the position had fallen through.

Dean Schumer, blinking spasmodically, now handed out folders to committee members. "Here are dossiers for our top three candidates from last year," he said, his cherub's face clenching each time his eyes shut. "We can save time by revisiting these applications."

"But wouldn't they have found jobs by now?" Jane's eyes fluttered, the lids rising and falling again and again. She couldn't control her compulsion to blink back at Martin. Horrified that he might think she was mocking him, Jane fumbled for her sunglasses and slipped these on.

Martin popped knuckles of all ten fingers in rapid succession. "I've checked, and they're all available," he said. "The market is tough for candidates in this field."

Lucinda opened her file sleeve and scoffed. "I'm not surprised Brain Fart is still available." She'd formed a grudge against a candidate who during a conference call interview had drawn a blank in response to one of their questions, saying, "I must be having a brain fart." They had all traded dubious looks over the speaker-phone, and afterward, Lucinda, who cursed with abandon, claimed to be deeply offended by this utterance.

"I thought she was one of our better candidates," Dr. Caspar said, damning Brain Fart with the other committee members. "She displayed keen interest in honors."

Jane flushed, her eyes batting behind dark lenses as she recalled Caspar's attempt to get her to change that honor student's grade. The girl couldn't draw a convincing circle, but then she never *tried*. Like many of Caspar's honors students, she considered art courses "fluff" and said so when she met with Jane before enlisting Caspar to intervene. "It's all so subjective," the girl had said. She'd pointed to a Chagall print hanging in Jane's office. "Why is *that* art? Why isn't what I draw art? Just because you say that I don't spend enough time on it?" Such students failed to comprehend that creating art ought to take all of their time, all of their lives. That was what Jane loved about her work, that she would never finish solving its problems or confronting the challenges it posed.

"She even talked about developing a studio-art course for honors," Caspar said with a pointed look in Jane's direction. "I think that's an idea whose time has come."

Lucinda eyed Caspar in the way a mountain lion might regard a brain-damaged squirrel that had stumbled into its lair. Oh, she'd dispatch him in due time, but first, she would enjoy whatever amusement the addled creature might provide.

"Let's invite Brain Fart for a campus visit." Frank issued his automatic grin, a rectangular flash of bleached teeth.

"Doesn't she have a name?" asked Hailey, a puzzled look on her Flemish maiden's face as she paged through the file. "Oh, here it is, Regina, Regina Barresi. Wasn't she the one with those dark and depressing slides?"

Jane nodded. The candidate's portfolio consisted of greenish-gray and muddy brown images. "Swamp-scapes, she called them. She claims to be 'anti-color.'" Her gaze arced toward Lucinda as if tracing the trajectory of a softball lobbed in her friend's direction.

"*Anti-color*?" Lucinda drew back, wearing the expression of one who has trod barefoot on dog droppings. "¡Carajo! We can't have *that* here. Who's next?"

"I think we ought to go back to the drawing board then," Caspar said. "Maybe place another ad and look for someone who balances things gender-wise in the art department."

Jane shared a glance with Hailey, and they both turned toward Frank Means. The ceramicist was the only male in fine arts. His antipathy toward other males was on par with his dedication to doing as little as possible, and Jane wondered which would win out. Frank did not disappoint. "Are you suggesting we renew the search, that we read a ton of applications and then conduct a slew of phone interviews? Are you out of your mind, man?"

Martin popped his knuckles again. "Besides I don't think it's appropriate or legal to—"

"It's actually a good idea," Lucinda said, astounding Jane. "We ought to diversify by gender across the board, alternating male and female program directors. We could start with honors next semester."

Caspar, blanching, at last apprehended his peril.

"In fact," she continued, "I will call the motion at our next full faculty meeting."

Dean Schumer's cellphone buzzed. He grabbed it and held up an index finger before bustling out of the conference room.

Jane turned on her phone to check the time. It was only three-twenty. How was it that time passed more slowly during these meetings? Why, if Jane learned she had a terminal disease, she'd attend meeting after meeting to stretch out her last days infinitely. She snapped her phone shut and excused herself for a drink of water. Lucinda was chatting with Hailey and Frank, while Dr. Caspar fiddled with his phone. No one glanced up when Jane left the room.

In the empty hallway, Martin Schumer's soft tenor gained resonance with reverberation. "Sure, I can pick her up, no problem. How's the new yoga class, sweetie?"

At the endearment, envy again twisted in Jane. Dean Schumer's muscular back to her, she paused before the water fountain, a few yards away, vicariously enjoying the warm tone he used with his wife.

"It's always rough in the beginning," Martin said, "but they'll get better." He sighed before speaking again. "Same old, same old here. Caspar's burying himself deep, Frank's a fool, and Jane . . . You know Jane." He laughed. "She's good, so good that when Lucinda speaks, you never even see Jane's lips moving."

Stricken, Jane crept away. She slipped back into the conference room. Again no one looked up until her phone chimed with a call. At sight of the displayed number—the Wyoming area code—her heart tripped, a coronary hiccup, and she flipped it open. "Hello?"

"Hey, I'm here," he said. Static crackled like cellophane crumpling in her ear, and an announcer's voice blared unintelligibly in the background.

"Where?"

"Here, in Georgia. I'm at Hartsfield in Atlanta."

"What are you doing here?" Jane gripped the phone with both hands now

"Tall Drink?" Lucinda asked, and Jane nodded. If Lucinda knew of her phone call to him last night, those incoherent tears, she would think this more manipulation, a ploy to get him to come to her and to fortify her against the machinations of those who would play her for everything she had, those she could no longer outmaneuver on her own. *We do what we can,* as the now-retired Kerry Fujimori used to say when confronted by impossible tasks coupled with insane deadlines, *and somehow we find ways to do what we can't.* For the first time, Jane longed to read Lucinda's book and draw inspiration from her fictional self.

Lucinda, Hailey, Frank Means, and Dr. Caspar stared at Jane, openly eavesdropping.

"You sounded like you could use some help last night," Tall Drink told her, "so I took the first flight out of Sheridan. Should I rent a car or can you pick me up?"

"I'm in a meeting right now," Jane said. "But I'll come for you as soon as I can. Just wait for me. It's nearly rush hour, so it might be an hour or more."

"I'll grab a bite then and read the paper. Call me when you get close and I'll meet you curbside near baggage claim." Not one for goodbyes, he hung up again.

Martin returned and adjourned the meeting to collect his daughter from soccer practice. As the group consulted calendars to schedule the next meeting, a curious glow skittered across the ceiling, a rainbow splinter of refracted light. Jane tracked this to its source: Lucinda's left hand. Was it a diamond ring glinting in the sunlight slanting through the blinds? Jane lowered her sunglasses to see the rhinestone pen Lucinda, a southpaw, clutched as she scribbled on her agenda. Of course, Jane would have had misgivings about an engagement undertaken in the aftermath of Lucinda's job offer. But what did she know? If someone as odd and off-putting as Lucinda garnered a position at a prestigious university, why shouldn't she become a bride, too? Strange women would do strange things. There was a peculiar sense to this.

Jane clapped her datebook shut, jammed it into her bag. "Oh, I don't *care* when we meet again," she said with force, astonishing herself and startling the group. "I have to go. I *can't* . . ." She rose from her seat, wondering if she should explain she meant more by this than just excusing herself from the room, but Jane didn't know how to end the sentence she'd started—*what couldn't she do?*—so she gave a tight smile and turned for the door, catching one last glimpse of the prism strand hovering now on the ceiling like an iridescent hatpin, a dragonfly suspended for scant seconds over the lake before darting from sight.

Fifteen Beads More

In memory of the Master of Time and Space

I

*I*f only the doctor had told Kerry that actually, no, she'd never borne children. Her nipples—just look at them now!—again blush-colored, her hymen still ballet-slipper pink, the satiny membrane intact. "There's been a mistake," he might have said as he snapped off gloves. "This body, your body has never given birth." But how could that be? Susan and Scott say she sometimes misses things. They'd not be her children anymore, would they? Kerry could regard them as—no, not friends—but, say, neighbors. Her married daughter's preoccupation with Percy would amuse, rather than trouble Kerry. ("That gal's just wild about her cat!") Her son's faith would make him a conscientious neighbor, the devout fellow next door. Kerry could say to them, "Those darned white blood cells," and release a self-deprecating laugh. Their neighborly faces would lengthen with concern. They might draw her into a clumsy embrace while wondering who will keep up her yard and what will happen to property values if squalid tenants move into her house? As though preparing for a long trip, Kerry could ask them to collect the mail, to water the fig tree, and they would be glad to oblige.

Pressure, is what the doctor really said. Kerry would feel intense pressure on her tailbone for a few seconds. But this was beyond pressure: the blunt-nosed needle piercing flesh and bone, the scraping and suctioning of marrow. She didn't cry out. Surely, most patients must yelp and clench fists. But Kerry's long fingers unfurled, rippling like the translucent tentacles of a sea anemone. In a week, the doctor told her, his office would call with results of the biopsy. Two days later, he phoned Kerry himself. "You'll have to come in as soon as you can."

II

WHAT IF, WHEN KERRY HAD been married to him, Takashi had spoken to *her* in whole sentences? What then? Instead, he would rely on fragments, elliptical phrases that twisted away like smoke. "If only . . ." "Just suppose that . . ." "What if . . . *hmm*?" So when Arlene, an art restorer, appeared one morning to examine paintings Takashi, a dealer, hoped to sell, paintings he kept in their basement, Kerry was stunned by the full paragraphs that floated from the stairwell. She was in the kitchen topping strawberries when these wafted up, like a suspicious smell. Word upon word upon word—yes, full paragraphs. Kerry approached the door at the top of the stairs, nudged it wide. The voice rumbled, deep like Takashi's, but not Takashi's. Arlene, the restorer, issued these streams of sentences, her voice low and insistent, as Kerry toed the door shut.

After Arlene had driven off, Kerry penned a vellum drawing, a human kidney rendered as an aerial view of a tropical island. She'd started the series of such images way back then, sketches she now calls "Organs as Islands." Kerry was developing contours of a kidney shaped like Cuba, when paragraphs again rolled toward her. This time they resonated from Takashi's office. Kerry pressed an ear to the wall. Was he speaking on the phone? He must be, the unbroken ribbon of his words flowing into the mouthpiece. Though Kerry couldn't make out much, she recognized two syllables that punctuated most of his sentences: "Arlene," Takashi said, again and again and again. "Ar-*lene*."

III

JUST SUPPOSE THAT KERRY HAD chosen to work in watercolors instead of oils. Kerry considers this as she massages lotion into the veiny dermis sheathing the backs of her hands, the loose skin that remains fluted like piecrust long after she's pinched it. Since she's heading out to the prison, Kerry applies extra moisturizer. They like to shake with her, the men do. At the start of each session, they clasp hands with her and with Fred Royce, her co-teacher, sometimes reeling Kerry close for a shoulder bump. This makes her self-conscious about her raspy skin. When she uses oil paints, Kerry must wash with turpentine, which pickles her fingertips and makes her nails brittle. She envies Fred, a watercolorist, who needs no more than warm water and soap to clean up. Kerry now flaps her hands about like a large flightless bird to air dry them before reaching for her canvas carryall and keys—ready to teach the men on death row to paint.

She opens the door to the carport, and the phone trills. Kerry stops short. Her son? Her daughter? Some crisis with the cat? What mother can ignore a ringing phone? She backtracks into her tidy kitchenette and sets her bag on a chair, drops her jangle of keys on the table.

IV

WHAT IF KERRY COULD FIND the missing poem that has eluded scholars for centuries? In twenty-five years of marriage, she's picked up only a few words of Japanese from Takashi. She can't read or write a lick of it, so there's no point in flying to Japan to scour archives there, even if she had the time for this. Really, beyond searching the internet Kerry has no idea where to look.

Takashi and Arlene belong to an organization supporting reincarnation research, Kerry's son told her. Years ago, Scott ran into his father in the airport, near baggage claim when returning from a trip. Arlene was nowhere in sight, so Takashi spoke to him while they waited for their suitcases. He and Arlene are convinced they have lived past lives and when they die, they will be born into new ones. Takashi told Scott that he believes he was a priestess in twelfth-century

Japan. Specifically, he was once Princess Shikishi, the third daughter of Emperor Go-Shirakawa. Takashi as Shikishi was appointed High Priestess of Kamo shrine in 1159, at just six years of age. A decade later, he/she gave up the position due to illness. Shikishi then became an accomplished poet, who composed 400 poems. All but one remains in print today. Curious about this, Kerry ordered a volume containing the former priestess's verses—translated, of course—that she now keeps in her handbag. Perhaps reading the poems will help her make sense of the quarter century—days, weeks, months, years—she poured out like water streaming from a pitcher onto a patch of sand.

Since running into Scott at the airport, Takashi has had no communication with either of his children. Arlene insists he cut off all ties to that past life, though she encourages him to investigate others. She had not even allowed Takashi to attend Susan's wedding. Kerry's former colleague Lucinda, once a victim of domestic violence, says isolation from family is a classic sign of abuse. At this, Kerry shrugged. It's not like she can report it to social services. "I think my sixty-year-old ex-husband is being abused." Though Takashi's silence troubles her on behalf of their children, she has no desire to speak to him. Even so, Kerry is curious about the missing poem. *Where could it be?*

V

IF ONLY KERRY HAD OPTED for caller identification when she purchased her landline service plan, then she would know whether or not to pick up the ringing phone. Too late for that now, she supposes. She clears her throat before lifting the receiver. "Hello?"

"Kerry?" A phlegm-coarsened falsetto sounds in her ear. It's a singular voice, the disappointingly recognizable voice of Leah Caspian, an abstract painter who was hired to teach at Birnbrau Women's College with Kerry nearly four years ago. Leah, though, was released from her contract before she taught a single class due to her failure to produce work at an arts residency and also due to some funny business involving the internet. "Kerry?" Leah says again. "Have you heard?"

"Heard what?" Kerry resists the impulse to be brusque with Leah, though the poor woman is likely still jobless, caring full-time for her wheelchair-bound husband.

"Leon Russell! He'll be in Athens next month!"

"I know." Kerry has set an auto alert on her computer to notify her of Leon Russell performances within a hundred-mile radius. She's bought tickets for herself and for Lucinda and Jane, two colleagues from Birnbrau, the first day they went on sale.

"Turns out, I can get us really great seats through a friend of mine who *knows* Leon Russell," Leah says in her sweetly grating voice. "She's actually friends with one of the roadies, and there was even some naughtiness between her and—"

"It's kind of you to offer," Kerry tells Leah, "but I can't make it."

"Come on, Kerry," Leah says. "I mean, it's *Leon Russell*. What could possibly—"

"My grandson Percy is ill." Kerry clenches her face, bites her lower lip. Though she's been practicing for months, Kerry's still a terrible liar. Small lies of commission are far more complicated to pull off than her one whopping lie of omission. Now, she can't recall if she's told Leah about her daughter's troubled marriage and problems conceiving, about her own frustrated longing for a grandchild. Leah, though, rarely listens to what anyone says, and her memory is about as retentive as a rotted volleyball net. "He's scheduled for surgery the last week of April," Kerry says. "I have to fly out to Connecticut for that."

"Oh, my gosh, I am *so-so-so-o-o-o* sorry! I had no idea. Why didn't you tell me?" Leah's tone upshifts from compassionate to mildly scolding before sharpening with suspicion. "What's *wrong* with him anyway?"

Percy, her daughter's cat, suffers from feline kidney disease, an ailment that doesn't sound right for a human child, and Kerry regrets stirring Leah's sympathy, however performative and brief it is. "Tonsils," she says. "He's having his tonsils out."

"Why, that's nothing," Leah tells her. "I had mine removed when I was six or seven. It's no big deal. How old is he?"

Kerry calculates her grand-cat's age. "Twelve," she says.

"I didn't know you had a grandson. *Say*, didn't you tell me that your daughter—"

"Percy's adopted," Kerry says. "Listen, I'm just on my way out the door."

"At least, *think* about coming with me to the concert. *Leon Russell*, for heaven's sake!"

"Leah, I really have to go. Talk soon. Bye." Kerry re-cradles the receiver.

VI

JUST SUPPOSE THAT KERRY COULD have loved Takashi. She tried, didn't she? Kerry calls up a montage of images like paging through a well-worn photo album: the trips to Panama City Beach, Susan's tap-dance recital, Scott's underbaked banana bread presented as a Mother's Day gift. The brightest of these feature their children. She can't pull up a single shiny snapshot from before Susan was born. Kerry mostly remembers the apartment they rented back then, that terrible mantel clock—whatever happened to it?—click-click-clicking to mark the day's inexorable progression into night. Just after signing the marriage certificate, she and Takashi sat on a sunny bench outside of city hall, holding hands. Buttery warmth caressing her face and honey-scented breezes ruffling her then-long blond hair, Kerry startled herself by speaking a reflection on love aloud. "Now I'll never know what it is."

Takashi dropped her hand. "What did you say?"

"Nothing." She gave him a sidelong look, smiled. "It's nothing."

After hanging up the phone, Kerry closes her eyes, blacking out the yellow walls, stainless steel fixtures, snowy curtains and dishtowels in her kitchen to envision her former husband, her *was*-band as one friend calls her ex. She says his name out loud, something she lets herself do just once each day. *I have sounded your name*, as one of Shikishi's poems ends, *which I miss*. With eyes shut, Kerry conjures Takashi's boot-black hair, his dark eyes, and wide mouth, the expression of a discontented toad on his face. The last time she saw him, more than two years ago, he stood before a bin of ginger in the DeKalb Farmers Market. He held up a scabby knob, gazing at the beige root as if at last confronting the finality of death. His jawline had lost its precision, his cheeks had softened and sunk, his complexion the color of cream in a zinc bucket. Kerry steered her cart away before he noticed and then pretended not to notice her.

She regathers her belongings and heads out the door, careful to key the knob, then slide the two deadbolts—*snick, snick*—behind her.

VII

WHAT IF, WITHOUT FINDING THE missing verse, Kerry could crack the code of the love poems, instead of being flummoxed by most of these? The translated collection of Shikishi's poetry, *String of Beads*, contains three one-hundred poem sequences: A, B, and C, followed by D with just ninety-nine miscellaneous poems. Sequence A's fifteen love poems, or "beads," are somewhat clear to Kerry, but in Sequence B, the writing grows vague and strange, confusing her. Several pieces mention sleeves in a baffling way. One goes like this:

> *Desperate, I picked watercress in Shallow Marsh Field: if I could show him my decaying sleeves*

And another reads:

> *My sleeves are wet and I keep this secret, yet how would I deal with the safflower?*

What is going on with those sleeves? And the safflower, for that matter? As Kerry waits in the prison's parking lot for Fred, she skims the poems again for references to sleeves. She flips to a page where sleeves are lodged with evening dew; then they are an abyss that is "much deeper than yesterday"; a few poems later, they are "unknown to Princess Tatsuta" and they begin to color; in a final mention, sleeves are shower sprinkled. A kimono sleeve can be voluminous, but can it really be called an abyss? Kerry fingers the frayed cuff of her painting smock.

Fred soon glides his compact car into the space alongside Kerry's car. He smiles and waves an orange tube of sunblock in greeting. A redhead, Fred burns easily, so he slathers his skin with high SPF unguents throughout the day. He's an earnest man, a bit younger than her own son, yet already married to a woman who is expecting their first child. He now swings his car door open and stretches his bare legs to apply cream clear up to the hem of his cargo shorts. Sunblock streaks his face and glistens on his rust-colored arm and leg hair. By day, Fred manages an office supply superstore, and he volunteers either at the homeless shelter or the prison in the evenings. He longs to institute a program that offers college credits to the inmates. Though inspired by his sincerity, Kerry can't see how college credits, even if these accumulate toward degrees, will benefit the men on death row.

Fred caps the tube and tosses it into his glove box. He reaches for his materials and climbs out of his car. Kerry and Fred trudge across the blacktop toward the main entrance to the prison, chatting about Fred's wife, her morning sickness. The complex itself consists of a central structure, surrounded by five separate units, squat concrete buildings, all of which are enclosed by tall fencing topped with spirals of razor wire. Kerry imagines the chain-link is electrified, though no signs warn of this. The only signage she sees prohibits weapons, drugs, alcoholic beverages, and smoking. Once Kerry and Fred step into the building, they must hand over art supplies for examination by a guard and empty their pockets. They drop change and keys into a blue bowl where they will remain at the desk. Then they step through the metal detector and turn all the way around within a red square taped to the floor while a guard waves a paddle-shaped wand over them. Usually, this is enough, but today, a guard says they must be patted down.

VIII

IF ONLY KERRY KNEW WHAT she was supposed to feel when a uniformed black woman runs hands along her torso and pant legs, then maybe she wouldn't flinch in a way that likely seems racist or even anti-gay to the mannish guard. Apart from the handshaking and shoulder bumps, this is the most physical contact she's had with another human being in months. She doesn't know whether to be sad or relieved about that. In fact, Kerry loses the thread of her thought when the woman releases her to rejoin Fred after he has been frisked. They collect their materials and make their way to the next building, another checkpoint, where they exchange their driver's licenses for an ultraviolet-light stamp on the back of their left hands.

Next, they head through a short corridor with doors on either end. One door can't be opened until the other clicks shut. This door leads outside to a caged passageway, where again, the second chain-link gate doesn't buzz open until the first locks. Then they step into the third structure. This is death row. It's a labyrinthine setup through which they must continually move to the right. Kerry, though her sense of direction is not bad, would be lost in this maze of corridors and rooms without the simple rule to keep right. Right turn from the corridor to the first enclosure; right door out of the enclosure; right turn to the visiting area with its plastic scoop chairs, crates of grubby toys, and coffee tables piled with tatty magazines; right entrance to the next common area; and right door to the workroom.

Keeping right and right and right, Kerry and Fred pass khaki-shirted guards, many blank-faced or hostile-looking, as well as inmates milling about in white T-shirts and pants. Sometimes prisoners wear their T-shirts inside out. While Kerry's sure this is significant, she has no idea what it means. A few drape T-shirts over their heads, rolled up in front and long in back like legionnaire's caps. Now and then, she and Fred recognize a student from their class, and the handshaking, the shoulder bumping ensues. The men, who are only allowed to shower every other day, sometimes smell musky and sour. Even so, their embraces, though brief, feel cushioned and sturdy, cozy as nudging against well-padded recliners.

The workroom is a former conference room with a battered rectangular table in the center. The men must sit in mismatched chairs around it or stand and stoop to paint atop it. Kerry and Fred usually stroll about the room examining student work. It takes several minutes for the prisoners to be summoned for the class. During this time a loud and reverberant cacophony fills the high-ceilinged chamber: chairs scraping, overhead fans flapping, door slamming, laughter and raised voices: *Hey, Akeel. Hi, Abdul. Where's Ronnie? How've you been? What up, Fred? Hey, Kerry, how's it going, gal? Isn't Tico coming today? How are you? Doing okay? How you?*

IX

SUPPOSE DEWAYNE DOESN'T ATTEND TODAY. That he isn't among the stragglers cheers Kerry. Last week, he presented her with an envelope at the end of the session. "Read this," he insisted. DeWayne has rightly targeted her as an apologetic white woman, who—if she can't do exactly what he wants—will feel terrible about this. Apart from DeWayne, Kerry likes most of the men, even has her favorites. Akeel, a squat and muscular young man from Memphis, is one of these. His twangy voice is melodious, so comforting that Kerry's shoulders loosen when he speaks. Though she's not from Memphis, not even from the South, Kerry experiences Akeel's smooth drawl like a glowing porch light on a wintry night, the promise of food, music, and laughter within—a homecoming.

Today, Akeel, in wire-framed glasses, looks professorial, despite his long sideburns, his Fu Manchu that tapers into a long skinny beard, and his Māori warrior tattoos. He slips Kerry a poem he's written. She reads it while Fred distributes paints and brushes. Akeel's piece consists of three meticulously printed stanzas, each a rhymed couplet posing a rhetorical question that asks what has become of an innocent boy.

"It's heartfelt," Kerry tells Akeel. "I can see you put a lot of emotion into this, and it's very moving." Her son Scott, before accepting the Lord Jesus Christ as his Personal Savior, was a poet with two published collections, and Kerry herself composes sonnets and sestinas, though most often haikus and tankas in her daily journal. Apart from Princess Shikishi's verses, she reads a lot of poetry and even belongs to a group wherein members share their favorite poems each week. So of course, she finds Akeel's piece trite and clichéd, though she would never say this to him. It *is* heartfelt and she does feel moved by his impulse to write it and to slide it shyly over the tabletop for her to read. "It's much clearer than the poems in the collection I'm reading now," she says, thinking of Shikishi's beguiling sleeves.

DeWayne, at last, breezes into the workroom to claim a center seat, and Kerry reaches into her bag for the envelope he gave her last week. It contains a sheet of notepaper filled on both sides with elegant cursive—a piece titled "The Wonderment of God's Love." *The wonderment of God's love is absolutely heart-possessing,* it begins. Just four paragraphs, the thing seemed to go on and on for Kerry. *My heart is awakened to an overwhelming indulgence of seemingly boundless titillation, creating an explosion of intoxicating feelings throughout every aspect of my existence, giving me countless reasons to undoubtedly believe in my destiny . . .*

Like Akeel, DeWayne is scheduled for execution as soon as officials settle upon a way to handle the controversy and protest this will cause. Both men may be gone before she is. Though it would be rude to ask, Kerry wonders what crimes they have committed to wind up on death row. She's far more interested in the irony of a condemned killer's undoubting belief in his destiny, than in the four platitudinous paragraphs DeWayne has produced. Still, she's affixed small yellow Post-it Notes to the piece he asked her to critique. *Great vocabulary! Terrific energy! What lovely handwriting!* Kerry now hands the envelope to him, and the big man's dark face splits with a grin. He slips it into the waistband of his bleached scrubs.

After a quick watercolor lesson by Fred and a demonstration on using kosher salt and cellophane to create the effect of texture, the men dip their brushes in water jars and commence daubing paper. Kerry and Fred wander among the student painters, pausing to comment on the work. In the periphery, she glimpses DeWayne opening the envelope she's handed him. The men paint images from magazine pictures that Kerry and Fred clip for the workshop, since they are not allowed to bring in objects for still-life painting. Most of the paintings are crude as elementary school efforts, but each week, Kerry sees improvement. Figures in the background of the prairie Akeel is working on now resemble creatures—buffalos or perhaps bears—and not boulders after all. Gary's bowl of fruit looks much less like a blurry bunch of balloons, and Abdul's fish, while still blobby, now sports an unmistakable tail fin.

X

IF ONLY DEWAYNE PAINTED AS blithely as he wrote, then Kerry could glance over his shoulder, murmur encouragement, and drift on to the next inmate. But DeWayne has an uncanny gift for perspective, light and shadow, a keen sensibility for color. He paints from memory to render his grandfather's truck. Kerry pauses as he mixes blue with yellow and red to produce a dull gray for a shaded section of chrome in the grillwork. The truck is nearly done, and the image stuns Kerry in its depth of detail and accuracy. From a few feet away, the watercolor resembles a well-composed photograph of the barn-sheltered Ford.

"I wasn't sure," he tells Kerry, "whether to show you my writing or not."

"Oh?" she says.

"I didn't think you'd understand."

"Really?" Kerry is more puzzled, than offended. "Why not?"

"Don't get me wrong. I'm glad you read it." He strokes the paintbrush's bristles on the jar's rim, drawing its fine hairs to a point. "But it's like playing music for the deaf, isn't it? It's like showing this to a blind person." DeWayne indicates his painting with the brush. "You don't believe, do you?" His deep brown eyes bore into hers, and the amber-tinged sclera prompts Kerry to wonder if he is jaundiced. As if mirror-gazing, she sees illness a lot these days.

"Believe?"

"In love, not even God's love."

"Well, I'm not really—"

"See, I knew that." DeWayne nods. "I could tell."

Kerry's face fills with heat. "Still, I enjoyed reading your writing."

"I feel sorry for you," he says.

"I believe in the possibility of love." Kerry keeps her tone even, though heat now pulses in her ears. *Here you are*, she thinks, *basking in the light of love for God. Here you are, DeWayne. Alive. Here. In this place. Because another human being is not.* Kerry shakes her head to shed the thought the way a dog flings off water. In her last sticky note on his piece, she wrote: *I'm curious about the context for such conviction.*

She hesitated to use that word—conviction, but now, she hopes the double-meaning nettles him.

"I feel bad that you can't open your heart to love." DeWayne strokes the underside of the chrome grill with the tip of his brush, creating a precise pencil line.

Kerry smiles at him in an encouraging way, certain that this will be the last time she sees him. She'll tell Fred that she must move to Memphis next week. "Nice shadow," she says.

XI

WHAT IF SHE COULD CONTROL her dreams? Then Kerry would never dream she is still married to Takashi. The recurring nightmare feels more dreadful than it would be to dream of herself behind bars alongside Akeel and DeWayne. In it, her children are sometimes their young selves—the bright and affectionate children she lost when they grew up—and she's thrilled to see them. But then there's Takashi, stubborn as a wart and blanched with silent fury. He never raised a hand to Kerry or the children. He rarely raised his voice, but night after night, he would pull her knees apart, waking her once, sometimes twice. She doesn't miss it, doesn't miss it at all. That clicking mantel clock, the sun's last flash of flame at dusk, the welling shadows—these no longer send the walls spinning, her heart banging against her ribcage like a frantic sparrow.

Now, her bed—a nest of flannel linen and soft quilts—offers more comfort, more absolution than the people she loves best. In it, Kerry leans against her many pillows, her raw-looking hands often holding open a book of poems. Sometimes the book drops to the floor when she drifts to sleep. Safe, she tells herself, I am safe and I belong only to me. Kerry sometimes dreams of flying. Clouds misting her forehead and cheeks as aerial images of islands appear below like the sequence of drawings she's penned. Now and again, she dreams of Leon Russell, his lustrous white hair, those dazzling sapphire eyes. *To count on nightly dreams,* Shikishi wrote in a bead more comprehensible than most others, *to know someone faintly, the one I think of but have yet to meet.* Kerry throws back the covers to invite him into her bed, and in the morning she finds the quilts clumped on the floor, though she rouses from sleep—even on chilly mornings—warm and buzzing with contentment.

But when she dreams of herself in the past, married to Takashi, Kerry wakes with her throat raw as a wound, her pillow damp and salty.

XII

IF ONLY KERRY HAD HAD the foresight to hold onto a few of the many orange vials she'd turned over to the DEA authorized collector when her parents passed away, then she could have packed up the garage today, separating photos, trophies, and mementos into cartons for Susan and Scott. The last thing she wants is for her children to squabble over the sentimental debris of their lives. Now she has little choice but to visit Leah. Since calling about the concert, the woman's phoned to invite her to lunch at her house, and Kerry's put this off until a month before the Leon Russell concert. She's run out of excuses at the same time that she sees a purpose for the visit.

Though she's dropped Leah off after running into her at an art show, Kerry has never been inside her oversized house. From the street where she's now parked, Leah's "mansion" resembles a convent for especially wayward nuns. She yanks up the brake, and her cellphone pings—a text from her daughter. The last time they spoke, Susan talked about leaving her husband, about taking the cat and moving to Georgia. She intended to move in with Kerry and to find a job teaching art. But that was weeks ago, and though Kerry was sympathetic and open to Susan's plans, she heard nothing more from her daughter, and Susan has not returned her calls. Kerry lifts her sunglasses to read the message: *Percy's tumor benign!*

Tumor? While Kerry's large hands manipulate toothpick-sized paintbrushes with ease, her fingers fumble on this tiny keypad. Kerry begins typing in one word: *Great!* Surely, she can manage that, though her fingers, now filmed with perspiration, have swollen in the heat, bulbing at the tips into slippery little clubs. Still, she touches G and R. Then, *oops*—another R! Kerry's thumb slides, pressing SEND. She's texted her daughter a message that reads: *Grr . . .* As if she is angry, growling at the good news about her grandcat's tumor. She phones Susan, but she gets voicemail. Unable to explain her mistake succinctly, Kerry asks her daughter to call her back. She slips her phone into her bag and opens the car door to climb out.

From the sidewalk, Leah's house, with its narrow grilled windows and fanglike columns, resembles a predatory beast, crouched and ready to pounce. The balmy Atlanta neighborhood of ranch-style homes and neat lawns throws Leah's malevolent mansion into sharp relief. Kerry struggles to recall Leah's husband's name as she paces the cement walkway unspooling like a lascivious gray tongue from the porch. She met him at a tea for new faculty, before Leah was fired. The man was a shrill abomination, a gargoyle with so many lumps, pocks, and blemishes that he looked barnacle-encrusted, like part of a shipwreck propped in a wheelchair. He'd boasted and griped, interrupting and insulting others as if his advanced age and debility, his near-death status gave him license for dispensing abuse. "You don't know shit from Shinola!" he'd crowed at Leah again and again.

Kerry lifts the knocker, an oxidized hasp that stains her fingertips. She thuds it against the thick door, wondering how on earth anyone will hear it from the bowels of Leah's vast abode. And no one seems to. A mower putters in the distance, and a dog barks nearby. Leaves on the desiccated magnolia in Leah's yard rattle like maracas with a steamy gust. Kerry knocks again and again. After several seconds, the front door yawns wide, and Leah appears, wearing a black apron with white lettering that reads: SHUT THE FRONT DOOR! Kerry steps over the threshold to oblige.

"You're here! You're really, *really* here!"

Kerry succumbs to Leah's cigarette-smoke scented embrace. "Well, you invited me, and I accepted, so here I am." She follows Leah through a shadowy corridor that opens into a furniture-stuffed parlor. Leah reaches behind a sofa to haul out a small collie by its ruff. "This is Shelley." Wild-eyed, the dog whimpers, writhing to get free. This room is so cluttered and dank, so flocculent with dust and fur that Kerry hesitates to draw breath. The sharp tang of urine spoils any appetite she might have had for the fatty foods—pimento cheese, buttery crackers, olives, macaroni salad—displayed on the coffee table.

Leah draws the dog, trembling as if demented by cold, to her bosom and kisses its narrow head. She then releases it, and the collie scrambles back behind the couch. "Don't you just love dogs?" she says. "But you're a cat person, aren't you?"

Kerry draws breath to mention Percy, his tumor, before remembering her excuse for not going with Leah to the concert. "I *am* fond of cats," she says, after a pause.

XIII

IF ONLY LEAH HAD BOTHERED to run a Dustbuster over the upholstery, then Kerry would plop down without a second thought. Instead, she glances at a discolored seat cushion shaggy with dog hairs and then at her newish black capris. Oh, what the hell. When Kerry sinks into the sofa's lap, a poof of dust whooshes out. Leah sits across from her on a wicker chair and spoons macaroni salad onto a Styrofoam plate. Leah's straight reddish brown hair is much thicker than Kerry remembers it being. It's synthetically glossy under the glow of the overhead fixture. Why, Leah's wearing a wig! And she's applied coral lipstick and blushing powder to her cheeks. Kerry's heart softens at the preparations made for this visit, even if Leah didn't quite break out the broom, and dust rags.

"What about your husband," Kerry says. "Isn't he joining us?"

"Oh, he's not here." Leah plunges the serving spoon into the pimento cheese. "He wasn't doing too great, so I put him in hospice care."

Kerry sits upright. "I had no idea." The man is gone, no doubt taking with him . . . well, *everything* she needs. Plans dashed, Kerry ransacks her mind for an excuse to leave at once—a sudden migraine, hives, appendicitis? But she doubts she can pull off an impromptu health crisis. "How awful," she says at last, "for *you*, I mean."

Leah waves her spoon, flinging a clot of cheese onto the floor. "It's fine, really."

Kerry wept when her father was admitted into a hospice center, knowing that he would not be coming home again. "Isn't that just palliative care?" she asks. "Doesn't hospice mean—"

"He's better off." Leah grins again. "Believe me, he's lucky he made it to the hospice."

"Still . . ." Kerry concedes that she must at least have a meal with poor Leah. "This has to be hard for you. You should let me take you out for lunch and save all this for dinner." A brownish scrim crusts the tub of pimento cheese and the macaroni salad emits a sour smell.

"You're joking!" Leah tilts her chin at the coffee table. "Everything's ready. I've even got wine. You still like Chardonnay?"

Kerry nods. If she can't eat—and she can't see herself digging into those greasy tubs—she will at least drink. Leah produces a dewy bottle from an ice bucket nearby. As she uncorks and pours the wine, Leah talks about a psychic she's been seeing. "I'm going to find love, Kerry! Can you believe it? At my age, I'm going to find love!"

"Not on the internet, right?" Kerry says.

"I'm not pretending to be people, if that's what you're asking." Leah sniffs. "I don't do that anymore. Enough about me! I want to hear what you're up to these days, now that you're a lady of leisure. Have you cleared probate yet?"

Kerry again draws a deep breath, opens her mouth. This is a chance to correct that small lie she told when she retired from Birnbrau, when she claimed to have inherited enough from her parents that she no longer had to work. Why not tell Leah, who remembers little and who, when she speaks, is rarely believed? Plus, none of their former colleagues still talk to Leah. It would be like whispering into a kimono sleeve or shouting into an abyss. *I really didn't inherit anything,* she could say, *but bad blood.* Instead, Kerry summons her version of an enigmatic smile. She stands, resisting the urge to brush off her backside. "May I use your restroom?"

Leah points the way with a spork.

The pink-tiled room reeks of mildew and wood rot. Kerry parts the shower curtains to find a ten-pound sack of dog food, a small TV, a plunger, two fishing rods, a tarnished statue of Ganesh, a dartboard, an empty aquarium, a basket of what looks to be unopened mail—all in the tub. Kerry drops the curtain and tiptoes to the sink. She glances at the reflection of her large freckled face before easing open the medicine chest. The row of orange vials causes her to gasp. Kerry lifts a plastic bottle, turns it to read the label. Raymond Caspian. Of course, *Raymond* is his name. He gets constipated with opioids, Leah said, complaining of the difficulty in getting his pain meds right. Kerry takes the vials, one after another, from the shelf: OxyContin, Darvocet, Fentanyl . . . "Hello, my pretties," she whispers.

XIV

WHAT IF LEON RUSSELL SPOTS her way out here in the cheap seats? He's cupping his eyes—those arresting blue eyes!—to gaze out and greet the crowd. She can barely see him, but what if he glimpses her between Lucinda and Jane, a trio of women well past forty at a rock concert given by a man in his seventies? He'd most likely notice Jane first, with her wide eyes and well-shaped face, though Lucinda, her black eyebrows magnified behind large horn-rimmed glasses, might arrest his attention with the accusatory look on her face. In such company, he'd overlook Kerry, her complexion as washed out as her sandy gray hair. For him to see her, she'd have to stand, wave her arms about, shouting. *Yoo-hoo, Leon! Here, I am!* Instead, Kerry remains seated, beating her palms together with others in the audience and beaming at the thumb-sized figure on stage as if he were connected to her in a secret but powerful way.

As the band launches into "Tight Rope," Kerry perches at the rim of her seat, peering at the stage as if gazing through a window into another world, a vibrant and shimmering place where, yes, if she wanted, she could tremble with love for a man. But the off-key sing-alongs in the audience distract her. "Oof," she says. "Why can't people just listen in silence?"

Jane shrugs, and Lucinda says, "Fuckers." She glares at a sunburnt woman nearby who's shrieking, "'Flanked by life and the funeral pyre!'"

For too long, Kerry has been balancing that whopping lie of omission with small and clumsy falsehoods of commission as if on a high wire. *One side's ice and one is fire.* No, no, nothing as thrilling as that. She shrugs off the song's influence. It's as if she's been alone in a small space, holding the hard news close the way Scott would cling to his terry cloth dinosaur. What did he call that thing? *Boolie*, wasn't it? Scott would cling to Boolie, fingering its button eyes like worry beads. "Words," Kerry would urge him. "Use your words to *tell me* how you feel." As Leon Russell performs, his miniscule form in the distance seems to exhort, even to challenge Kerry to do the same. This is the subtext undergirding his lyrics and gestures, exactly what he means when he whips ropy strands of sweat-drenched hair from his face.

XV

WHAT IF KERRY PRETENDS NOT to see Leah? But there she is bumping a wheelchair toward the concessions area during intermission. Just as Kerry recognizes the glossy auburn wig with a jolt, Leah raises her head, a puzzled look on her face. Then she wrenches the chair away, steering it back toward the auditorium. "There's Leah," Kerry murmurs, stunned that Raymond Caspian has recovered enough to be released from hospice care.

"I know," Lucinda says. "Just act like you don't see her."

"Look away," Jane tells her.

"I can't do *that*." Kerry breaks from the line and dashes through the crowd to catch up with the barreling wheelchair. She opens her handbag, fumbles for her checkbook. She will at least offer to pay for the pills she's taken. "Leah! Leah!" she calls.

Leah thrusts the chair forward, but a wheel catches, stalling her. As she jostles the chair, struggling to free it, Kerry reaches her side.

"I thought you had to go out of town," Leah says. "I thought your grandson was supposed to be having surgery."

Kerry's face flames. "Oh, yes, well, they rescheduled things. There was a—something even *more serious* that came up, for the doctor, I mean, and so . . . *Postponed*, it was postponed."

"I see." Leah squints at Lucinda and Jane, still in line for the restroom. Lucinda, who was cruel to Leah when they were at an artists' retreat, gives a jaunty wave.

"It's great that your husband's doing better." With her checkbook, Kerry indicates the blanket-bundled figure in the wheelchair. Even if he appears to enjoy the oblivion of sleep, Kerry deeply regrets what she's done. If she'd known he would return from hospice, Kerry never would have tossed entire vials into her purse.

"My husband *died* last week," Leah says. "Not that you care."

"Oh, my god!" Relieved and horrified, Kerry backpedals. So, a *corpse*? Has Leah wheeled a cadaver to the concert just to avoid wasting a ticket?

The man in the wheelchair stirs. He opens one eye, revealing a slimy half-moon of sclera, and Kerry cries out.

"This is Neil," Leah says, her voice softening. "Remember what the psychic told me?"

"Psychic?" Kerry's head swarms. Voices break apart, words separating from meaning. A dense and dizzying heat rises from the milling concertgoers. Along with the stench of cologne and sweat, the odor of problematic plumbing wafts from the restrooms nearby. Kerry clamps the wheelchair with one hand, worried she might faint.

"You don't ever listen to me, do you?" Leah says. "I told you the psychic predicted I'd find love, and I have." She smiles down at Neil. "I *really* have."

"But he's . . ." Kerry releases the wheelchair and steps back again. No polite way to complete her sentence, she closes her mouth.

Leah leans in to say, "Completely mute. Oh, he hears everything, but since his stroke, he can't speak a word." She straightens up. "He writes the sweetest things on Post-it Notes."

Neil closes his eye, and Leah kicks the wayward wheel straight. "We'd better get back to our seats." She winks at Kerry and thrusts the chair forward. "We're all the way in front—the handicapped section!" she calls over her shoulder.

Kerry blinks, and Leah vanishes into the crowd now streaming back into the auditorium. She admires how deftly Leah maneuvers the wheelchair out of sight, but then she's had lots of practice. Kerry returns to the line where Lucinda and Jane still wait. Perhaps they have moved up a foot or so; it's hard to tell. Lights flash, signaling the end of the break. Kerry doesn't have much time. First, she makes them swear never to tell a soul and then she blurts it out, in a rush like an impossibly long word that corrects the big lie of omission and the smaller ones of commission and ends with Kerry admitting she's told no one, not even her children about this.

Jane searches her face. "What will you do?"

"Nothing," Kerry says. Not chemo, not radiation, not a single ghastly thing that will only make her sicker longer, like her parents in their last months—her mother milky-eyed and bald, her father silent and sunken, his blue-veined hands ceaselessly raking the bedcovers. This is why she can't tell her children: They will want her to do things. They will want her to start now. She thinks of the orange vials, the fifth of vodka she bought days ago—not for tonight, not for this week or next, but for a time she knows will come.

"Fucking white blood cells," Lucinda says, "You could have told us sooner."

"But I didn't want you to feel . . ." From the way Lucinda cocks her head, from the perplexed look on Jane's face, Kerry sees that they have *always* felt sorry for her.

"What can *we* do?" Jane asks.

Kerry shrugs. There's nothing anyone can do.

Then Lucinda turns to Jane. "Are you thinking what I'm thinking?"

"No one's ever thinking what you're thinking," Jane says

"Make a wish!" Lucinda rummages in her outsized handbag.

"Why?" Takashi's name rises like a burning gulp at the back of Kerry's throat, and a fragment from one of Shikishi's poems surfaces in her thoughts: *The moon in its vagueness gives a glimpse of his loveless face.*

"Not why, *what*—the Make-A-Wish Foundation." When they are again seated in the auditorium, Lucinda produces a trio of nametags, remnants of academic conferences she's attended, from her voluminous purse.

"Don't you ever throw anything away?" Jane says.

"I guess not." Lucinda hands Jane a Sharpie. "You know what the logo looks like?"

"I can look it up on my phone."

Lucinda takes a nametag and removes the rectangle of cardboard from its plastic casing. She reverses it—blank side up—before giving it to Jane, who's uncapped the marker.

Kerry looks from Lucinda to Jane. "What are you doing?"

"We," Jane says, "are getting backstage passes."

A terrible idea, Kerry insists as Lucinda pins the badge to her blouse, a stupid thing that can get them all in trouble. Though Jane is a gifted graphic artist and the nametags *do* look authentic, someone is sure to see they are fakes. A personal assistant will know this is not on the itinerary. They will be turned away in derision or worse— detained until police arrive. Yet after the last encore, staff members, weary and likely high, are bemused by the superannuated Make-A-Wisher. "I'm not doing this," Kerry says, and Lucinda elbows her gently. The first layer of security, beefy men in tight T-shirts, waves them through to the next. One formidable giant wears the same arrogant scowl that DeWayne often adopts. Even so, he raises a braided rope for them to pass. "I just *can't*," Kerry hisses, but soon they face a harassed-looking blonde, fortyish and wearing skinny blue jeans and a concert T-shirt. She squints at them, examines the sheaf of pages affixed to her clipboard, looks at Kerry again, and sighs. "Come with me," she says.

Heart hammering her throat, Kerry trails the blonde's heart-shaped denim buttocks. The woman leads her away from Jane and Lucinda and through a long steamy corridor. At last, they stand before a wooden door with a peeling red star appliqued on it. The woman taps the door with her knuckles. "Mr. Russell," she says, "Mr. Russell, your Make-A-Wish person is here." She turns to Kerry. "Ten minutes, okay?" She checks her watch and strides off. Several seconds pass, during which Kerry detects no sounds from behind the door.

What if she slinks back through the corridor to where Jane and Lucinda are waiting? She could tell her friends that he is kind and funny, that he has smooth skin and straight teeth, soft eyes and a quick smile. Kerry can say that up close his eyes are bluer than the Aegean Sea, bluer than lapis lazuli, bluer than even blue can be. She winces at such rhymed doggerel. Oh, she's so close. *What to do?* Shikishi asks in one poem, an un-sequenced bead at the end of the collection. *I'd die of love if I did not think of meeting him, prolonging my life until then.* Kerry's right hand curls into a fist. She raps once, then twice more.

The knob rattles, hinges squeal, and the door at last swings wide.

Truffles

With apologies to Susan Glaspell

"**B**ut, Professor Aragon, that girl sounds just like Dracula," Randall said. After Lucinda had dismissed her last class of the day, Randall Ripley trailed her across campus into her office. They'd crunched over frozen grass, power walking and huffing into their hands to keep warm. As a consequence, they'd been unable to say much to one another along the way. Now Randall, still wearing his fleece-lined jacket, plonked into one of the folding chairs facing Lucinda's cluttered desk, his orchidaceous cheeks dewy with perspiration. "The audience will wonder what the heck a vampire's *doing* in Nebraska."

"Maybe so, but Nadezhda's learned the part." Lucinda shrugged off her coat, draped it on her chair behind the desk before sinking into the seat. Winter, late in arriving, had dawdled this year. Snow still sifted over Birnbrau Women's College in northeast Georgia well into the first week of March, and Lucinda was glad for her full-length wool coat, even if it smelled of barbecue potato chips—a thrift store find, she was proud of the price, too.

"She knows *all* the parts." With his pellucid eyes, high cheekbones, full lips, and that single obsidian curl arranged on his forehead like an upside-down question mark, Randall would make a stunning Mrs. Hale. But a cross-dressing—albeit gorgeous—Midwestern farmwife circa the early 1900's would be nearly as incongruous as a vampirish one. When students first performed the play in Composition and

Literature I, she'd assigned the role to Nadezhda, a Romanian exchange student. Nadezhda had delivered Mrs. Hale's many lines with precision, even if her voice was accented and oddly deep for a nineteen-year-old girl. Now that the class prepared to stage Susan Glaspell's *Trifles* for the entire student body, Lucinda proposed that Nadezhda continue in the role, embittering Randall, a drama major.

"She knows the entire play," he continued. "It's nothing for her to switch with me, and—think about it—people can deal with a sheriff who's an outsider, say, someone who moved from Transylvania for the job. But Mrs. Hale's supposed to have lived in Nebraska her *whole* life!"

Covertly, Lucinda admired Randall's glacial eyes, the glossy black lashes fringing these. Every now and again, a young man would turn up in classes at the women's college, but none as comely as Randall. These were the sons of faculty and staff, taking advantage of tuition discounts offered to dependents of fulltime employees. Usually, such young men had the sense to apply at peer institutions sharing reciprocity with Birnbrau, rather than enroll in the women's college that advertised on billboards featuring a fluffy-haired blonde clutching a similarly fluffy Yorkie, billboards promoting Birnbrau *'cuz girls just wanna have fun!* Randall, in fact, was Lucinda's first male student at the college, a sweetly incompetent plagiarist whom she liked, despite the off-topic essay—easily traced to Cheapresearchpapers.com—that he'd turned in at midterm, earning him a zero on the assignment and exacerbating the hard feelings between Lucinda and his mother, the registrar.

"I already asked Nadezhda, and she says she doesn't mind," Randall claimed.

The product of a rigorous Central-European educational system, Nadezhda proved capable of memorizing just about anything, so she was often tapped for monologue performances and extended recitations. For February's convocation, she'd unfalteringly delivered the "I Have a Dream" speech, but when Lucinda closed her eyes, she pictured the Count from *Sesame Street* at the podium issuing Martin Luther King Jr.'s unforgettable words.

Randall scanned Lucinda's face with a hopeful gaze. "She said she'd be fine if we switched." No doubt Nadezhda, an art major, would have preferred being left out of the play altogether and having more time to paint. The girl was like Lucinda in this way, though Lucinda was a writer, not a painter. Her first book had been accepted for publication, and the previous week, the press sent revision notes. Due to teaching and other Brinbrau nonsense, Lucinda could only work on the manuscript in fits and bursts. She now regretted offering to have her class perform the play; the time-consuming trouble this entailed had already commenced.

"Why do you want to play Mrs. Hale anyway?" Lucinda asked Randall. What was it with these males who coveted female roles? When she taught middle school, her class staged an abridged version of *A Raisin in the Sun*, and two thirteen-year-old boys nearly got into a fistfight over who would play Mama. Lesser conflicts erupted when it came to casting Beneatha and Ruth. While the eighth-grade girls appeared neutral about the roles they were assigned, the boys competed fiercely for the chance to don the cast-off dresses, skirts, and blouses, to rock the outdated pocketbooks parents had contributed for the play.

Randall gave her an exasperated look. "That's the *lead*."

Lucinda raised an eyebrow. Was Mrs. Hale really the protagonist? She hadn't counted lines, but the play's dialogue seemed evenly distributed among four of the five characters.

"She's the dramatic core of the story," he said. "You're always talking about choice and change. Well, Mrs. Hale's the one who makes the choice and change. This is a dream role for me, Professor Aragon, something I can put on my resume."

Surely, Minnie Wright, the character who strangles her joyless and punitive husband, exercises the most significant choice—one that catalyzes the greatest change for all the characters, especially, of course, for Mr. Wright. But Minnie, locked in a jail cell, remains offstage for the duration of the one-act play, and Lucinda had zero desire to go into this more with Randall now. She was hungry and tired, eager to collect her granddaughter from daycare, pick up dinner from a pizzeria not known for contributing to pro-life causes, and return home to her revisions. "You'd have time to learn the lines?"

Randall closed his eyes, held a fist to his heart. "She used to wear pretty clothes," he said, his voice a histrionic falsetto, "and be lively, when she was Minnie Foster, one of the town girls singing in the choir. But that—oh, that was *thirty* years ago—"

"All right, all right," Lucinda said. "I'll think about it . . . But you'd better not ham it up like that when it comes time to perform the play."

"Of course not!" He shook his head with force, but his ivory cheeks and the tips of his ears grew quite pink.

Footsteps pounded in the stairwell, a pair of shadows soon welled near the threshold to her office, and Lucinda groaned inwardly. She'd hoped to leave a few minutes early, or at least on time, for once.

"Well, I won't keep you." Upon issuing her tried-and-true phrase for dismissing students who lingered after their business had been concluded, Lucinda stood. But Randall remained seated, so she stepped around her desk to approach him. "Thanks for stopping by." She hauled him to his feet with a handshake, then cupped his elbow, and steered him toward the door. "We can talk about this more after class on Thursday."

Lucinda released him with a mild shove and peered into the corridor, where she spied her friend and colleague Hailey Linder. Hailey, Director of the Women's Center, had accepted Lucinda's offer to have her class perform the play after Dean Cheek had slashed the Center's budget just days before Women's Her-story Month, preventing Hailey from hosting the textile artist she had invited. This meeting wouldn't take long, since Hailey should be as desperate as Lucinda to bolt from campus at the end of a long day. Alongside fair and compact Hailey stood a swarthy and even more compact man, with an oversized and absurdly handsome head. In fact, Lucinda, whose sister had sent her a YouTube link to Pedro Infante singing "Las Mañanitas" for her birthday, was startled by this man's resemblance to the iconic Mexican actor.

"Oh, hi," Lucinda said. She nodded at her friend's companion.

"Do you have a minute?" Hailey asked.

"I'm about to leave, but sure, I can spare a minute." Lucinda returned to the chair behind her desk as Hailey and her companion filed into the office to sit in the folding chairs facing her. These wobbled and creaked. Their flattish cushions sighed, emitting the familiar gassy sounds that filled Lucinda's entire being with dismay.

"Do you know Jesus?" Hailey indicated the Pedro-Infante-headed man seated beside her.

Lucinda smiled at him and shrugged in a noncommittal way.

"He's the supervising groundskeeper."

"Oh, right, right, *right*." Lucinda flushed. Of course, she knew Jesus. He had an uncanny knack for having his crew blast leaf blowers directly under the windows of her classroom during oral presentations. Jesus usually wore khaki coveralls and a safari hat with a mesh veil that obscured his face, while his crew members wore olive-green uniforms, though they, too, curtained their faces with snowy mesh. Cursing under her breath, Lucinda had flown from her classroom to confront him one afternoon in the fall semester. He'd nodded deferentially, his face no doubt contrite behind the netting, and he signaled his men to stop, but soon after she had returned to the class, a soft-spoken undergrad stepped to the podium and the leaf blowers roared again. "I didn't recognize you without your, your . . ." Not veil or scarf, not hijab—what *was* the word she wanted? Lucinda waved a hand before her face. "Mesh thing."

"Is for yellow jackets," he said, his voice a thin tenor.

"Oh, I *know*," Lucinda said. "They're everywhere, aren't they?" But surely, not in March, with snow on the ground. Earlier that day, she'd glanced out the window at a pair of groundskeepers revving snow blowers, both men's faces obscured by netting.

Hailey beamed at the groundskeeper. "Did you know Jesus is from Guatemala?"

Lucinda nodded. She'd expected as much—most of the groundskeepers were from Central America.

"But I bet you didn't know he was in a community theater group in Guatemala City." Hailey's faint eyebrows rose, as if she herself were astonished by the information she imparted.

Lucinda checked her watch. "Really?"

"He played Krogstad in *A Doll's House* once, and he was the main understudy for Sancho Panza when they performed *Man of La Mancha.*"

Jesus grinned, a gold tooth glinting.

"I had no idea. How interesting." Maybe Lucinda *would* get pizza from the place that gave money to pro-lifers. It was closer to her granddaughter's daycare, and stopping there could save ten, even fifteen minutes.

"Anyways . . .," Hailey said.

Lucinda pushed her chair away from her desk. "Well, I won't keep—"

"I told him about the play," Hailey said in a rush, "and it turns out, Jesus would love to perform in it. He wants to be an actor, so he has to stay limber, you see, as an actor . . ."

Jesus tapped his lips. "My ingles is very good."

"It'd be great," Hailey said, "if he could audition for a part in the play."

"But there are only five parts. It's just a one-act play."

"I will be the sheriff," Jesus said.

"See, he's read the play, and—"

"I've already cast the sheriff," Lucinda said, thinking of Nadezhda, but also not enjoying such presumptuousness and remembering again the episode with the leaf blowers.

Jesus shrugged. "Then, the abogado?"

"Let me think about it." Lucinda rose from her seat. "Long day," she said, looking at Jesus. "You must be exhausted from all the groundskeeping, so I won't detain you . . ."

JESUS SHOOK HIS huge and handsome head, now refusing the role that he'd cajoled Hailey into asking Lucinda to give him. Of course, he had no idea that after meeting with Lucinda, Hailey had sought out Jane Ellen Klamath, a colleague in fine arts who was a grand master at getting people to do what she wanted. Hailey had taken Jane a dozen clementines and promised to cover her classes on the day that Jane had to appear in court with her son, if she'd speak to Lucinda about Jesus. "No problem," Jane had said, and the next day, Lucinda emailed Hailey to offer Jesus the role of the county attorney. He didn't even have to audition for it.

On this unusually warm afternoon, Hailey and Jesus spread a drop cloth in the copse behind the groundskeeper's Quonset hut, where Jesus sometimes slept overnight in a cot amid the lawn maintenance equipment. They settled a red-and-black plaid flannel atop the tarp for the picnic—baguette, cheese, and wine—that Hailey had packed. She'd expected Jesus to reward her for this news with a gold-tooth flashing grin, his ears twitching as they often did when he was pleased. Instead, he hiked his buttock to pull a Spanish/English dictionary from the back pocket of his khakis. "She is so . . ." He flipped through the pages, overshot the mark, and paged back to find what he was after. "She is impertinent, rude, discourteous. To *me*."

Hailey reached around to rub the small of his back. "That's just Lucinda," she said. "She's like that to everyone. Why, if she were ever polite or tactful, we'd think she'd suffered a brain injury." Hailey explained again that—impertinent or not—Lucinda had kindly suggested the play after an art show by Hailey's mentor, a famous weaver, had fallen through, due to lack of resources to install the work and to pay the stiff honorarium the artist demanded. When she'd called with this disappointing news, Hailey hoped her mentor would agree to the visit without being paid. Here, she'd banked on her personal connection to the well-known weaver, recalling how the older woman used to have her collect dry cleaning, walk her Schnauzer, even mow her lawn, back when Hailey was her research assistant. But the artist, a tempestuous woman far more impertinent than Lucinda, had flat-out refused, before hanging up on her.

"I know, I know," Jesus said at last. "I understand." He lifted Hailey's free hand and brought it to his lips to gnaw gently on her thumb. Then he held her hand to his chest. "For you," he said. "I will perform in the play for *you*, but that woman, la profesora Aragón, she knows me not at all. She thinks I cut grass, sweep leaves. I have been to university. I have studied to be an actor. I love my country. I want to stay in my country, but I have to leave. I am the last of my brothers, and I have to leave for my mother, so she will not lose me, too. I am here because the people of this country, they have been in my country, making struggles so no one can stay . . ." He continued, lapsing into Spanish and telling about United Fruit Company and its nefarious practices, covert military involvement, assassinations, and civil war . . .

When he finished speaking and they'd eaten most of the bread and cheese and drunk all the wine, Jesus drew Hailey into his arms and whispered, "What means 'lap dance'?"

"Let me show you." Though she wasn't sure she could pull this off while he was seated on the ground, Hailey soon lost herself in excruciatingly slow movements, grinding and rubbing against Jesus. She shut her eyes, wondering if it was warm enough to slip off her blouse, a violet button-down she often wore. Hailey began unfastening it when droning sounded like a far-off lawn mower that was drawing closer and closer. Could Jesus be purring? Her eyes snapped open and a black-and-yellow blur bobbled in the periphery. A yellow jacket! Allergic to bees, Hailey would leap into swimming pools fully dressed, dash into strange houses, even charge into traffic to avoid being stung. The hornet grazed her ear, and she shot to her feet.

"¿Que pasa?" Jesus said.

Hailey's blouse flapped open, exciting the insect, the way a matador's cape inflames a bull. The yellow jacket revved its motor and zoomed off for momentum before charging at her head. She ducked, and it missed, but the fierce little thing circled back. By this time, Jesus was standing. He snatched at the blanket, no doubt preparing to make a dash for the hut. Just leave it, Hailey wanted to say, but she was busy batting the insect away. Jesus now snapped the red-and-black flannel like a whip, this way and that. The yellow jacket grew crafty and began hovering behind or just above Hailey's head.

She couldn't pinpoint its insistent vibrato, so she waved her arms and kicked her feet, wheeling about like a dervish.

Likely confused, the hornet turned its attention to Jesus, who'd dropped the blanket to twirl, likewise jerking out his limbs as of seized by the Holy Spirit. In this instant, Hailey glimpsed movement in the bushes bordering the copse—a winking light. She then caught sight of Jesus flailing alongside her, and they both laughed before throwing themselves into impromptu dance moves that kept the yellow jacket at bay. Hailey imagined the two of them as Sufi dancers, spinning with strange and mystical grace, their arms and legs flung out to release desire and to embrace the divine as they whirled like a pair of planets orbiting the sun.

"I THOUGHT PROBATION was just for students," Devorah Grisham said after Lucinda told her that Dr. Caspar had reported to Dean Cheek that Hailey had been canoodling with the head groundskeeper behind the Quonset. "And what kind of word is 'canoodling' anyway?"

"Dated, for sure." Lucinda selected a pistachio from the bowl on Dev's desk. The two English professors enjoyed cracking the nuts with their teeth, a habit that released impassioned speeches concerning tooth enamel from Devorah's mother and served as one of the reasons in a long list that Lucinda's live-in boyfriend cited in breaking up with her the time before last. Like banished smokers, Dev and Lucinda sequestered themselves every now and again to gossip over a bowl of pistachios, molar-splitting shells with impunity.

That afternoon, Devorah, who kept large bags of the nuts in a desk drawer, had poured some into a bowl and rattled this at the threshold to Lucinda's office, summoning her while both waited to attend a faculty meeting. Though she had a favor to ask, Dev took her time, watching Lucinda's bony face and monitoring the tension ebbing from it as they shared the nuts. "*Canoodling*," Dev said again. "Doesn't it sound like something you'd have to do on a lake?"

"Or on notepaper," Lucinda said.

Here, Dev pictured their colleague Jane Ellen Klamath idly sketching a series of dugouts in the margins of her program during a drawn-out convocation. "And which was it—canoodling or satanic dancing? I don't see how they could have been doing *both*."

"*Pagan* dancing, Snoop-and-Snitch. called it pagan dancing, which makes me wonder where he's seen pagans dance before." Lucinda tossed a pistachio into her mouth and parted its shell with a joint-popping sound.

"YouTube, I bet," Dev said.

"What's he doing watching pagans on YouTube?" Lucinda asked. "That, along with lurking in the bushes, seems far more suspicious to me than any kind of dancing."

"Did you get a look at the picture he took?" Dev hoped to see it for herself.

Lucinda shook her head, spit shells into the trash. "Jane saw it. She says it's mostly blurred. If not for that purple blouse Hailey wears, you wouldn't be able to tell she's in it at all."

"Imagine that man photographing people in private moments . . ."

"Of pagan dance," Lucinda said, and they both laughed.

"Just the idea, though, of him skulking around gives me the yips," Dev continued. Any of them might be photographed without their consent, the images used against them by wicked sprites like Caspar. She winced when she considered what might have happened if he had been in Common Grounds the day Karla returned her key to the apartment they'd shared.

Lucinda shrugged. "Well, he *is* a skulker."

At this, Devorah sprang from her seat to swing her office door shut.

Lucinda laughed again. "Relax. Caspar's at the Godwin Center, sitting in a budget meeting for Dean Cheek—another migraine."

"That woman," Dev said, "has more migraines than—"

"Hey, don't knock the migraines. The day's coming when we will all be very grateful for Muriel Cheek's headaches."

After exhausting this topic, Devorah asked Lucinda, in a casual way, how the play was coming. It was Dev's fault really that Lucinda had to put on the play. This obligation forged the latest link in an inexorable chain of events that started when Dev, fearful of repercussions from administrators at the conservative women's college, handed off to Hailey a student who planned to start an LGBT . . . and Q—Dev was always forgetting the Q—newspaper at Birnbrau. Hailey, Director of the Women's Center, embraced the idea, providing resources for the nascent group to print their first issue, a publication that easily outshined the lamentable *Birnbrau Outlook*, produced by Caspar's chuckleheaded crew of honor students. But then, Dean Cheek had shut down the paper and defunded Hailey's Plan A, an art show for Women's Her-story Month, triggering Lucinda's Plan B, the play.

"Fucking nuisance," Lucinda said. "People better learn their lines over the weekend. We start rehearsals on Monday, and I don't want to see *anyone* holding a script."

The time was right, so Dev feigned a yawn before asking, "Who's directing it?"

"I hadn't thought about that. Does someone have to direct it?"

"It *is* a play," Devorah pointed out, "and plays generally have directors, so yes, I think you do need a director to tell people where to stand and how to act, to oversee rehearsals—"

Lucinda's angular face softened, glowing now as if in apprehension of divine light. "If there's a director, then I wouldn't have to go to rehearsals, would I?"

"Well, you'll probably *want* to go to them anyway." Dev glanced up at her framed master of arts degree and considered the Hippocratic oath: *First, do no harm.* Too late for that. She'd done harm by not supporting the student who wanted to start the LGBT *and* Q newspaper, and as a consequence she'd harmed Hailey, and Lucinda, too, who now had to put on the play. Of course, the Hippocratic oath was really intended for physicians, not poets. Still Devorah resolved to atone for the harm she'd done, if possible, by assisting students who henceforth came to her for help, instead of passing them off to others.

"But if the director oversees rehearsals, why should *I* have to go? It'd be redundant really." Lucinda's dark brown eyes tracked back and forth, as if scanning names. She snapped her fingers, pointed at Dev. "*You* should be the director."

"I have no idea how to direct a play," Dev said.

"But you suggested this. You even know what a director's supposed to do."

Dev shook her head. She cracked open a pistachio, dropped the shell into her hand, and bit into its desiccated nutmeat—tough and bitter as burnt cork. She leaned over the wastebasket to blow it out of her mouth. "That was nasty."

"You have to eat a good one now to get rid of the taste." Lucinda tilted the bowl so Dev could fish out a more promising nut.

But Dev waved it away. She plucked a Kleenex from the box on her desk, wiped her tongue with it, and then raked the tissue's fuzz from her tongue with her front teeth. "You know who might make a good director, though?"

"Who?"

"April Madison." Dev sat back in her chair, nodding as if the idea had just come to her, as if April herself hadn't petitioned her to speak to Lucinda about this. "She took that stage-management course over May-mester, and remember, she was going to be a teaching assistant in drama last summer?" Dev didn't mention that the latter had fallen through due to April's arrest for indecent exposure. After all, her probation was nearly over by now.

"Doesn't she have some kind of Sylvia Plath-related Tourette's?"

Dev emitted a snort. "Oh, *that*."

"The last time I saw her, she looked me right in the eye and said, 'I shut my eyes and all the world drops dead. / (I think I made you up inside my head.)' Couldn't have been more than a few weeks ago," Lucinda said.

"That's the end to 'Mad Girl's Love Song,' a villanelle—*six stanzas* long," Dev pointed out. "And April knows it by heart. She's memorized most of the poems in *Ariel*. Some are pretty extensive. Why, she'd learn the play in no time and be able to help people with their lines. Plus, she's on Haldol now."

"I can't have a director randomly spouting Sylvia Plath," Lucinda said. "I really can't."

"She doesn't do that anymore. I swear she doesn't," Dev insisted. "The Haldol has been *very* effective, and since she's working at the library again, she has access to the color copier. She can make flyers for the play, even print programs at no charge."

"That *would* help," Lucinda said. "But is she even interested in directing the play?"

Dev shrugged. "I could ask, see what she says." The scorched bark residue of the rancid nut still soured her tongue, so Dev reached for the bowl, examining its contents for a pistachio that looked likely to contain a plump and sweet-flavored nutmeat. Maybe Lucinda was right about the bad nut, and Devorah shouldn't stop after a bitter one.

JANE ELLEN KLAMATH had arranged plywood panels, paints, and brushes on plastic sheeting at the back of the Loft, a small performance area with a stage on the second floor of the building that housed the campus coffee shop, a place students called The Swill. The acrid odor of over-stewed coffee clashed with heady paint fumes as Jane and Nadezhda, who'd tied a kerchief over her nose, knelt painting the sink and cupboards penciled onto the plywood. Though Hailey had booked the university's main auditorium months ago, planning for the renowned weaver to hold her pre-exhibit talk in it, word came from Dean Muriel Cheek's office just days ago that the main auditorium would be closed the last week of March to service its HVAC system. Hailey had scrambled to find another place, and Jane, friendly with some of the Buddhists who met on campus, helped her to negotiate for use of this, their meditating space, for the play.

As Jane worked, trepidation fluttered in her stomach, a queasiness not caused by the paint and coffee smells. Lucinda had asked her to proofread the flyers before these were sent out to the Birnbrau mailing list. But when Jane asked to see a draft, April, the play's director blithely told her that she'd delegated the task to Kayla Martin, a work-study student known for a level of incompetence that was striking, even at Birnbrau. "Don't worry," April had said. "I gave her my copy card and the code for the postage meter in the library. These aren't going to cost a penny!"

On stage, April now crouched near the floorboards, affixing masking tape *X*s to indicate, as she'd told Jane, where the actors would stand. "For blocking," she'd said. The platform moaned with the girl's movements, and Jane wondered how it would hold the weight of the five actors who would perform on it, actors who would soon appear for their first rehearsal on this stage. Now, Jesus, no doubt eager to be relieved of groundskeeping duties for the afternoon, bustled in— first to arrive, if Jane didn't count Nadezhda. Jesus set his headgear on a folding chair and stepped out of his coveralls, wearing newish jeans and a polo shirt under these. He pulled the script from his back pocket to go over his lines. Simeko Tyler, a short junior with a loud voice, appeared next, and moments later, Alexis Shearer, a vegan known for being on time, turned up at 2:00 sharp.

Including Nadezhda, Jane counted four performers. Who was missing?

"Where's Randy?" April called from the stage.

Of course, thought Jane, Randall Ripley, the little twit—just as inconsiderate as his mother, the registrar. He *would* make everyone wait for him.

"Does anyone know where Randy is?" April said.

The cast members traded perplexed looks. A few shrugged. How should they know?

"'You do not do, you do not do,'" April muttered.

Jane set her paintbrush down. "You okay?"

"Fine, I'm fine," April said. "Well, let's start without him . . . Mrs. Hale doesn't turn up until page three. We can go over props before the run through." April hopped off the stage with a thunderous crash and lumbered for the folding chair that held her backpack. She pulled out a clipboard and pen. "Who can bring in a few pots and pans?"

Simeko, who worked in the campus dining room, called out, "I will."

April jotted this down. "How about bread and a bread knife?"

Simeko nodded.

"The birdcage?"

"I can bring," Jesus said.

"Does anyone have, like, any access to taxidermy? Can anyone get ahold of a stuffed bird with a twistable neck?"

Alexis Shearer raised her hand, and Jane, who'd read the play online, wondered what on earth a vegan was doing with such a thing.

"Great," said April. "Now all we need are dishrags, the sewing basket, and a quilt of some kind. I guess it's too much to expect any of you to have one with a log-cabin pattern."

The actors nodded—that *was* too much to expect.

"I have dishrags and a sewing basket," Jane called out. "I can even bring a quilt. You don't have to have it flapped open for all to see its pattern."

April made note of this and glanced over at Nadezhda. "What are you going to bring?"

The Romanian girl looked down at the panel she was painting in a pointed way, and Jane said, "Nadezhda's been painting scenery since noon! She shouldn't have to bring props, too. What about the Ripley boy? Shouldn't he bring something?"

April shot Jane an impatient look. "Randy's bringing the flowers."

Flowers? Jane didn't remember there being flowers, or anything remotely cheerful, in the dolorous drama about a woman driven to the edge, a farmwife who strangles her sleeping husband before the play's action begins, and whose motive for the crime is covered up by the women who come to her dismal farmhouse to collect the belongings she will need while in jail.

Randall burst into the Loft, winded, as if he'd just galloped across campus. Instead of apologizing for holding up the rehearsal, he said, "You better not have started without me."

He really was his mother's son, Jane thought as she coated the sink she'd drawn with a dull metallic gray. The brush slipped from her hand, splotching her knee, the one place where her smock had parted to expose her capris. "Son of a bitch," she murmured.

Gazing at Randy, Nadezhda nodded.

ON HER WAY to campus, Kerry Fujimori stopped at Kroger to buy several packages of LINDOR candies: milk chocolate, strawberries and cream, caramel with sea salt, almond, hazelnut, and something called stracciatella—she would have to try one of those. They were literal-minded, the girls at Birnbrau, and so Kerry would have her sacks of sweets to distribute *after* the play, as a treat for those who did not stomp off upon realizing they'd been misled by the colorful flyers decorated with images of candies that read:

TRUFFLES

by Susan Glaspell

Most would assume Glaspell was an expert chocolatier and the cast members, whose names appeared under playwright's, without reference to their roles, would be taken for assistants. Though the date and time for the event were correctly presented, nowhere on the flyer did the words *play* or *performance* appear.

And sure enough, as Kerry strode through The Swill toward the stairwell, she overheard two students in conversation.

"I'm going to that candy thing," one said.

"What're you talking about?" asked the other.

"Upstairs—they're giving out truffles."

"Aren't truffles, like, fungus that pigs dig up?"

"*Ew*—seriously?"

Since Kerry arrived early, she was treated to the pre-play drama, which featured Lucinda ejecting meditating Buddhists from the performance space. "I'm sorry," Lucinda's voice sailed through the open door to the Loft. "A scheduling error. I am so sorry but you have to leave. Yes, you need to go. You, too, and you. Take your pillows, *please*." Hands, likely Lucinda's, clapped—two sharp smacks. "Okay, okay, time's up. Everybody out!" Furious Buddhists—who knew there were so many in Turley?—filed past, wearing expressions that telegraphed deep desire to curse. "Oh, dear," Kerry murmured. How hard life must be for Buddhists!

"Whose gong is this?" Lucinda called out, after snapping on the lights. "You can't leave that here. It will be in the way."

Jane Klamath appeared at Kerry's side, likewise bearing a Kroger sack of LINDOR chocolates. The two women embraced, plastic bags crinkling between them. Jane, then, pulled back to regard her former colleague, as if preparing to compliment Kerry's appearance, but instead she asked, "*What* are you wearing?"

Kerry had not been back to campus since her retirement luncheon, and she'd dreaded having to drive in for the play. These days, she spent most of her time working on her house—painting, even retiling floors on her own—and gardening in the hopes that her children would sell the property at a good price when the time came. Most days, she wore flannel shirts and sweatpants. She avoided shoes, but when she had to, Kerry shoved her feet into bubblegum-pink Crocs. That afternoon, she'd rummaged through her closet, trying on slacks, skirts, and blouses—all of them too constricting, too oppressive to bear. She'd hoped to lose weight with her illness. But Kerry had grown thicker since leaving Birnbrau, partly due to increased muscle mass, but mostly from eating too much. At this point, Kerry wasn't about to invest in a new wardrobe, or go on a diet.

"I've just come from yoga," she told Jane. "I didn't have time to go home and change."

"Well, you look great." If Jane were Pinocchio, her nose would have shot out at least a foot from her face. "What's going on in there?" She indicated the open door to the Loft, where the ruckus was just subsiding.

"Lucinda's throwing out the Buddhists."

"Stupid Buddhists," Jane said. "I told them and told them that we needed the Loft tonight. I even sent it out in a message to their list-serv." She reached for her phone.

Now, it was Kerry's turn to cast a skeptical look. Well-known for her struggles with all things numeric, Jane was far more likely to transpose a number, confuse a date or time, than she was to get such things right. She now scrolled through her emails, pausing to read one. "*Oh* . . ., well." She slipped the phone back into her purse.

"Sounds like Lucinda's setting up chairs," Kerry said. "We should go in."

After greeting Lucinda, who also blasted the Buddhists, Kerry began pulling folding chairs from their stacks to set these up for the audience. As soon as she'd arranged a row of seats, Frank Means, the poufy-haired ceramics instructor, arrived with his wife, a gaunt Amish-looking woman in a long calico-print dress. At first, Kerry assumed she was one of the actors costumed for the play. Now, she couldn't remember the woman's name, though Kerry did recall that Frank's wife attended a seminary, studying to become an Episcopalian minister. She now gave them a friendly wave, wondering why Frank didn't help out with the chairs.

"It's our anniversary," Frank said.

"Congratulations." Kerry cast a sympathetic look at his wife. How cheap of Frank to bring her to this free play that was bound to be bad. Surely she deserved better than that. Frank Means made for a heavy cross she was obliged to bear. How difficult to be Christian!

"You're looking well-fed these days." Frank would often comment on the amount Kerry ate at shared meals, expressing surprise—with underpinnings of castigation—when she enjoyed her food. No wonder his wife was gaunt and hollow-eyed.

Of course, he knew nothing of her illness. Still, how far along would Kerry have to be before she could—like Frank—spout unmediated thoughts, heedless of boundaries inscribed by discretion and tact? She looked forward to a time when she could say to him, *You are not the fucking food police!* And: *This thing you call honesty—this habit of saying whatever you're thinking—is a luxury born of mindless male privilege.* For now, Kerry nodded in silence. There would be times when she'd need his help—a vote, a recommendation, a signature—for friends, former students, maybe even for her daughter Susan, who was moving to Georgia where she hoped to find a job teaching art. Jane once said that people lie at least fourteen times a day, but surely those who lack power *must* lie more often than that.

"*Very* well-fed," Frank repeated, as if to be sure she absorbed the insult.

Kerry bared teeth in a wide grin. "Thank you," she said.

Soon all the chairs were arranged, and the Loft filled to capacity. Students flocked to the event, most, if not all, likely expecting to eat chocolates. Kerry and Jane took chairs near the door, grocery bags at the ready in their laps. Devorah sat in the row in front of them with her mother, an unpleasant woman that Kerry tried to avoid. Moments before the play was scheduled to begin, Lucinda's live-in boyfriend—a bearded ginger-haired fellow—ambled in to claim the seat she'd saved for him up front. The lights flickered and dimmed, and Hailey stood at the podium to welcome the audience and remind people to turn off their cell phones. Then April Madison, with her face heavily powdered, tramped to the stage to deliver the invocation.

"I'd like to open this event with a poem titled 'Morning Song' by the world's greatest poet, Sylvia Plath. I'm dedicating this to my daughter Faith who's in the audience tonight." At the sound of her name, the toddler, who'd been fussing in her grandmother's lap a few rows in front of Kerry and Jane, froze to regard her mother in silence. April's face glowed, bobbling against the dark stage like a blanched balloon. "Love set you going like a fat watch," she began. With that, Faith unleashed a mind-mangling wail, after-echoes of it buzzing in Kerry's skull long after the child had been borne away by April's mother.

This departure triggered an attempted exodus; students were beginning to suspect that candies might not be involved after all. Chair-scraping, whispered voices, and rustling sounded in the loft as April recited the poem. Kerry and Jane, armed with their Kroger bags, leapt for the door. They barred the exit, displaying their grocery sacks and promising to distribute the truffles *after* the play had ended. Almost all returned to their seats, but one fast-thinking girl claimed she had to pee, saying she would only be a minute. Of course, she never came back.

Kerry and Jane returned to their seats, and April finished reading the poem. Stage curtains parted to reveal a card table holding a basket, pots and pans, a loaf of bread and a knife arranged before a realistic-looking backdrop. "Nice work," Kerry whispered to Jane.

"Nadezhda helped," Jane said.

A short man with a large handsome head strutted across the stage, rubbing his hands together. "This feels good," he said in an accented voice. "Come up to the fire, ladies." Then he raised a fist in the air and shook it as if to make an impassioned point, calling to mind newsreel images of Mussolini addressing Italian throngs from a balcony.

Little Simeko Tyler stepped out in the role of Mrs. Peters, wearing a long skirt and a shawl. "I'm not—cold," she said in a startlingly loud voice.

Nadezhda, in trousers and a blue Oxford shirt with a tinfoil badge pinned to it, soon appeared, and Alexis Shearer, the prompt vegan, followed her onstage in overalls, as Mr. Hale, a neighboring farmer. So far, so good—except for the fist-waving, perhaps a Latin-American style of acting with which Kerry was not familiar. The players seemed to know their lines, so she allowed herself to relax and enjoy the story. Then Randall Ripley burst through the door behind Kerry and Jane and barreled at the stage, clad in a yellowing wedding dress. As he passed, Kerry, who now smoked medical marijuana, caught a dizzying whiff of hemp.

Jane cupped her mouth, leaned to speak into Kerry's ear. "That little turd is late *again*."

"Why the white gown?" Kerry asked.

Jane shrugged, and Dev's mother turned around to shush them.

From the stage, the county attorney, wound up a long passage of fist-waving dialogue, by saying of the jailed Minnie Wright, "Not much of a housekeeper, would you say, ladies?"

At this, cast members looked at Randall, and Simeko, standing nearest to him, nudged him with her elbow.

Randall closed his eyes, held a fist to his heart. "She used to wear pretty clothes," he said in an artificially high voice, "and be lively, when she was Minnie Foster, one of the town girls singing in the choir. But that—oh, that was *thirty* years ago—"

A thumping silence filled the auditorium, and except for Randall, the performers tensed, their faces creased in confusion. Finally, Nadezhda cleared her throat and said, "I think Mrs. Hale wants to say, 'There is a great deal of work to be done on a farm.'"

To which the county attorney, fist in the air, said, "To be sure. And yet . . ."

The play progressed with Randall staring at the floorboards and standing mutely on stage, the large-headed man punching the air each time he spoke, and Nadezhda delivering her lines as the sheriff, along with Mrs. Hale's, which she'd preface by saying, "I think Mrs. Hale wants to say . . ." This meant that the sheriff had to remain onstage throughout the play, including when the two women are alone together, plotting to deceive the men and especially the sheriff. This incongruity, though, was eclipsed by the large rabbit hutch hauled onto the stage and slammed atop the card table by April, just in time for the farmwives and the sheriff to examine the "birdcage," noting its broken door. And that bit of strangeness was trumped by the discovery of the songbird's body in the sewing basket.

Here, Nadezhda, as sheriff/interpreter for Mrs. Hale, handed the cloth-wrapped bundle to Randall, saying, "I think Mrs. Hale will open this up and say, 'Oh, Mrs. Peters—its—'"

Randall unwrapped the bundle, and a stuffed animal—Tweety Bird, in fact—rolled onto the stage, its head twisted backwards. The audience gasped. Kerry and Jane rocked and snorted with stifled laughter, and Devorah's mother again whipped around. "You are grown women. *Act like it.*" Poor Simeko, undone by the appearance of Tweety Bird, succumbed to giggling each time she attempted to speak a line. She gave up and clapped a hand over her mouth, her cheeks puffing and eyes streaming. The sheriff had to speak for her, too, and Nadezhda, as if in the throes of schizophrenia, commenced full conversations with herself onstage, until at last, the county attorney reappeared to wave his fist and provide some dialogue-relief.

But worst of all, when the play at last ended, and all the actors appeared center stage to bow—Randall in the middle as if he had been the star—Mrs. Ripley, the registrar, rushed the stage, a dozen wine-red roses cradled in her arms to present to her son. This provoked Lucinda to likewise charge up front. She snatched the bouquet from Randall to divvy it up, handing roses—two apiece—to each of the players and then summoning April to receive the remaining pair of blooms. Mrs. Ripley, who was returning to her seat, whipped around to race back. Voices rose, petals flew, and scuffling ensued, but Kerry could no longer see the stage for the gaggle of girls gathered before her. The students had waited, enduring the entire performance, and now they wanted their truffles. Certainly, they'd earned them.

THOUGH THE PLAY was bad—well, worse than that, a debacle, really—Kerry still hoped to go out for drinks with her former colleagues afterward. She anticipated laughing over the disaster of it with them, but Hailey, like a shrewd felon, had seen an opening early on and made a break for it, towing the large-headed man who'd played the county attorney along with her. No way would Kerry invite Devorah, who would have to bring her disagreeable mother along, and Jane, when asked, claimed exhaustion from working all night to finish the set. "Raincheck?" she said. After her tussle with the Registrar, Lucinda—red faced and wild-eyed—looked downright combustible. Kerry didn't dare ask her out.

Instead she gathered up truffle wrappers to toss into the trash bins, thinking about the play and the production of it. Women helping women—the two farmwives colluding to hide the reason for Minnie Foster's murderous rage, thus supporting her claim that a random intruder had entered the farmhouse to strangle her cruel husband in his sleep. And then there was Hailey helping the LGBTQ students with their controversial newspaper, and Lucinda bailing Hailey out with the play. Jane had lent a hand, too, with the set, and Devorah no doubt had something to do with April Madison's involvement. Kerry gazed out at the sea of disarrayed chairs. No way would she collapse and restack these, though too soon Kerry would be done with helping and being helped by women like herself—the beautiful and irksome mess of this. She folded up her plastic bags.

As Kerry emerged from The Swill into the cool evening, she thought of Lucinda's boyfriend, the practiced and patient expression on his bearded face, when he finally took Lucinda's arm to lead her out. She was likely filling his ears with her wrath as they made the long drive to their home in Athens. He was Jewish, so he no doubt knew what it was to suffer. Still, how challenging to be Jewish. Buoyed once more by her lack of faith, Kerry slipped off her Crocs and stowed them in one of the empty grocery sacks.

She strolled across the lawn to the parking lot, blunt blades of grass pricking the soles of her feet in a pleasurably painful way.

Campus Tours

*P*lease. Call me Hailey. Professor Linder is what the students call me. Here at Birnbrau Women's College, they'll call you whatever you want. Since I'm not that tall and kind of youngish, I go with "professor." And with this nevus on my face—

What? Nevus? *N-E-V-U-S*. The British spell it with an "A" before the "E." A birthmark, of course. You must have, like, *noticed* it. What did you think I meant?

Anyways. With my nevus—birthmark, whatever—I don't like to encourage too many jokey nicknames. Not that being called *professor* really prevents this, but for me, it's definitely a step in the right direction. Older folks on faculty usually go by their first names. It makes them feel young. If you hear a girl call an instructor *Sally* or *Joan*, you can bet Sally, or Joan, is pushing seventy. There's a dean in nursing who makes everyone call her Tristan, though her name is actually Amy. She says she's always felt like a Tristan, and who can argue with that?

No surprise that most PE faculty like to be called *coach*. Folks with PhD's usually insist on being called *doctor* to distinguish themselves from those of us with just Masters or MFAs. If you wind up here, I recommend you go with *Professor* Barresi. In fact, you should encourage all of us—including colleagues—to call you *professor*, because an unflattering nickname attached to you after that first phone interview.

What's that? Not even close. And actually, *chatterbox* isn't half bad. Sorry. I shouldn't have brought it up. We're not supposed to talk about what happens on our end of things. Still, if you cast your mind back to that first conference call interview—a certain un*apt* phrase that you might have used. If nothing comes to mind, trust me, it's better to be known as the person who insists on being called "professor." *Way* better.

Okay, so, I suggested we start at this gazebo thing because it's easy to find. There's a name for it—can't think of it now. Some alumni group donated the thing, dedicated it with a ceremony and whatnot. You'll notice the four portals of learning, which are kind of wordy for portals and mainly show that we need better editing skills around here. What? The *statue*? Hardly. More like plaster sprayed with some metallic paint. See the flaking near the nostrils and again where the arms bend. It does look kind of bronzy from far away.

Nope, not a clue. Could be Clara Barton or Harriet Beecher Stowe, could be Oscar Wilde in drag, for all I know. Most likely it's just some random nineteenth-century gal holding a fan. Or maybe a mirror. On a day like this, I imagine it's a fan. The hair's kind of nice, all abundant and swooped up like that. So, gazebo, statue, and four portals of learning. Please don't write them down. Seriously, put the notepad away. This will only make the nickname situation worse. It's more than enough to remember they're to do with science and math, art, society or culture, whatever. You can probably find them on the website.

Nah-uh, that's not it. Again, see, a person wouldn't mind being called *eager*. *Beaver*, though, has an unfortunate connotation. Let's move on, yeah? Oh, and watch out for yellow jackets. They nest here in the lawn. Those men in padded coveralls with the mesh headgear, they're our groundskeepers. That's what we call maintenance people here, like they're straight out of *Lady Chatterley's Lover*, when mostly they're straight out of Mexico, with a few from Guatemala and El Salvador.

Okay, here's the fountain. Sure, it's mildewed and stinks a bit, but listen. Sounds cheerful, doesn't it? And from here, it *looks* cool and refreshing. Tradition is, when a student gets engaged, her soror- ity sisters throw her into the fountain for good luck, which wouldn't

be too bad this time of year, but pretty much sucks in January or
February. Even March can be bad. Supposedly, one girl got shoved
into the fountain in wintertime years ago and she developed pneumonia. Supposedly, she died on the exact day she was to be married.
Supposedly, she's now one of the ghosts that haunt the campus. And
supposedly—

Just two: the pneumonia girl and Agnes. That's an even sadder
story. If you wind up teaching here, you'll hear a few versions of it.
If you don't, well, you'll be better off in the long run. It's *that* kind of
story. Anyways, we need to move on to get you to lunch on time.
While we're not usually sticklers about promptness, those who teach
at one tend to be put out if anyone's late to a 12:30 lunch.

Right behind the fountain is Anhoy Hall. Like most buildings
here, it's named for some deceased guy no one remembers now. This
is where new hires go to fill out tax forms and sign stuff. When we
refer to the building, we pretend we're from Liverpool and drop
each *H*, so it's always *Annoy All*. Around here, we amuse ourselves
however we can. No surprise, the registrar's office is in Annoy All.
Mrs. Ripley is the registrar, and I wouldn't say she's cruel or exactly
evil—which takes energy, even creativity—but she's for sure vengeful.
Think of Annoy All as paperwork central, the place we submit the
endless stream of forms we complete to meet the endless flow of
deadlines. We copy everything we turn in because just as sure as
stars in the galaxy collapse pulling whatever's nearby into emptiness,
the paperwork we turn in will get sucked into oblivion as soon as
it reaches Annoy All.

Oh, and here's something about deadlines, and that is most of
us never, *ever* do anything before the day it is due. That's what's kind
of magical about the college. Things change from moment to moment,
and the work we put off, we are always glad to have deferred. At
Birnbrau, we have little sayings like "procrastination is next to godliness
and "last minute is the best minute." Here's an example: Muriel Cheek,
the former dean of something—the moon, for all I know—demanded
we complete detailed assessments of graduating students, something
beyond the nonsense we already do for accreditation. Some of us, like

Lucinda Aragon (you'll meet her at lunch) hopped right to it, but others wisely (or lazily, in my case) put this off, and guess what? The very day assessments were due, Dean Cheek suffered a massive stroke. Nowadays, her roommate, who used to be her receptionist—*long* story—visits her daily at a rehab place called Fairview Plantation, where Dean Cheek can barely swallow applesauce, let alone demand overdue reports.

I'm not from the South, so it's hard for me to wrap my mind around all the good-timey feelings suggested by the word *plantation* these days. In fact, it's hard for me to use an adjective like *fair* to modify a noun like *plantation*, much less use both to name to a convalescent home. Think about it: No one would dream of calling the place Fairview Internment Center or Fairview Concentration Camp. I mean, *sheesh*.

What's that? Nope, not even close. Seriously, let's drop the nickname thing? Like I said, I shouldn't have mentioned it in the first place.

Huh? Where? That's just Dr. Caspar. He directs the honors program and teaches lit courses. Wave him off—like this—instead of waving back. You'll get your fill of Caspar at lunch. We despise him, but he's ultra-popular with the students. He's interviewed at least once each semester in *The Birnbrau Outlook*, which—no surprise—his numbskull honors students run, and he's had the yearbook dedicated to him twice, and that's something usually reserved for students or faculty who *die* during the school year. His courses, especially the Neglected Agrarians and Contemporary Confessional Rhymed Verse, are standing room only each semester, and the waitlists are mind-blowing.

You'd think, *right*? But no, not at all. Fact is most students don't care a lick about poetry. They do, though, enjoy getting A's in their classes, especially when little to no work is involved, and Dr. Caspar hands out high grades the way the free clinic dispenses condoms: come one, come all—*oops*, bad pun. But that's why *The Birnbrau Outlook* makes us sort of cringe, and some honor students can't read or write that well. They're bad at speaking, too, and slow to understand what we say to them. Not *all*, of course. It's wrong to generalize. Some are very bright, but the bright ones don't last too long. One semester and—*whoosh*—they're out of here.

Uh-oh. He's heading this way. Don't look, don't look. Keep walking, sharp right here. Whew! That was *close*. Caspar came to us from the Air Force Academy, where he taught insignificant military poems or some such thing. He likes to say that Birnbrau made him an offer he couldn't refuse. More likely, the Academy gave him an ultimatum he couldn't ignore. Jane Klamath—you'll meet her at lunch—says she burst into his office late one night and caught him watching cheerleader porn on his laptop. Who even knew that was a thing, right? Granted, Jane's not always the most reliable narrator, but that's the kind of story we tend of believe. Also, confidentially speaking, Caspar's a great champion of yours. In fact, he's offered to be your mentor, so if you take this job, I suggest you have someone else in mind.

What? Me? That's actually not a great idea. I'm sort of on probation for what happened to the Women's Center while I was the director, even though Dean Cheek was the one who slashed the budget before actually shutting it down, like *immediately* after we published an LGBTQ newspaper. *Coincidence?* You tell me. With no funding, I had to cancel the art show I'd planned for Women Her-story Month in the spring. I was lucky (or unlucky, as it turned out) that Lucinda Aragon got her students to put on a play about women at the end of March. Plus, I'm accused of oversharing, which—okay—fair enough.

And though no one says it outright, I'm also in trouble for hooking up with Jesus, who's in charge of the groundskeepers. Weirdly, for us, it kind of *is* like *Lady Chatterley's Lover*. There's even this wooded area behind the Quonset where tools are kept, but no one tells a person up front that *canoodling*, as Snoop-and-Snitch called it, with custodial staff is frowned upon. So—words to the wise—hands off the groundskeepers, especially Jesus. Haha.

Snoop-and-Snitch? That's Caspar, of course. What? *No-o-o.* I mean, well . . ., yeah. It actually *is* a bit worse than Snoop-and-

Snitch—in fact, *way* worse, but we're not going to talk about that, remember?

Ah, there's a question I'd be comfortable answering . . . *if* I knew the answer. Truth is, no one's running the Center now. The office is vacant, the windows always dark. Not even a groundskeeper has set foot in it since it was shut down, or went "under reorganization," as the website says. I feel kind of bad because I left a tuna sandwich in my desk drawer on the day Dean Cheek made me turn in keys to the office.

Good question, and honestly, that's something I haven't figured out. I, for sure, never *applied* to direct the Center or even expressed interest in this. How could I when I didn't even know such a thing existed until I was appointed the director? Funny story, actually. Before I sort of settled down with Jesus, see, I used to like a good time, and by good time, I mean blackout binge-drinking and waking up with men I swear I'd never seen before, men I couldn't pick out the next morning in a police lineup if my life depended on it, men who sometimes barely looked human. I'm talking great hulking, hairy beasts snoring to shake the walls, know what I mean?

Well, early in my first semester at Birnbrau, Kay-Kay, my college roommate, came to visit me. A little background here: Compared to Kay-Kay, I am a nunnish sort, sober and reserved, despite the oversharing. Kay-Kay, on the other hand, won't go anywhere without a flask and back-up flask, along with a Ziploc full of pharma. Lucky for her, she's a drug rep, and not just for the company car. So when Kay-Kay picked me up on campus, I happened to be wearing this white denim number I'd bought with my first Birnbrau paycheck. Snowy pencil skirt, crisp little jacket—I'm talking perfect fit. That suit looked sharp, if a bit phosphorescent in dim lighting. Instead of stopping at my apartment to change, we headed straight for a gastro-pub near the Square. While you're in town, you should definitely check this place out. The food tends to be rubbery and tasteless—inedible, actually, but hey, full bar!

So we were pounding down vodka martinis—which is, by the way, the reason I only drink gin martinis these days—when Kay-Kay decided we should go dancing. Of course, no self-respecting nightclub would ever find itself in Turley, so we had to haul to Atlanta, Kay-Kay driving the drug company car with one eye shut. For focus, she said. We wound up in this gay bar, and somehow got thrown out, and then ended up in another, and another. I vaguely remember line dancing, salsa dancing, and I *know* we did the Macarena. At one point, Kay-Kay and I waltzed to Celine Dion. *I'm everything I am/ because you loved me!* And later some dude, or gal—who can say for sure?—stomped my toes while we're doing the Hustle. But pretty soon after that the curtain just . . . *dropped.* My brother, who's a therapist, says memory works like a tape recorder and when you blackout from drinking, the tape stops running, though you can still do stuff like say regrettable things, stagger around, even drive, though not spectacularly well. My brother calls it temporary amnesia, losing the ability to create memories for a while. Whatever it is, at one point, everything sort of went blank for me.

You know, if you keep that up, those folds in your forehead will become permanent, and you'll have to wear bangs all the time like Lucinda. Anyways. This *isn't* a sad story. It's kind of hilarious, really.

Okay, so, here's the library. Yes, it's small and low on books. The lighting's bad for reading. And like most buildings around here, it tends to be overheated in winter and fiercely air-conditioned in summer, but in an *extreme* way, even for the South. If you see someone bundled in a parka in July or prancing around in shorts in February, you can bet that person's headed for the library. Also, we have an erratic, sort of bat-shit student worker there who goes off on library patrons, as in shouts poetry at them. At first it was just Sylvia Plath, but now she quotes Ann Sexton and Sharon Olds, too—really loud and kind of in your face. It can be unnerving. She was fired for a while and hostessed at DiColo's, over in the Square, in a fairly sane and capable way, so the library took her back. Since then she regressed, *big-time.* Devorah Grisham, who teaches poetry, often has to be called in to calm her down. You'll see her, Dev, I mean, at lunch, too—

Didn't you get the itinerary? Someone was supposed to get it to you. The itinerary tells who all will be at lunch and when to meet them. I'm guessing it'll be at 12:30, and you'll meet about five or six people. Let's see. Snoop-and-Snitch will be there, along with Frank Means. He's our narcissist-in-residence. Just kidding! Frank's actually too slothful to be a full-on narcissist. We just call him one, in an affectionate way. You'll also meet Mildred Haney, our office manager. She's another difficult, bordering-on-bat-shit person. My first day of teaching—now, this is funny—my first day, she accidentally locked me in the supply closet for nearly an hour! Said she couldn't hear me banging on the door, even though the closet's just a few feet from her office. I actually had to climb on the copier to pop open the transom, squeeze through the window, and jump onto the porch where I landed on a pinecone and sprained my ankle. When I hobbled around to the front entrance, Mildred said, "Where *were* you?"

Takes getting used to, but that's how Mildred greets people. See, she has to work Monday to Friday from nine-to-five, so she expects all of us to put in the same kind of facetime, even if we are professors, even if we have work to grade, conferences to attend, projects to complete. "Where *were* you?" she always wants to know. And she's all scornful and suspicious, even if you tell her you were *teaching class*. Then she has you repeat your reasons for not being around, like, to check for inconsistencies. In Mildred's book, if you're not in the building, if you're not where she can find you to sign forms or meet with some student who's mixed up about your office hours, then, basically, you're goofing off, and she won't have that.

At lunch, Mildred will be sure to sit by Lucinda, who taught five composition courses last semester, who grades papers around the clock, who was ticketed not too long ago for scoring quizzes while driving. A traffic violation—who knew? Lucinda, by the way, earned her master-of-arts *and* doctoral degree in a record five years, because basically all she does is work. (No surprise, she's leaving for a better position.) Any chance she gets, Mildred ponies up to Lucinda to mention someone she knows (always some guy) who earned a PhD in, like, one weekend. This drives Lucinda to a special zone of rage, the sort of choked fury of someone who's privileged through education (though a minority and a first generation college grad from a lower-income background) toward this white woman, who's just a high-school graduate and literally lives in a double-wide, with meth-head sons and a disabled husband.

"Yup," Mildred will say. "He done his dissertation on a Sunday afternoon while watching *The Golf Channel*," and Lucinda will get purple in the face and shoot off a slew of questions to disprove this, but Mildred just goes, "I don't know *how*, but he done it in time to take his wife to supper at the Red Lobster." None of us dares to get involved. There's no limit to the tricks Mildred can pull to get even, so no one will say a thing, except maybe Jane Klamath, who's moving to Wyoming in December, so she doesn't care too much about winding up on Mildred's bad side.

Good question, but no, you're not exactly replacing Jane, who only recently gave notice. You're actually replacing two other painting instructors. One of these was fired even before she started, which even around here is kind of impressive, and the other—Kerry Fujimori— retired last year. Kerry *said* she'd inherited a lot of money from her deceased parents, but really she quit because she found out she has this blood disease. Turns out, Kerry's got a daughter named Susan. Turns out, Susan's an artist, too, teaches painting in New England, or she did until her marriage broke up when her cat died. Turns out, Susan and her husband were just staying together for the cat. Digression—big-time! I talk too much, as if you hadn't noticed, and I go on too many tangents, saying stuff I really shouldn't say. *Over*sharing, again.

About the position, though, it's a full course load. See, I just teach design, textiles, Weaving I and II, and Frank Means covers the ceramics lab and sculpture workshops, so basically we have no one for 2-D, at all. If you get this gig, you'd be teaching drawing, watercolor, oil painting, and color theory. *Oh*, I thought you knew. Don't most painters have some coursework in color? Surely, you must have—

Anti-color, *hmm*. Anyways . . .

What's that? Right, right, right—where was I? Okay, so early that morning I woke up, not in bed with Australopithecus, as is my custom, but alone on the floor of this vast office in an Atlanta high-rise. I was curled up near a desk, still wearing my white denim skirt and a sports bra, so I'm like, what happened to my blouse? Not a clue. But my new jacket's wadded under my head—a pillow! I shook it out, and even in the thin light of dawn, I could make out this dark shoeprint across the back, a large oily one. By the tread, and the logo, I'd say it was made by a man's Nike, size elevenish. I was trying, uselessly, to rub off the stain, when Kay-Kay—an early riser thanks to her Ziploc— turned up with two mugs of coffee.

No point in trying to figure out how we wound up in a vacant office building, so we drank the coffee, headed down to the parking garage, and Kay-Kay drove me back to campus, where I was just ten minutes late for Design I. Of course, I had to teach all my classes in the same outfit I'd worn the day before, only with a huge footprint stamped on the jacket. Without my blouse there's no way I could take it off, and that day, I taught back-to-back classes, so no time to run to the bookstore to buy a T-shirt or hoodie to wear with the skirt. Thank god, students here tend to be oblivious, or else they're used to seeing people in trod-upon clothing. No one mentioned the footprint. It didn't even come up in my end-of-term evaluations or at all affect my three hotness chili peppers on ratemyprofessors.com!

Kind of weird, yeah—in a women's college.

Here's the Godwin Center. It's where liberal arts classes are held— English, religious studies, philosophy . . . Smells nice, doesn't it? This is one of the newer buildings. No mold yet, and radon just barely exceeds acceptable levels. Uh-*oh*. Don't look. *Quick*, in here. Spacious, huh? I mean, for a ladies' room, and also not too bad smelling. Minty, really. Feel free to use the facilities, if you like.

What's that? Sure, a little strange, I guess, but that burly guy heading our way, that's Otis Jenks, the chaplain. He teaches the Bible as literature. Word to the wise: Keep your distance. You may have noticed that he looks a little *moist*. Fact is, he sweats like a quarter horse. He likes to give these super-*unwanted* back rubs and hugs, lots of hugs, especially now that he's been accused of sexual harassment and needs more comforting than usual. If you wind up here, you'll

have to come up with a way to keep him off you. Lucinda claims she's
a germaphobe. And Devorah, who actually *is* a germaphobe, tells him
she's been traumatized by sexual assault at an early age. And Jane,
who really was molested as a kid, well, she's the plaintiff in the sexual
harassment thing. Me? All I had to do was mention that Jesus is the
jealous type and that he's wanted for manslaughter in Guatemala City,
which is really only half untrue.

Never could snap my fingers, but—*leprosy*. That could work for
you.

Coast is clear. Come on, this way. I'll show you the mailroom.
Just down these stairs and around the corner. *Voila*. Faculty get assigned
cubbyholes for receiving mail. Each day of the week, my cubby will
get crammed with all kinds of junk: inter office memos, forms, flyers,
notices. Hence the nearby recycling bins. I just pull everything out
and dump it into recycling, like so, unless of course it's plastic. We
have a separate bin for plastics.

If it's anything important, I'll get an email reminder. If it's anything
crucial, Devorah will tell me about it. That's another handy tip: Make
friends with someone who pays attention to stuff. Also, and this is
crucial mailroom advice, do not ever buy anything online and have
it delivered here. It's tempting, I know, since most of us are here all
day and not available to sign for things at home. But never, ever have
packages delivered here.

See that door? That leads into the office of the director of online
instruction—a total joke, if you ask me. She's the other Hailey, here,
Hailey Blenkinship, and she's a mail thief. But we fondly call her the
Forger. If a package comes here for you and the delivery person needs
a signature, she will be the one to sign for it. And she will keep whatever
it is you've ordered for herself. Jane once bought a nice wall hanging
from the online distributor that handles my weavings, and she paid
quite a bit for it, too, though—truth be told—I only get a smidgen
of that. So, the postal records show the piece was delivered and signed
for just days after she placed the order. But Jane never received the
wall-hanging. *Never*. This is not an isolated incident. I only mention
it because my own weaving's involved.

So, we don't speak to that Hailey, and we avoid eye contact with her. She's now under investigation by the US Postal Service, but the administration's defending her pretty staunchly because, frankly, no one else here knows how to run online instruction, which is a huge cash cow for the university, even if it is, as mentioned, a total joke. Even if eight out of ten students who enroll in online classes—some of whom will go into lifelong debt to pay for these—will drop out because the coursework is too confounding and irrelevant, not to mention burdensome, especially for those poor folks who don't have time for regular college instruction. And, let's face it, prestigious companies and reputable academic institutions aren't exactly headhunting folks with flimsy online degrees.

What's that? *Oh.* Sorry—my bad. Seriously, I had no idea . . . You can actually earn a bachelor of fine arts online? *Hmm.*

Okay, okay, though there's really not much left to tell. Just before my last class on that endless and shameful second day of the white denim suit, a work-study student turns up to hand me a pink slip of paper—just a Post-it Note, it turned out, but still, *pink*. It was a message from Dean Cheek summoning me to her office. I'm thinking, for sure Caspar's told her I reek like I survived a distillery explosion, or else he snitched about my being late, the footprint on my back. Still, after dismissing class, I splashed water on my face, brushed my hair, and trudged over to the admin building. Like dead woman walking, right?

Once inside, the air-conditioning needled me all over, releasing this wave of sour smells, and Dean Cheek's assistant—the one who now visits her at Fairview Plantation—ushered me into an inner office (not half as luxe, mind you, as the one I slept in the night before). Even so, I deeply wanted to plant my face in that flat industrial carpet, so Dean Cheek could add her orthopedic print to the gym shoe mark on my back. Instead, old Cheek swooped around to grasp my clammy little claw, congratulating me. I'd been appointed Director of the Women's Center.

Yeah, I'm still trying to figure that one out. Maybe I accidentally said something intelligent in a meeting one time. Maybe I used the word *vision*; they like hearing that around here.

Now I don't tend to overanalyze stuff, and that's partly why I drifted into weaving, instead of say, philosophy or even cultural studies. But it seems that at Birnbrau, a person can be rewarded for doing unwise, even self-destructive things. I spent the entire day hungover and wearing a footprint on my back, like some human doormat. And what happens? I get promoted. But when a person does something that's, say, *right*, something that actually benefits others—here, I'm talking about the LGBTQ newspaper—that certain someone might find herself kind of screwed. If you're okay with what some might call oppositional, transgressive, or even flat-out hypocritical systems, then this might just be the place for you. Or maybe you won't exactly be down for what goes on here, but like me, you'll be inclined to stick around, to see what comes next. And, of course, for the paychecks.

Cloudy all of a sudden, might even rain. It's like that a lot here. You'll find yourself whipping sunglasses off and on all day. I got these aviators at a yard sale. They cover part of my nevus fairly well, but steep the world in shadows, pretty much blinding me when it gets overcast like this, so I have to keep jamming them back into my bag.

What's this? Ho, ho—the itinerary! Had it all along. Shoot, you *are* late for the lunch. I mean, *really* late. That will not sit well.

Again, with the nickname? Yeah, so, I'm not going to tell you what it is. If you get this job, someone at some point *will* tell you. All I can say for sure is that it won't be me. And here we are again, back at the gazebo, the four portals, the flaky nineteenth-century gal. That salmon-colored building, just past the gazebo, that's the dining hall, also known as The Gag. There's a nickname that's self-evident, as you'll see. Head down the path to your right? What's that? No, I really can't. I've got to meet Susan Fujimori in a few minutes. That's right—Kerry's daughter. I'm going to take her somewhere decent for lunch, since we have to endure The Gag for dinner, and then show her around campus. Huh? Yeah, another one, just like this.

Nice to meet you, and good luck with . . . um, *everything*. I'd get a move on, if I were you. Cut across the lawn to save steps. Look out for yellow jackets in the grass. *Bees*. Watch where you—

Hey, *hey*, where you headed? The Gag—it's the other way, over there. *What?*

Okay, yeah, I get that. Sure, I'll let them know. So, bye, then? And take care!

Postcards from the Gerund State

*L*ucinda stood in the doorway, blinking as her eyes adjusted to the dim and smoky diner. She and four other women were waiting to be seated in the Silver Spur on Main Street in Sheridan, Wyoming—thirty miles from the arts residency that housed them for the month. All five women looked forward to an undisturbed breakfast away from Leah Caspian, an annoying abstract painter in their group. Apart from the silver spurs depicted on the awning out front, no further references to this motif appeared inside the diner. Instead, it was decorated with roosters: paintings, posters, and prints, as well as ceramic statues of these. Lucinda, who liked renaming things, considered *Cock-a-Doodle-Do* for the place, or maybe it should just be called *Cocks*. Many leather-faced men, a few with beards to their bellies, sat around the bar, sipping coffee, sopping up yolks and ropy albumen with biscuits, working their whiskery jaws as they chewed. Some diners had gone still, as the women stepped over the threshold, gawping until Lucinda broke the spell by shutting the door behind her. Then the men resumed eating, while keeping wary eyes on the newcomers.

"It began with the internet shutdown," Lucinda said, resuming the conversation started on the drive to town. She closed her eyes, casting her mind back to reconstruct clues. "We blamed clouds for the interference, but Leah was day trading. I know it. And we were told not to stream anything."

"I knew," Kerry, a pointillist, said, in her fluty voice, "within minutes—the constant name-dropping, that gushy baby-doll voice. Within five minutes, I knew that woman would be a thorn in my side." Here, she clutched her ribcage and grimaced, as if lanced by a sword, instead of pricked by a thorn.

"I didn't know right away," said Hailey, a petite blond weaver often bemused by her own shortcomings. She issued a deep-dimpled grin. "I was too open with her. My mistake—I trust people too soon, and now she thinks she's my best friend."

"For me, it was the pill bottles, the ailments, the on and on about bunions and blood pressure. That's how the elderly talk." Jane, a plein-air painter in her early fifties, shuddered, her fine-featured face tightening with distaste. "Then there's that rash—*yecch*—those splotches she keeps showing me."

Dev, a slender and fastidious-looking African American poet, told the others that she just wished the woman wouldn't touch her food. "Who knows where her hands have been? Has anyone ever witnessed her washing up? Has anyone actually *seen* Leah with soap?"

"A *thorn* in my side," Kerry said again. She turned fifty that day, and the five women had come to town that morning to celebrate her birthday.

Lucinda glanced about again. Would she and her colleagues have to take seats on the stools available among the masticating men? Oh, she hoped not to have to eat alongside the one wearing stained long johns under bib overalls. She could see crumbs in his beard from where she stood at the entranceway. Now, the door behind her flew open, banging into her backside. Another bearded man, long-haired and wizened as a biblical prophet, thrust his head inside the diner to shout, "Tommy just got acquitted!" Someone whooped, and applause broke out among those seated at the bar. The hirsute messenger then withdrew from the threshold, no doubt to broadcast this glad news elsewhere.

The hostess at last appeared to lead the women through a door to a back room, where—thank goodness!—they were all seated together in a booth. The rich aroma of coffee and smoky scent of bacon suffused the diner's two rooms, and Lucinda scanned the menu planning to order both, along with biscuits and some form of non-runny eggs, perhaps an omelet.

After the waitress poured coffee, Jane said, "We should toast."

Kerry hefted her mug. "To what?"

"Freedom," Dev said.

"Peace," suggested Hailey.

"Women artists, those who manage to prevail despite obstacles." Lucinda included Leah Caspian among such obstacles.

"To Hedda Sterne!" Kerry's cup clattered into Lucinda's, sloshing hot coffee on her knuckles.

"To Mary Cassatt," Dev offered, and Lucinda caught Jane trading a glance with Kerry. The well-known painter of mothers and children was an obvious choice.

"To Berthe Morisot," Jane said.

"To Camille Claudel." Hailey touched her mug to Jane's and extended it toward Kerry's.

"Oh, dear." Kerry withdrew her cup, her freckle-spattered forehead seamed with doubt. "With the alcoholism and insanity, can we really count her as *prevailing*?"

Lucinda, who had seen a film about the artist's troubled life, felt that, if anything, poor Camille deserved *extra* credit for coping with Rodin, dog that he was.

"The work is the measure of an artist, and her work endures." Jane clicked crockery with Hailey again. "To Camille Claudel!"

To Frida Kahlo. Lucinda thought of her cousin Carmen, who embroidered the Mexican artist's image on pillows and handbags that she sold online, but Kahlo, like Cassatt, was a usual suspect when it came to women artists, so she said, "To Jane Austen, to Virginia Woolf."

"Hear, hear." Jane raised her cup again.

Encouraged, Lucinda added, "To Margaret Atwood and Alice Munro."

The faces ringing the table pleated in puzzlement.

"To Frida Kahlo," Dev said, and the others swiftly bumped mugs one last time.

THEY WERE ALL new to each other and to the university in Georgia where they would teach together that fall. In August, the administrators at Birnbrau Women's College planned to inaugurate a creative arts program at the behest of a wealthy board of trust member—Ariadne Warwick Murdoch, the great-granddaughter of Aaron Thaddeus Warwick, III, a railroad tycoon and founder of the college. Recently, Ariadne Warwick Murdoch had made a large donation to finance the new program. Murdoch, a visual artist herself who now lived in Wyoming, earmarked some of the funding for sending newly hired faculty in the creative arts program to a month-long residency, so they could produce work for presentation at the program's inaugural ceremonies. Murdoch had offered the retreat house she owned in Wyoming as the place for the women to stay as they developed their projects.

Lucinda, hired to teach composition classes and an occasional section of creative writing, had earned her PhD with an emphasis in fiction writing. She was marginally lumped with the arts faculty since the residency had space for six, and only five women were engaged to teach creative arts full-time at Birnbrau. Lucinda would round out the number, so the university could take full advantage of the heiress/artist's generosity. Now, sipping her coffee, she winced, disappointed in her powers of observation, and she was supposed to be the fiction writer—well, marginally—ever attuned to peculiarities of personality, the human heart in conflict with itself and all that, yet it had taken her longer than the others to get the lowdown on Leah Caspian. To be fair, at first, Lucinda had been blindsided by her luck in being included among the artists and then distracted by the unfamiliar pleasure of introducing herself to the others as a writer.

Usually, when she earned no income from teaching, Lucinda worked editing community newsletters and tutoring high school students for college entrance exams, all the while cobbling together enough money to send her daughter (from a disastrous early marriage) to the various arts camps that she enjoyed. This time, she had borrowed money to fly Anita—now nineteen, supposedly at the end of a gap year that Lucinda feared might turn into a "gap life," before starting college—to Los Angeles to stay with her aunt, Lucinda's sister Bertha. Lucinda still glowed with triumph over wresting her daughter for a month from work in a fast-food restaurant, where Anita was being fast-tracked by Diego, her overeager supervisor for store management. Even though traveling to Wyoming entailed debt, Lucinda considered this not to be a sacrifice, but an investment in her writing. She was heady with expectation, thrilled, really, and more unwilling than unable to detect early signs of trouble at the residency.

Apart from this, on the first day, she had been enthralled by Wyoming, its weirdly lunar landscapes—buff-colored rises, burnished fields, the indigo mountains etched with ghostly traces of snow in the distance, and she'd been awed by the residency itself—the great house with its unique angular architecture, its abundance of original, if peculiar, art created by Ariadne Warwick Murdoch, and Lucinda's own well-decorated room with its tall feather bed. Just outside this room, in the hallway, hung a self-portrait of the artist/heiress herself: a black and white rendering that resembled Lucinda's cousin Carmen, also something of an artist, though in no way an heiress. (Carmen cleaned houses for a living when not stitching Frida Kahlo's face onto purses and pillows.)

Lucinda's powers of observation had also suffered due to elevation sickness, a condition not improved by sipping the Sauvignon Blanc provided with turkey chili by the staff for their first supper. After this meal, they would cook for themselves.

"I'm no leader," Jane had declared that first night, before telling the group that she had been to a few artists' residencies. She suggested they take turns to prepare dinner, whereupon the women chattered about dietary fads and food allergies—Kerry avoided dairy and gluten, Dev disliked spicy foods, and apples and asparagus caused Hailey's buttocks to itch—before divvying up meal preparation and kitchen clean-up over the weeks to come.

Under these conditions, Lucinda found Leah Caspian to be no more than a dumpy-looking abstract painter with wispy auburn hair and florid jowls, a middle-aged woman who perhaps tried too hard to impress others. While she picked up on Leah's tendency to boast and name famous people she knew, Lucinda had attributed this to the posturing that insecure people perform when first in a group setting, and it stirred compassion in her. But later, she remembered that on the ride from the airport, Leah had asked if she would be able to do some day trading while at the retreat. "Nope," said the ranch manager, a Wyoming woman wrangler named Merle, who was driving. Merle had then explained that streaming of any kind would shut down all internet access for everyone at the retreat.

The next day when Lucinda was in her writing studio, she added pages to the manuscript she had been writing for the past five years, a monstrously long work that she suspected might really be two or three novels or maybe two novels and a short story collection, though she didn't know quite how to break it up yet. Despite this, months ago she'd mailed a draft for her agent to send out to various publishers. Editors were now reporting back, and the news had not been good. Still, there was one publisher, with a reputation for receptivity to nontraditional works, a press in which Lucinda placed great hope for the epic-length narrative that her agent—a novice in her profession with a graduate degree in French literature—was spinning as "a Proustian, yet female and fictive, perspective on contemporary life in the Southern U.S."

Even so, Lucinda revised paragraph after paragraph, occasionally going online for information about recreational lakes in South Carolina (part of the story was set near one) or trivia about side arms (the main character's ex-husband being a paranoid gun collector) or tips about dealing with ticks (rampant in Wyoming) and rattlesnakes (also prevalent here), as well as to check her Facebook page (to "like" a picture of a friend's cat sleeping in a basket), and then—nothing. No internet at all. After several futile minutes spent trying to reconnect, Lucinda peered through the slatted bamboo shade screening her studio/office. She didn't know how to raise the thing but could see out through gaps in its weave, and there was Leah Caspian, strolling by. *She was smoking.*

This was not the smoking area! If Lucinda had figured out how to raise the screen, instead of peeking through the bamboo slats, the window was supposed to provide a vista to inspire her creative work. Instead Leah Caspian paraded by like a derelict queen, puffing on a cigarette. How was *that* supposed to be inspiring? The side of a barn had been designated for smokers, a rinsed tuna can had been provided for ashes and butts. Why wasn't Leah in her assigned smoking place near the trash bins?

At once, Lucinda *knew* that Leah Caspian, the rule-breaker, had crashed the system. All of the women relied on the internet for staying in contact with friends and family at home. Though outgoing long-distance phone service was blocked, they could receive outside calls through the landline at the residency, but without the internet, there was no way to schedule these so the women would know to be in the retreat house, and not in their studios, when calls came through for them. To use their cell phones, most had to hike a mile or more away from the retreat house for a signal, and Lucinda, with her bargain service plan, had no reception at all outside of Sheridan. She'd put off replying to her live-in boyfriend's message of the previous day. Now she had no idea when she'd be able to answer it. On top of this, Lucinda had promised to email her daughter each day. Her throat tightened; her eyes stung.

And yet, at dinnertime, mellowed by a glass of Chardonnay, Lucinda found herself speculating that the few tags of cirrostratus scudding overhead had caused the interference, when the others discussed being inconvenienced by the outage. Hailey and Dev also chimed in. "Cloud cover, yes!" "What a pain!"

"Ah, the internet," said Leah Caspian, in her little girl's voice. Its high-pitched and artificially softened tones gushed forth like the over-treated tap water at the residency, water that left a slimy residue on Lucinda's skin no matter how she tried to rinse it off. Then Leah talked about people she knew at Microsoft and Apple. Bill Gates, she claimed, once had dinner at her house. He'd offered to buy her miniature collie, a sheltie, really. "He just loved Shelley! It was the funniest thing." Leah punctuated her anecdotes with a phlegmy laugh that often devolved into a coughing fit. She launched next into a story about the two Steves—Wozniak and Jobs—telling how she met them at a party years ago, where they all traded ribald jokes.

Kerry sighed. Jane raised an eyebrow, shot Lucinda a look. The topic of the internet amply covered, Leah embarked on a story about her husband. "He looks a lot like Richard Gere, you know," she said. Tipsily, Lucinda struggled to picture the silver-haired movie star in this jowly woman's embrace, then his tinsel-downed form mounting Leah's pallid and blotchy body. This distracted her from Leah's anecdote that had to do with her Richard-Gere-lookalike husband's drunken confusion after a party given by Ted Turner the previous month. Lucinda lost the thread of the thing several sentences back. She stifled a yawn, glanced at her wristwatch. Only eight o'clock, yet Lucinda was ready for bed.

When Leah sensed her audience's focus fading, she launched a barrage of questions, calling on others by name to snag their attention and sometimes confusing Hailey, a blonde, with Dev, who was black. Leah asked where they were all from, where they lived, what kind of houses they had. Upon learning that Lucinda lived in an A-frame, Leah asked how old the house was. "I don't know," Lucinda said. "It's just a place I'm renting. It's not like I celebrate its birthday." Of course, this—like all roads and Rome that night—led to something quite interesting about Leah. She and her husband owned a grand old home that she bragged about by complaining—it was too big (baronial really), too old-fashioned (nearly registered as an historic residence), and too expensive (worth well over two million dollars). Oh, what an inconvenience that vast, venerable, and valuable mansion was to Richard Gere's twin and to Leah!

"Well, I'm going to bed," Jane had said with a yawn that first night. "Again, I'm not trying to be bossy, but days start earlier than you think on retreats."

When they'd assigned kitchen tasks, Dev had made a chart. It was not Jane or Lucinda's night to clean up, so Lucinda sprang from her seat, too. "Exhausted," she'd murmured, before saying good night and trailing Jane from the dining area. In the hallway, outside their bedroom doors which were next to one another, Jane—a mature woman, the mother of two adult sons—whispered to Lucinda, "I just want to slap that woman."

"Make sure when you do," Lucinda said, "that I'm there to watch."

"*LUCINDA*," LEAH SANG out when she found Lucinda in the kitchen before breakfast, when she encountered Lucinda returning from her studio during the daytime, and when she saw Lucinda in the evenings, all evening it seemed—"*Lucinda, Lucinda, Lucinda*." In fact, Lucinda couldn't count the number of times she entered the retreat house with a specific intention that was flushed from her brainpan by the relentless flow of Leah's chatter, and Lucinda, after surfacing from the gibbering depths, would find herself outdoors, even back in her office without whatever it was that she'd set out to retrieve. She'd have to slip her coat on again, wind her scarf about her neck, crunch-crunch-crunch over gravel, returning to re-face the yak.

It didn't matter to Leah if Lucinda was in a jigging rush to pee, absorbed in a book, or engaged in conversation with Jane or Kerry. Calling out Lucinda's name, Leah would burst into whatever common room of the house she occupied. That breathy, unctuous voice oozed from Leah like clotted oil extruded from a pustule: "*Lucinda!* What're you up to? How's it going, *Lucinda?* Where are you headed, *Lucinda?*" Only her bedroom and the bathroom Lucinda shared with Jane provided sanctuary from Leah, though both smelled of the woman's cigarette smoke.

ONE MORNING, A few days after they ate at the Silver Spur, Lucinda, sleep-dazed, wandered into the kitchen for coffee—coffee that Kerry, Hailey, and Dev did not often drink; coffee that she and Jane chipped in to buy after breakfast in Sheridan; coffee that Lucinda prepared in the evenings, setting the coffeemaker on delay brew for the morning; coffee with which Leah filled her thermos, draining the pot before Lucinda or Jane could pour a second cup; coffee that Leah never bothered to wash out of the carafe when only the dregs were left after she filled her thermos, let alone empty the grinds out of the filter—and there she was: Leah standing before the sink, guarding the coffeemaker like some chatty deity to be propitiated with time and attention.

"*Ooh*, I had the raunchiest dream." Leah gave Lucinda a wink.

"I dreamed of my father," Lucinda said. "He passed away in December, and in my dream, he came back, and he was younger, much younger, and he looked . . . *so well*. He looked healthy and strong, a young man. He wanted me to know he was fine. That's what he said in my dream, 'I'm fine, honey. Don't worry about me.'"

Lucinda paused, gazed out the kitchen window. A pair of feral cats lounged on the patio chaise, one gnawing at the other's ear. She emitted an exhalation accompanied by a low moan, something sadder than a sigh, and with a shake of her head, she filled her cup and wandered back to her room. Lucinda regretted using her father, killing him off—he was actually quite well, retired now and living in a condo in Riverside—and then bringing him back in a made-up dream just to nip Leah's nastiness in the bud. But, hey, it worked.

Despite the day trading, the Richard-Gere-like husband, the famous friends, and the historic mansion, Leah Caspian wore the same black polyester button-down shirt each day, with tight and faded black pants, and dingy white gym shoes. Sometimes she threw on a bleach-splotched dark hoodie just to mix things up a bit. Leah was clearly a person-in-black or a PIB, thought Lucinda, using graduate-school shorthand for a thick-bodied person more reliant upon the slimming effects of black than those that result from diet and exercise. In the coming weeks, Lucinda had no trouble recognizing Leah's faded and threadbare underthings—yellowed bras and panties with elastic that was shot—in the laundry room. As if the woman's unsavoriness could be transmitted through contact with her garments, Lucinda stuffed Leah's clothing back in the dryer, though she didn't mind folding shirts, slacks, pajamas, even underwear belonging to the others.

Mornings, Leah sometimes tried to embrace her—as if they were close family members separated for years, instead of new acquaintances parted for just eight hours by sleep—and Lucinda would shrink away from the woman's loose nightgown, those uncontained and roaming breasts, the foul nimbus of cigarette smoke that trailed Leah wherever she went. "I'm not a hugger," she'd say, again and again.

"Oh, okay. Gotcha." And Leah winked.

Then: "Lucinda, I bet you speak Spanish, Lucinda."

"Not a word," Lucinda lied.

Next: "You like to cook, right, Lucinda?"

She shook her head, another lie.

And: "Lucinda, what are you working on now, Lucinda?"

A shrug. A pointed glance at her watch, as if out here at the retreat in Wyoming, Lucinda had fast-approaching deadlines, places to be, and things to do.

Still later: "Lucinda, where's Lucinda? Has anyone seen Lucinda? There you are, Lucinda. You're so quiet in that corner. Oh, were you napping, Lucinda? Oops! Sorry I woke you, Lucinda. Lucinda! Lucinda? *Loo-sin-dah!*"

ONE AFTERNOON NEAR the end of the first week, Lucinda struggled to compose a tricky scene involving many characters in a social setting. She worked to reveal and juggle their various agendas while trying to maintain fidelity to the perspective and groping to find a better word for "provocation," when the entryway to the writers' workspaces flew open and slammed shut. Then *rap-tap-tap*—knuckles pecked on the inner door to her office. Lucinda cursed before yanking the door open, and there in the threshold stood Leah in her Grim Reaper garb, a vapid smile playing on her puffy face.

"What's up?" Lucinda said.

Leah peered over Lucinda's shoulder into her office as if hoping to be invited in.

Lucinda stepped into the vestibule she shared with Dev and pulled the door to her workspace shut behind her. "Is everything okay?"

"You have a phone call," Leah told her. "It's your agent."

Coatless, Lucinda barreled past Leah and out into the icy wind toward the retreat house. Leah's gym shoes rasped over gravel close behind her. Once inside, Lucinda dashed through the mudroom and hallway to snatch the receiver lying atop a kitchen counter.

"This is Lucinda," she said into it. "Yes, yes, okay, so what happened?" She turned her back to Leah, who'd followed her into the kitchen and now stood nearby leafing through a newspaper and eavesdropping so intently that Lucinda sensed suction from her ears. At first, Lucinda gripped the receiver tightly, but her fingers grew numb with this pressure. Digit by digit, she loosened her hold as her agent explained that her manuscript had been rejected by an editor at the publishing house for which she'd had great hope. This editor—like the others—found the main character unlikable.

"I see," Lucinda said, not seeing at all since the fiction was autobiographical. She coughed to clear her throat. "I see. Well, this isn't the best news in the world."

At her back, the newspaper ceased rattling.

"Thanks for letting me know," she told her agent, who promised to send the editor's notes to Lucinda by email. "Okay, sure. Bye." Lucinda re-cradled the receiver.

"What happened?" Leah knitted her pencil-drawn eyebrows with concern, though prurience shone in her inky eyes. "What did she say?"

In a moment of human weakness and self-dramatization that Lucinda regretted almost as soon as she opened her mouth, she told Leah what her agent had said and about the other editors who had rejected her manuscript, even alluding to the hopelessness that now pervaded her, and Leah, was *so, so, so-o-o-o-o sorry*.

"Oh, how horrible!" Leah cried. "Those awful people, stupid, stupid, *stupid* people! What do they know about books anyway?"

"Well," Lucinda said, "they're editors. Books are pretty much what they do know."

Leah clasped Lucinda's hand with moist and chilly fingers. "Listen to me," she said, the pupils of her eyes scanning Lucinda's face as if a miniature ping-pong match were being played upon it. "You're going to show them all. I just know it. You are an *awesome* writer!"

"Thanks." She wormed free of Leah's clammy grip. Though aware that Leah had never actually read a word she'd written, Lucinda's next statement was nonetheless heartfelt in this moment. "That means a lot to me."

Lucinda would have remained sincerely touched by Leah's passionate, if baseless outrage on her behalf, but Leah—like Hailey picking at her weaving projects—couldn't leave it alone. Nearly every time she saw Lucinda, Leah stopped to pat her shoulder or offer a sad smile, along with words of consolation. Leah behaved as if the phone call were a secret between them, as if her expressions of sympathy were somehow cryptic to the others. In fact, Lucinda soon confided in each of the women, disclosing the rejection with more anguish than she'd mustered when informing Leah of it. Lucinda had even allowed a fat tear to waddle down the side of her nose as she told Jane about her agent's call. But Jane hadn't bothered to pretend that platitudes would make disappointment sting less. She'd simply said, "So what are you going to do about it?"

"Good question." And Lucinda began to consider this.

Or she tried to, when not waylaid by Leah. The woman now lurked about the retreat house, ever ready to spring out at her. "Lucinda, oh, Lucinda! You hanging in there, girl? Such a shame, such a sad, *sad* shame! But it's always darkest before the dawn. And you know what? Let me tell you something, girlfriend, something I have learned the hard way. Time—*it's true!*—time heals all wounds. But, oh, *Lucinda*, how dreadful this must be for you! Those stupid editors! They just make me sick, you know that, Lucinda? *Sick*."

"I HATE MY name," Lucinda told Jane one afternoon as they ambled along the unpaved county road toward the highway into Sheridan. This was the only way to evade Leah, who often enumerated her many health problems, ailments that prevented her from exercising and for which she took a variety of medications. The side effects of these caused her to eat rich foods, compelled her to imbibe vast quantities of vodka followed by tumblers of red wine on ice each evening, and somehow induced her to smoke.

"I used to not mind my name. But now, I hate it. I hate hearing my own name."

Jane turned to squint at Lucinda. "What's wrong with it?"

"Leah's taken it away from me, don't you see? She's turned it into a device for hijacking my thoughts."

They hiked up a biscuit-colored incline, their boots rasping over the gravelly road. Few vehicles rumbled past on this road, and these were usually trucks. Now, an engine puttered in the distance. The women fell into single-file to make room for a rust-colored pickup. They gave the cowboy-hat-wearing driver a two-fingered salute. He grinned and waved back. As the old truck rattled by, a chain-tethered hound in its bed launched itself at the tailgate, barking explosively at Lucinda and Jane.

"Holy Christ," said Lucinda as Jane cupped her ears.

Then they trudged on savoring the profound silence in the truck's wake. On both sides of the road, herds of cattle grazed beyond barbed-wire fencing. A brown-and-white cow, cudding grass near a fence post, glanced up at them, an incurious yet disdainful look on its bovine face.

"She's taken my name, too," Jane said.

THEN THERE WAS the note: a handwritten sheet of binder paper that appeared in Lucinda's mailbox soon after she'd begun avoiding Leah in more obvious ways. In the note, Leah apologized. But for what? It was unclear. *I know I can be loud,* the note read. *I take too much joy in life. I have some serious health problems, though I don't like to talk about these. Knowing I have a rare heart condition, and hearing from my doctors what my future holds, finds me really living each day like it's my last. Laughter and wit are my friends. The way I express myself is an affirmation that I am here on earth. I know I can be too exuberant by trying to make every moment shine. So forgive me, Lucinda. I hope you can forgive me for that. Love, Leah.*

Pah-*leeze*, thought Lucinda, who—in fact—had heard many times about Leah's serious health problems, including the rare heart condition. Early on, she'd been given, along with the others, the grand tour of Leah's prescription medications—a futuristic micro-city of orange-vial towers, squat salve rotundas, and brown-glass high-rises for containing an array of capsules, tablets, ointments, and syrups— assembled for display on the dining room table. How she'd raved about the expense of these drugs! Leah—historic mansion owner and close personal friend to Bill Gates and both Steves: Jobs and Wozniak— had sputtered in outrage, "*Seventy dollars!* Look, *look*. See that?" She'd pointed to the price printed on a vial. "Can you believe I have to pay seventy dollars *each month* for these caplets?"

"The note was supposed to be an apology," Lucinda told Jane during another afternoon hike. "But it was really an accusation."

This time they'd turned left after crossing the cattle guard, heading in the direction of Cloud Peak set deep in the blue-black mountain range. Again, the road cleaved golden-grassed meadows that rolled, cresting and sloping like a tawny sea, and on the far left, a hillock writhed and twitched, blooming before their very eyes with . . . *What on earth?* Could those be *snow blossoms?* Lucinda removed her sunglasses to squint at the dun-colored mound, aboil with movement as it transformed from hillock into a herd of white-tail deer skittering for a vanishing point in the distance. Seconds later, the rusty truck chugged past, and both women braced themselves, covering their ears against the hound's deafening salvos. This time the dog punctuated these by baring teeth and snarling, glistening loops of saliva swinging from its jowls. The truck disappeared from sight, and the women again enjoyed a few minutes of silence, after which Jane pointed out layers of color in the sky, bottom to top: cerulean, cobalt, and ultramarine. Then she asked Lucinda about Leah's note. "An accusation, of what?"

"I'm apparently some kind of killjoy who's diminishing her happiness over being alive, in what could be her last remaining days."

"Oh, *right*," Jane said, "she's dying. I forgot about that. So what are you going to do?"

"That's on her. If it's a sincere apology, then she should stop bothering me, right?"

Jane issued a doubtful look.

"In the meantime, I plan to treat it like an unwanted email." Lucinda had a hyperactive delete-key finger, a hair-trigger reflex for reporting messages as spam. "I *hope* she doesn't expect me to write back. The last thing I want is to start a pen-pal thing here." She then told Jane about a former friend from grad school, with whom she'd had a falling-out. During this conflicted time, the friend was diagnosed with lupus. "Oh, why must I have such trouble with the infirm?"

"I don't know, but on a windless day like this and when the sun is high, I think I see a fourth color." Jane pointed at the sky just above the mountain range foregrounding Cloud Peak—jagged white-capped fangs zigzagging in the distance. "Look," she said. "Just beneath the cerulean, there's slate."

THE NEXT DAY a trip to town was scheduled. The heiress wrote the women weekly stipend checks to buy groceries and supplies. On shopping days, they had to vacate the residency from nine in the morning until one for housekeepers to clean the place. Lucinda and Jane, joined by Kerry, wandered around the downtown area for a couple of hours, dodging Leah as best they could by ducking into a boot shop, the JCPenney, and even a storefront Pentecostal church. In between, Jane photographed the banner strung across Main Street, promoting the National Day of Prayer, and then she snapped an image of Kerry and Lucinda in front of the Mint Bar. They wandered into galleries and shops, where Jane bought turquoise earrings, Kerry purchased a T-shirt, and Lucinda picked up a few postcards. At the designated time, they headed to meet Dora, the staff driver who would transport them to the supermarket, at a coffee shop. There, they were accosted by Leah. She held a striped bag out to Kerry, saying, "Go on. Take one."

An apprehensive look on her face, Kerry fished out a small tissue-wrapped object.

"A little gift. Enjoy!" She offered the sack to Jane, who reached in and pulled out a navy blue kerchief. "Not *that*," Leah said, grabbing it from her. "That's mine."

Flushing, Jane withdrew a bundle similar to Kerry's.

Then Leah approached Lucinda, who waved off the bag. "I really don't eat sweets."

"There's nothing sweet in here, I promise."

Gingerly, Lucinda reached in for the last item.

"Open them up," commanded Leah. Jane, Kerry, and Lucinda tore off the paper to discover cowboy- and cattle-themed Christmas tree ornaments, no doubt discounted for sale in April. Lucinda's was a ceramic cow in boots, holding aloft a wire lasso.

They all thanked Leah before climbing in the van to head for the supermarket. Lucinda placed her ornament in the same bag with the postcards she'd bought, wondering if she owed someone she disliked a gift.

"Peace offerings," Jane whispered. "When what we really want is peace."

A thorn, Kerry mouthed, *in my side.*

She, Hailey, and Jane bore the brunt of it: Leah knocking on their studio doors to see what they were working on, to ask questions, to borrow staple guns, to return staple guns, to re-borrow and re-return staple guns, to apologize for bothering them about the staple guns, to ask a few more questions, and then to start in again with the staple guns. After summoning Lucinda for her agent's phone call, Leah, uninvited and having no legitimate business there, stayed away from the writers' offices in a separate structure from the hangar-sized building that housed the visual artists' work spaces. Both Lucinda and Dev felt grateful for that. But whenever she could, Leah paraded before their windows, chuffing cigarettes as if to send urgent smoke signals: *Pay attention, pay attention, pay attention to me.*

AT THE SUPERMARKET, Lucinda finally received a signal on her cell phone, and as she pushed her cart through the produce section, she managed to reach her boyfriend at work. She'd missed him deeply, but he was distracted, seemed to think there should be a specific reason for her call. Wounded feelings, a misunderstanding—not quite a quarrel—erupted between them during the staticky call when something bulbous and purplish black loomed into sight. Lucinda pulled back to focus. *Eggplant?* An eggplant was being thrust in her face. By Leah. Lucinda shook her head, indicated her cell phone and flicked a hand to shoo the woman.

"I found eggplant." An insipid smile tugged up the corners of Leah's thin lips. "Right over there by the turnips, there's eggplant, a whole bin of—"

Lucinda wrenched her cart away with such force that she crashed it into an onion display. She sped away from cascading onions that bounced to the floor like golden softballs. "*Leave me alone,*" she told Leah.

Someone gasped, nearby shoppers gaped, and Lucinda's boyfriend, on the phone, said, "Hey, you're the one who called me."

"You all right?" Leah followed her, still holding out the eggplant. She wore an avid look on her face, even if concern crimped her eyebrows. "Is everything okay at home?"

AFTER PACKING THEIR groceries in the van's storage bay, Jane, Kerry, Dev, Hailey, and Lucinda took their seats and buckled safety belts. The driver climbed aboard, adjusted the rearview mirror and released the parking brake, but Leah was nowhere in sight. They all watched the supermarket's entrance in silence. The glass doors parted wide again and again. Two cowboys emerged bearing sacks of dog food, next a harried young woman rushed out—surely no older than Lucinda's daughter—in pursuit of a toddler, and then a trio of teenagers sallied forth, sipping sodas. In the van, someone's stomach growled. Another roared back. Lucinda had not eaten since breakfast at seven, and now it was nearly one. As usual, hunger failed to improve her outlook on life. The cow ornament would make a *fucking fine* souvenir for her boyfriend.

"I am a grown woman," Lucinda told Jane and Kerry.

They both nodded, for this was true.

"If I want eggplant, I am perfectly capable of finding one in a supermarket."

"*Oh,*" Jane said, "the eggplant. Now, see, I told her not to bother you with that."

"Do I *look* like the kind of person who wants an eggplant shoved in my face?"

"It was me," piped Hailey from the middle seat. "I told her I might make eggplant moussaka, but I changed my mind. I'm going to do fish tacos instead on my cooking night."

Several minutes later, Leah trundled her cart toward the van. Her gait was unhurried, ever regal and remiss, and she took her time loading groceries in back. Finally, she slid into the front seat, slammed the door shut, and nearly buckled up before saying, "Forgot all about the Liquor Barn." With this, Leah clicked open the van's door. "I'll be just a sec."

Chin tilted skyward and shoulders back, Leah marched back across the parking lot in the direction of the liquor store, a few doors from the supermarket. The previous evening she'd peeled off her socks and treated all to the sight of her misshapen, fetid, and blistered feet, and now Leah limped with the dignified drag-step of someone leading a solemn processional, as if "Pomp and Circumstance" were playing inside her head.

Stomachs gurgled and moaned. Kerry sighed several times. Hailey drummed fingers on the armrest. In the back seat, Jane mimed loading a pistol, spinning the chamber, inserting the barrel into her mouth and firing it. Her head jerked back with the imaginary impact. No one said a word, not even after Leah returned. Lucinda and the other four women shared an elective muteness that lasted from Sheridan to the ranch. Their silence had no impact on Leah, who prattled all the way back to the retreat. "A *heron*," she said. "See that? I just love herons. Don't you love herons? Say, there's that barn we saw on the way in, same barn. There it is. And those horses—*look*! They're still there. I *love* horses. Just last year, at the Kentucky Derby, it was the most *hilarious* thing . . ."

Just as the van pulled into its parking space, Leah rotated to face the rear seat. "Oh, Lucinda," she said. "I bought eggplants for you. I noticed you didn't get any, so I picked up three. You can pay me for them now or later. Whenever you like—really, it's fine."

KERRY AND LUCINDA, this time, strode along the county road, again heading toward the highway into Sheridan, both tall women taking long, swift steps. Dense, iron-bellied clouds crowded out sunlight, dulling the sky to gray—a color not merely comprised of black and white, according to Jane. Instead it could be a combination of red and green or blue and orange or yellow and purple. Lucinda glanced overhead. The murky amalgam of colors comprising this gray suggested a blended protein drink involving blackberries and chalky whey powder.

"It's that voice," Kerry said. "That *voice*. I can't bear it."

On the road in the distance, a coppery smudge appeared, shimmering in the dust.

"Here it comes," Lucinda said. "Cover your ears."

"Why? What is it? That truck?"

Lucinda, leading the way, plugged her ears with her fingertips. She again experienced a heart-juddering surge when the frenzied dog lunged for the tailgate, slavering, snapping, and barking thunderously as the pickup chugged out of sight.

"What on *earth*? How did you know?"

Lucinda shrugged. "Every time I'm on this road—doesn't matter which direction—that truck passes by with the hellhound in back."

Kerry held out her hands, displaying knobby, chill-blanched fingers. "Look—my hands are *shaking*. That was dreadful."

"You're very sensitive to sounds."

"*Yes*, yes, I am, and that's why I can't bear that woman's voice."

"The high-pitched, little-girly sound of it?" said Lucinda. "Or the fakeness of it?"

"*Both*—the sound and the tone just drive me out of my mind. Listening to her is like having someone drill holes in my skull. *In my skull.*"

Lucinda winced. "For me, it's that congested laugh and those hacking fits as end punctuation to every sentence she utters. Nothing says I'm jovial though infirm like haw-haw-hawing that thickens into a wet cough. And she's not even funny. She has to laugh to signal she's said something that's supposed to be amusing. Otherwise *how* would we know?"

"I can't tell my son about her. Scott would be furious," Kerry said. "Just furious."

"Your son's a poet." Lucinda remembered Kerry's shy pride in showing her a chapbook written by him.

Kerry nodded. "He knows how hard it is for me to steal a few hours here and there to work, especially since my parents live with me. He's taking care of them now, and I can't breathe a word about Leah to him, but every morning I write the most spiteful things in my journal. I used to fill it with sketches, plans, poems. Now it's page after page of spite."

Lucinda issued Kerry a sympathetic look. One by one, the others had been approaching her privately, as if she were a Mother Confessor, capable of relieving suffering through listening to Leah's transgressions against them and absolving their unkind thoughts in the aftermath of these. Or else they rightly sensed that Lucinda enjoyed mean gossip.

"You notice," Kerry said, "how she talks like she's black when she's speaking to Dev?"

"I *know*, and Dev speaks Standard English." Lucinda pictured the set of chef's knives fastened to a magnetic strip above the coffeemaker, just to the right of the sink. "I would testify in court," she said.

"What's that?"

"If Dev stabbed Leah for talking that way, I would be a witness for the defense. I would swear it was a clear-cut—excuse the awful pun—case of justifiable homicide."

"Dev would *never* do that," Kerry said. "She's too good-natured. Besides, it would make a big mess, and Dev couldn't bear that."

Lucinda had to agree. Despite upkeep by the weekly cleaners, Dev often swept and mopped, wiped off counters, and took out the trash. She'd straighten, dust, and scrub with greater vigor whenever Leah was nearby. That morning, Lucinda had caught sight of her— Leah at her side, nattering—while Dev hauled the vacuum cleaner out of the front closet, her dark eyes searching the baseboards, somewhat wildly, for an electrical outlet.

"I might," Lucinda told Kerry. "I don't mind a mess. If she ever starts using a phony Spanish accent with me, I just might reach up for one of those knives in the kitchen—"

"I'd testify in court for you," Kerry said. "We *all* would."

TO GENERATE LOCAL interest in the artists' retreat, Ariadne Warwick Murdoch arranged for the women to present their work in Sheridan. The night of the presentation, all six boarded the van driven by Dora into town. Though she spent the day complaining about rheumatoid arthritis, tendonitis, nonspecific bum knee, and what have you, Leah ultimately lacked the nerve to back out. She, along with the other visual artists, packed the van's storage bay with unwieldy portfolios, while Dev and Lucinda climbed into the back, the coveted seats as far from Leah in front as they could get. Once settled, they traded self-satisfied looks, as if not having to haul bulky works of art had been shrewdly factored into their decisions to become writers.

On the way to town, Leah persuaded the driver to stop at the Loaf 'N Jug, a gas station/convenience store, ostensibly to use the restroom, but really—and they all witnessed this through the plate glass—to buy cigarettes. After disappearing from sight for a few seconds, Leah reappeared at the counter handing over a credit card for a pack of Marlboro Lights. Nonetheless, Dora said, "Well, when you gotta go . . ."

"*Really?*" Dev said.

Hailey turned to flash a wicked grin. "It's probably her medication."

Everything that went awry for her, Leah attributed to this. When she cracked the MOMA bowl, when she melted a spatula in the oven and filled the kitchen with noxious fumes, when she opened the dishwasher during the rinse cycle and steamy water shot out in all directions, when she left the door open on fish-taco night and feral cats entered the house—it was the meds, always the meds that caused her to do such things. But after the internet was restored, Jane investigated the drugs Leah had displayed. Not a one, she told the others, listed carelessness as a side effect, and none of the medication was typically prescribed for treating heart problems, rare or otherwise.

Kerry palpated her ribcage—the *thorn* in it—before glancing at her wristwatch. "Well, we're going to be late."

When at last Leah climbed back into the van and chunked the door shut, Lucinda couldn't help herself, and for at least the third time that day, she said, in a voice loud enough to carry to the front seat, "Now, we have just ten minutes apiece, am I right?"

"Oh, right," Jane said, also amplifying to be heard up front. "Heaven help you if you exceed your time limit. You're supposed to practice and time yourself to keep it to ten minutes or under. That's what Merle said."

"What happens," Hailey asked Dora, "if we go over ten minutes?"

At the end of the first week, they had shared samplings of their work with one another, and Leah had taken close to an hour to elaborate on computer-generated images of her art.

"We let you know," Dora said. "But it's not like we have a hook to pull you offstage."

A HOOK HADN'T BEEN needed for Leah, who flushed and stammered as she stood before the assembled group of about thirty local people interested in the arts. Despite the two glasses of Riesling she pounded down in the reception area before speaking, Leah appeared rattled, even chagrined, perhaps aware of the shortcomings of her work compared to that of the others. Lucinda experienced a twinge in her stomach—a flutter-kick of sympathy during Leah's shamefaced and rushed presentation. Jane cast her a sidelong look and shook her head.

Despite her bulky portfolio casing, Leah produced only two paltry eight-by-twelve-inch canvases. These were poorly painted, the lines shaky, the effect amateurish even to Lucinda's untrained eye. But on the computer screen, which projected its images onto a large sheet tacked to one wall, the designs Leah displayed, though not to Lucinda's taste, were bright in color and arresting—geometric shapes in yellow, red, and orange that reminded her of psychedelic posters popular in the seventies. In her presentation, Leah mentioned using an Adobe program, and Lucinda was awed by the transformative effects of computer software. After a few minutes of halting discussion of her work, Leah returned to her seat, without waiting for questions, as they were all instructed to do. She had to scramble back to the podium when one man in a cowboy hat asked for more information about the software she used.

Again, thought Lucinda, *no respect for the rules*.

Jane was next, and she'd brought one of the bird nests she'd sketched, along with the miniature pochade kit that she'd constructed for painting outdoors. She showed the audience how she stored her brushes, paints, and canvases within compartments of the wooden box that opened to serve as a small easel. Then she exhibited renderings of local landscapes that caused the audience to murmur in recognition. Jane fielded many questions after her presentation, most of these from a tall, rugged-looking man with a long iron-streaked ponytail, a fellow that Lucinda noticed at the outset of the presentation for his striking looks. Kerry and Hailey's presentations followed Jane's, and the local people, warmed by Jane's engaging demonstration, responded to their work with thoughtful questions and comments.

This was a no-frills group, thought Lucinda, eyeing the audience. Many women had their hair coiled in buns or braided, and the few sharp-featured men present had donned Levis and crisp long-sleeved shirts. Most wore scuffed brown boots. No wonder Jane, in a muslin blouse and denim skirt, connected well with them, while Leah, who'd traded her hoodie and faded trousers for a sequined black sweater and shimmery gold pants, looked and seemed to feel out of place. Lucinda was glad she'd opted for indigo slacks and a tan corduroy blazer, and she, too, had pulled on scuffed boots, though these were black.

When not displaying the visual artists' work, the projector showed an image of all six women, a photograph taken by Merle the first day they arrived. In it, Leah angled her head away from the lens so that only a slice of her profile had been captured. The other women, tired from travel and unsmiling, looked steely-eyed and grimly triumphant, as if the photo had been snapped nearly two centuries ago, after they had just robbed a bank.

Kerry's gray eyes seemed flinty and unrelenting, and Jane's pretty face was clenched in a scowl. Dev's shrewd expression conveyed cunning and calculation. Even Hailey looked like someone who relished a good fight, someone who might laugh while delivering a kick to the kidneys. Lucinda, dark eyebrows lowered and lips compressed, wore an expression on her face that suggested she'd welcome the slightest provocation to whip out a pistol. But snapped before she could swoop out of the frame, the blurred image of Leah—the sliver of her face and soft dumpling of her nose—told the world that she would be the one most likely to forget to tie horses to hitching posts or to leave a labeled vial of pills at a teller's window.

When the others had finished their presentations, it was Lucinda's turn, and she sidled up to the podium, her legs slightly bowed as if she'd just slid off a saddle, so powerfully had she envisioned that long-ago robbery. She cleared her throat, and her thoughts, to project an animated voice while reading her writing. Lucinda had chosen to present a freshly drafted excerpt of a new piece, a novella she'd begun just days ago. It was set on a ranch just outside of Sheridan, so she thought it a good choice for this venue, and she was proud of the comic potential realized by one obnoxious character. Lucinda, a bit of an amateur thespian, enjoyed performing her work. She read for exactly ten minutes—not a second more or less—as she'd been instructed, and then took questions from the audience, speaking with self-deprecating wit about her work. After it was over, the others congratulated her on the reading.

"I had no idea," Jane said, "that you spoke so well."

"You seem so reserved," Kerry put in. "But you looked totally at ease up there."

"You can tell you've had experience teaching." Having never taught before, Dev had confided being anxious about her appointment at Birnbrau.

"Nice," Hailey told Lucinda. "That was nice."

"I really need to work on presentation skills before the semester starts," Dev said. "Maybe I should join Toastmasters . . ."

"Teaching really isn't about presentation," Leah said. Like Dev, she had admitted being new to the profession, so Hailey, Kerry and Jane—all experienced teachers—drew near, no doubt prepared to scoff at whatever advice Leah had to impart.

"What is it about then?" Lucinda, with more than a decade of classroom experience, was especially curious to hear how teaching departed from presentation: the communication of ideas and skills. She wanted to know how teaching really wasn't about *teaching*.

Leah gave a sly look and crooked her finger, beckoning them near. "*Course evaluations.*" Her warm breath stank of sour wine.

Lucinda drew back, and Leah fixed her gaze on Dev, likely targeting her as the most credulous of the group. "I have a friend at Princeton," she said. "He's smart as a whip, and he's won just about every teaching award there is. He's practically a legend, and he's just crazy about me. He tells me *everything*."

Familiar by now with Leah's tendency to exaggerate and dissemble, Lucinda parsed this to mean that Leah perhaps made the grudging acquaintance of someone who'd claimed to have given instruction at the prestigious university—maybe an adjunct or tech support personnel engaged to show administrative staff how to use new programs. Quite possibly no such person existed. Still, Lucinda had to ask, "What's his name? What department does he teach in?"

Leah wagged an index finger. "That's confidential since he made me swear never to share his professional secret." She grinned, baring stubby teeth.

"You may as well tell us his name," Hailey said, "since you're divulging his secret."

Leah ignored that. "Anyway, he told me that the secret to great teaching evaluations is what he calls the Marie-Antoinette approach."

Kerry lifted an eyebrow. "Marie Antoinette?"

Leah nodded. "You know, Marie Antoinette. *Let them eat cake!* Well, that, my friends, is the secret to outstanding evaluations."

Lucinda's tongue separated from her soft palate with a clicking sound.

"Giving students *cake?*" said Dev, who enjoyed baking. "Like right before they fill out evaluations?"

"She's talking about grade inflation," Lucinda said. "Aren't you?"

Leah shrugged. "To-*may*-to, to-*mah*-to. You say grade inflation, and I say *positive reinforcement*. Give students what they want, and they'll love you to death."

Hailey wore a puzzled look on her face. "But wasn't Marie Antoinette, like, beheaded?"

The tall man with the ponytail approached the group to ask Jane about her landscapes, and a woman with a silvery braid coiled atop her head joined the group to discuss textiles with Hailey. Soon all of the women from the retreat were borne out with a cluster of attendees to the reception area in the foyer, a card table holding bottles of wine, a bowl of mixed nuts, and stacks of plastic cups, where they had conversations with attendees.

During the reception, Dev snapped many photos. As long as the flash didn't blind her while reading, Lucinda didn't care who took her picture. She wasn't bad looking or vain, so she didn't pay much attention to how she appeared in photographs. And Dev was something of a shutterbug. She especially enjoyed taking pictures of tables arrayed with food before they ate it. Lucinda had visited Dev's Facebook page when the internet was working, and there she beheld images of the more picturesque meals they'd consumed. But when Dev or Jane, another camera aficionado, tried to capture Leah's image, she would turn her head, duck, and dodge out of the crosshairs of any lens pointed in her direction.

Soon after the reception, they climbed into the van for the return trip, and snowflakes drifted onto the windshield. Within minutes, the wind kicked up, stirring great billows of snow. Despite her pitiable presentation that night, Leah regaled the others in the van with a number of obvious observations ("look it's *snowing*—it's really, *really* snowing") and another installment in the unending series of things she considered interesting about herself. This time, and perhaps triggered by mention of her teaching friend, the topic was People Who Like Leah a Whole Lot, and she discussed her various friendships by category—her famous friends, her gay friends, her intellectual friends—before pivoting to share an insight by one close pal, supposedly a don at Oxford, who declared that Wyoming, because it ends in I-N-G, is the only "gerund state."

Though she had rededicated her life that night—with a stern lecture-to-self in the restroom before leaving the presentation—vowing never again to rise to Leah's bait, Lucinda couldn't resist saying, "I would think an Oxford *don* would know there is more to a gerund than ending in I-N-G."

"What is a gerund anyway?" Hailey asked.

"It's an I-N-G verb," Leah told her, "I'm talking, it's snowing, Dora's driving and so on."

"Those are *not* gerunds." Lucinda shook her head with such force that the vertebrae in her neck popped. She experienced the nearly pornographic thrill of forbidden pleasure, a ticklish sensation at the back of her throat, from the punitive tone of her voice. "Gerunds are *not* verbs. A gerund derives from a verb, but functions as a noun. Some examples are: Irritating people is what she does best. Being pestered generates violent thoughts. Annoying others is what ultimately resulted in her untimely—"

Dev, seated beside her, clasped Lucinda's hand and applied pressure.

"Well, Wyoming is a noun," Leah said. "So there it is—the only gerund state!"

Lucinda released a slow exhalation like air hissing from a punctured tire. She curled her fingers around Dev's and squeezed these gently—as if to say, *give me strength*—while Leah continued to blather on about her many friends, establishing their fame, talents, and accomplishments before telling of their great devotion to her.

When the van delivered them to the residence, Lucinda rushed with the others into the house. She'd shed her coat and tugged off her gloves before remembering she'd left her laptop in her office. *Damn it.* She bundled up again and raced into the blizzard for it.

After she disconnected her computer in the dark, Lucinda parted bamboo slats to peer through the screen. Again tenderness twisted deep inside her. Leah stood smoking outside the window in a halo of motion-sensor lights from the nearby studio, as forlorn as an ever-solitary figure encased in a snow globe.

HAILEY, A FEW days later, trod the county road with Lucinda. It was late afternoon, and they timed the walk so that when they returned the rest of the group would have departed for Buffalo to listen to music.

Earlier, Leah had exhorted Lucinda to join them for the outing, and when she refused, Leah said, "I get it. You'd probably rather go out next weekend to celebrate Cinco de Mayo."

"Oh, really? Why is that?"

"Come on. You know. It's your holiday."

"How is it *my* holiday?"

They were in the kitchen, again, standing before the coffeemaker and the magnetized strip to which the chef's knives were affixed. Lucinda cast a surreptitious glance at these.

"Isn't it like the Fourth of July," Leah said, "for your people?"

"If by *my people*," Lucinda said, that irresistibly pedantic tone sharpening her voice, "you mean my family, then you might remember me telling you that my ancestors have been in this country since before Jamestown."

Jane stepped into the kitchen, wearing plum-colored lipstick and a tailored check shirt with jeans. She held out her blow-dryer like a gun. "Okay, you two," she said, "break it up."

"Why should *I* celebrate a holiday that commemorates a battle that took place in Mexico in 1862?" Lucinda's cheeks flared, and her throat throbbed with a now-familiar drumbeat. "That's more than two centuries after *my people* had been in the United States. And Cinco de Mayo isn't even Mexican Independence Day. That's actually September sixteenth."

Jane offered the blow-dryer to Leah. "Did you want to borrow this or not?"

"Gosh, I had no idea. I thought you still had family in Mexico—"

"You had *no idea?*" It drove Lucinda to the edge that Leah seemed incapable of wrapping her brain around anything that was not a cliché or stereotype.

Palms raised, Leah shrugged. Since Lucinda had a Spanish surname, nothing could convince Leah that Lucinda was not a recent and likely undocumented immigrant, someone to be treated with the solicitousness that reflected an open mind. Lucinda envisioned Leah, at some future time, boasting to others about how kindly she'd treated that Mexican girl at the retreat. She could almost hear the woman saying, "It's not my business how she got into this country. I treat everyone the same—illegals, blacks, even white trash. That's just the way I roll."

"I told you all of this in the first week." Lucinda labored to keep her tone even.

"*Oh*, okay. Gotcha." Leah winked.

Dev, then, appeared, wielding Windex and eyeing the countertops.

"Dev! There's my sister from another mister!" Leah approached as if to embrace Dev, but was fended off by the glass cleaner and sponge.

"I think I'm getting a cold," Dev told her. "You'd better not come too close."

As THEY HIKED, Lucinda and Hailey discussed this, shouting to be heard above the harsh wind whipping icy needles of rain in their faces, needles that pierced the knit caps they'd pulled over their ears. Frigid blasts ransacked Lucinda's many layers of clothing, tunneling into her nostrils, ears, and mouth and lashing her face with strands of hair that escaped from under her cap. Her eyes and nose seeped from the cold, yet she plodded with Hailey into the gusts, the two of them like driven cattle. Under the bridge they crossed, the creek roiled with uncommon agitation, and in the distance Cloud Peak was ringed by dense and shadowy tufts that resembled a thick corona of sooty mattress ticking.

Squinting at this, Lucinda said, "Leah's like this mass of toxic goodwill."

"Like some synthetic fiberfill substance that you can punch and kick," added Hailey. "You can sit on it, even flop on it with all your weight, and it just bounces back to the same unmanageable shape, again and again." She peered up at Lucinda. "Know what I mean?"

Lucinda nodded. "Have you noticed how Leah won't let anyone take her picture?"

"Maybe she's in witness protection."

"You mean maybe she's here under some ruse? That she's not really an artist?"

"I don't know about the ruse business, but do you think she's an artist?"

Unqualified to comment on Leah's work, Lucinda asked, "Do *you*?"

Hailey shrugged. "I think she's just this needy person who doesn't mean any harm."

"I agree with the first part," Lucinda said, "but not the second. I think she does mean harm. For whatever reasons, she's not painting much, so she's making herself an obstacle to prevent the rest of us from working. She's exactly what we came here to escape."

"It bugs me when she calls me *bitch*," Hailey said. "I have a thing about that word. I don't mind when it's used to describe a man. Then it's kind of edgy, ironic, you know, and usually apt. But when a woman's called a bitch, that really grates on me, like some poly-wool blend against bare skin. I mentioned this to her, and she keeps forgetting, so she calls me *bitch*, like nonstop. Have you noticed?"

Lucinda nodded again.

"But, she's just like that—forgetful and kind of obtuse," Hailey continued. "Leah probably remembers I said something once about being called bitch, and she's confused this in her mind, flipped it somehow so she thinks I *want* to be called bitch, or else she believes we are such great friends that *she* alone can call me this. She mixes things up a lot, but I really don't think she's malevolent or scheming, do you?"

Lucinda disagreed. The woman was positively hazardous, but reluctant to credit Leah with the requisite cunning for evil, she said, "Well, maybe not . . . Do *you* think she's an artist?"

"I have to say I don't get her work. I really don't."

Lucinda's eyes smarted and her ears, despite the cap, stung from the cold. When the maniacal hound trundled past in the rust-colored pickup, Hailey jumped, but Lucinda issued a curt nod of recognition. Hailey's hands, without gloves, reddened, though she huffed into these often to warm them. Lucinda's cheeks grew chapped and numb, yet she and Hailey marched for two solid hours that frigid and blustery afternoon, and when they returned, they were—like sinners who'd performed a hard penance—rewarded with the peace of mind that comes of absolution. The van absent from its parking space, the great house, with its curiously angled architecture, welcomed them with silence, with warmth.

After a serene meal of leftovers, Lucinda and Hailey separated to continue their work: Lucinda line-editing pages she'd drafted that day and Hailey distressing fabrics in her work studio. She brought an armload of broadcloth to continue with this when they rejoined each other upstairs in the media room to watch television later in the evening, a pleasure denied by Leah's running commentary interspersed with many questions about the shows they tried to enjoy. Plus, Leah filled whatever room she entered with the stink of cigarette smoke, inducing sharp headaches in Lucinda. So it was a rare treat to watch programs undisturbed for one evening. With no interruption from Leah, Lucinda even enjoyed the commercials.

She and Hailey watched a reality TV cooking competition episode, at the end of which a humiliated chef was eliminated for preparing an incongruous dish of salad and pretzels. Hailey, pulling threads from a scarlet square, sighed. "Ah, if only it were as easy as that."

Lucinda nodded, picturing Leah, her white toque bowed in shame, as she backed away. "If we could just tell Leah to please pack her knives and leave . . ."

"Sometimes I imagine this residency's a reality-show competition," Hailey said. "Who do you think would win, if it were one?"

"Oh, Jane, definitely Jane."

"Really? My money's on Kerry."

"Kerry's too nice," Lucinda said, thinking that Hailey was also too nice to triumph. They'd be inclined to eliminate themselves to save others the trouble. Lucinda, given her newfound delight in delivering punishing speeches, felt sure that she or Dev, whose constant cleaning implicitly indicted the hygienic standards of others, would likely be "on the chopping block," as the chefs on the show liked to say, soon after Leah's departure.

When the cooking competition ended, they watched the news, including clips from the royal wedding—Prince William and Catherine Middleton before and after exchanging vows at Westminster Abbey. Cameras panned the crowds of spectators, providing glimpses of famous guests with an emphasis on the racy new royal sister-in-law. Once in a while, the screen flashed images of the Queen herself, and then the television camera returned to the bride, lingering on her voluminous wedding dress.

"All that fabric," murmured Hailey.

"Think of all the threads you could pull."

Hailey had her lap filled with the fabric she picked apart, crimson tangles of thread now nesting on the armrests of the chair where she sat. "I *know.*"

"Look. There's the Queen again."

"She looks tired." Hailey yawned. "I can't imagine being the Queen, all that responsibility."

"The prime minister does the real work," Lucinda said. "The Queen just shows her face now and then, while the PM makes the hard choices and suffers for them." She thought of Tony Blair who'd paid publicly for his impulsive decisions and misplaced loyalties, while the Queen—now in a yellow suit and matching headpiece with fabric roses nested in orange leaves, a bucket-shaped thing the Mad Hatter might have designed—remained untouched by his poor judgment.

The others returned after eleven. First Jane climbed the stairs to the media room to tell them about the evening's adventures. "Great bluegrass music, and the food was fine, though Dev sent back her seafood Caesar salad—I guess—because the shrimp was on a kebob skewer. That was a little weird. And Leah," Jane said, lowering her voice, "was a completely different person. She was charming with the people there, and they seemed to like her, but best of all, she flitted around to other tables like a butterfly, and she left us alone. Can you believe it? We ate an entire meal in peace."

"She's supposed to be," Hailey whispered, "one of the social sparks of Atlanta."

"*Really?*" Lucinda said. "I can see how Leah's demeanor might fly in superficial situations, but after a while—"

"*Shh . . .*" Jane put a finger to her lips.

Footfalls sounded heavily on the stairs, those slow, processional steps.

Leah's hooded form manifested like a specter of death at the threshold, the odor of cigarette smoke wafting into the room before she did. "*Ugh,*" she said with a glance at the television screen. "Not the royal wedding. I despise all the pomp and pretension. My ancestors were patriots, you know, who fought in the Revolutionary War. But you won't catch me joining the DAR. Talk about sticklers for documentation, proof of this, proof of that! Still everyone knows that I'm all about democracy, and I can't stand that royal crap. I can't *bear* the Queen! If she were in the yard right now, I wouldn't take one step outside this house to see her. I'm sorry, but that's just how I feel."

Lucinda nodded, encouraging Leah to honor those feelings, to follow the democracy in her heart (right out of the room and back down the stairs). Why, if the Queen were—for some reason—loitering in the yard or even hanging out by the dumpsters, Lucinda would gravitate toward the one person capable of repelling Leah. Now, she found the Queen's hat quite novel and daring, the orange leaves a unique touch rather than a symptom of colorblindness.

"Can't we watch something else?" Leah approached the coffee table for the remote.

"I want to see this," Jane told her. "I love the Queen."

Lucinda grinned. "I'm a fan."

"God save the Queen," Hailey said, before biting off a thread.

Leah withdrew from the room. Her footsteps drummed, one reverberant beat after another as she descended the staircase. Lucinda, Jane, and Hailey traded triumphant grins. But cigarette smoke fumes lingered, a malodorous reminder that even this small victory had been compromised.

ON MONDAY, WHEN Lucinda returned to the residency house for lunch, Leah hunkered at the door to the mudroom, waiting to tell her the news. "Osama killed Obama," she said.

"*What?*" Lucinda's heart constricted as if squeezed in a fist. She struggled to picture the robed and bearded terrorist breaking into the White House. Then she peered at Leah, the notoriously unreliable narrator, the shameless attention-addict. "How?"

Leah's cheeks were drained of color, her kohl-rimmed eyes muddy, genuinely sorrowful. "Navy SEALs, a raid, just hours ago."

Lucinda couldn't fathom why on earth Navy SEALs would attack the president. "A raid on the White House?" she said. "How did they get past the Secret Service?"

Leah's mournful expression dissolved into bafflement. "The White House?"

Lucinda glanced over Leah's shoulder to see if someone else in the house might tell her—quickly and clearly—what had really happened. "Where was it then, the raid?"

"Pakistan."

"Pakistan?" Granted, getting news at the residency could be dicey, especially when weather interfered with satellite reception, but surely Lucinda would have heard about it if the president had traveled to the Middle East. "What was he doing there?"

Leah's face softened with sympathy, no doubt for Lucinda's naivety. "He was *living* there. It turns out he was there all along."

"Who?"

Leah gave an impatient huff. "Osama bin Laden. He was hiding out in Pakistan."

"But what was Obama doing there?"

"Where?"

"*Pakistan*," Lucinda said. "What was the president doing in Pakistan?"

Leah cocked her head, squinting at Lucinda. "Why would Obama be in Pakistan? It's the president who orders strikes, but the *military* carries them out. It was the Navy SEALs, not the president himself, who raided the compound."

"You told me Osama bin Laden killed the president."

Leah shook her head with vehemence. "I never said that."

"You *did*. You said, 'Osama killed Obama.'"

"Ah, the names," Leah said, nodding. "They sound alike. I get why you were confused."

"*I* wasn't confused, that's what *you* told me." As if reaching for a sweater in a dark closet, Lucinda groped for patience. "Was there really a raid? Did anyone even die?"

Jane appeared in the threshold to the hallway, holding a magnum of champagne. "Osama bin Laden was killed in a raid on his compound in Pakistan," she said. "I just saw the news on my laptop." She waggled the dewy green bottle. "I knew this would come in handy."

Leah gasped, cupped her mouth. She side-stepped Jane and scurried to her room in the back of the house, the door to which she slammed shut.

"Want to pull out the flutes while I get the others?" said Jane.

Soon, the five women sat before the fireplace, where Lucinda had built a crackling fire. They sipped the tart, sparkling wine after toasting the president and the Navy SEALs, and then sharing what they knew of the raid from radio and internet broadcasts. During a lull in their conversation, Kerry said, "Where's Leah?"

Devorah shrugged, Hailey glanced about, and Jane pointed to the hall. "In her room."

"I think the champagne upset her," Lucinda said.

Hailey placed her half-filled flute on the coffee table. "She probably has, like, qualms about celebrating the loss of human life."

Kerry set her drink down, too. "That makes me feel . . . *dingy*."

With wide-eyed solemnity, Jane nodded.

Dingy, yes, Lucinda felt it, too. Yet, after a respectful pause, she and Jane exchanged a look and drained their glasses.

THE NEXT SHOPPING day, Merle—the tough woman who worked with livestock when not overseeing the residency and sometimes hauling the women into town—spoke up as Leah pulled open the front passenger door of the van, already hoisting a haunch to climb in. "Now, see here," Merle said. "We need to take turns riding shotgun. Jane, why don't you sit front this time? And we'll switch off again next time. We have to be fair." Merle, Jane had told Lucinda, had been her student years ago when Jane taught at a community college in Florida, and the two women remained in touch since that time, enjoying a long-distance friendship. Merle, in fact, called Jane to encourage her to apply for a teaching position in creative arts at Birnbrau.

"Sure, of course." Leah withdrew from the front seat. "Gotcha."

Kerry had whispered to Lucinda that morning the sad news: Leah's husband—formerly Richard Gere's twin and now Matthew McConaughey's lookalike, after Hailey mentioned some prurient gossip involving a gerbil—had slipped from a ladder and hurt his back. "Poor thing," Lucinda had said, while hoping the accident might prove serious enough for Leah to depart from the residency to care for him. With this in mind, she determined to treat Leah, if not kindly, at least somewhat less coldly.

Injured husband or not, Leah held court in the van with her usual vigor. In fact, she unleashed a new weapon in her arsenal to co-opt Lucinda, who, unlike the others, no longer bothered to feign interest in her. Leah now used flattery, in place of interrogation, to command Lucinda's attention. When Kerry wondered aloud if they'd passed the junkyard—an eccentric woman's yard littered with broken-down cars, discarded appliances, machine parts, and lumber, as well as a mound of bricks heaped atop a dead horse—Lucinda pointed to the right, saying, "I think it's just over that rise."

"You always know everything," Leah told her. "You have the most amazing memory."

As they drove into town, Jane said, "What was that church we went into?"

"Pentecostal." Lucinda pointed out a storefront in the distance. "There it is."

"Phenomenal." Leah turned to her in back. "Your mind is just phenomenal."

And unable to control herself, Lucinda cleared her throat to say, "Isn't it funny how an experience like a retreat changes a person or causes one to discover things about the self? For instance, before this, I never realized just how much I dislike flattery."

"Oh, I get embarrassed with praise, too," Kerry told her, her voice amplified like Lucinda's for all to hear.

"Yes, praise can be hard to take," Lucinda agreed, "but flattery is egregious."

"Why? I thought they were pretty much the same thing," said Hailey, who—time and again—proved willing to underplay her intelligence to set the stage for yet another castigating, if indirect allocution by Lucinda.

"Praise expresses admiration, and flattery is excessive and insincere praise that's given to further the flatterer's interests. In fact, flattery has little to do with the person being flattered; it's all about the flatterer. The subtext is always the same: *Like me, like me, like me.*" Here, Lucinda made her voice as obsequious as Leah's. Over the past few days, Lucinda had come to embrace her nascent pedantry and openly enjoy issuing these punishing speeches.

"As a matter of fact," Lucinda said, "there's deceit in flattery and manipulation, a lack of regard for the intelligence of the person being flattered, as if false praise is all it takes to compel another to feel or behave in the way the flatterer sees fit. Flattery also skews power dynamics by placing the flatterer in a position of judgment over the person being flattered." To demonstrate, Lucinda lifted one hand just above the other, raising and lowering her fingers to her thumbs in a manner suggestive of talking puppets. "*From my perch of superiority, I judge your actions or words*"—Lucinda had her upper hand say to the lower one in a high-pitched and unctuous tone—"*to be praiseworthy to me.*"

"What a great observation!" Leah released a smattering of applause that sounded like the last kernels of popcorn bursting in a microwave. "You say the smartest things. You do!"

By the time they reached the supermarket, though, Leah wilted. Just as Merle parked the van, she sniffled and then released a shuddery sob. Dev and Hailey sprang from the van, so the middle seat could be lurched forward for Lucinda and Kerry to shoot out and join Jane, who already stood in the parking lot, slamming her door shut. She, Kerry, and Lucinda trotted for the store, with Hailey and Dev close behind. When Lucinda paused to look back, Jane clutched her forearm, propelling her toward the store. "You will be turned into a pillar of salt."

They approached a rusted pickup parked near the entrance that struck Lucinda as familiar. An earsplitting racket jolted the four of them as the chained hound thrust itself at the tailgate, barking as if unhinged by rage.

"That dog again," said Lucinda, impressed. "Damned thing sure gets around."

When they returned to the retreat, Leah was presented with a staple gun purchased for her by Jane, Kerry, and Hailey. And Dev handed her a box of industrial-sized staples. All Lucinda could offer was a hard look when Leah displayed these that afternoon, saying, "You're all so great to me. Today has been really tough for me, and when you do something like this to let me know you care, well, it just makes all the difference in the world to me."

Leah gathered the packaged stapler and box of staples to her bosom, beaming at the others through damp eyes. "You know what?" Her voice thickened. "I just might get a box frame to mount this in, a memento to the great friendship we've enjoyed here."

"Oh, don't do *that*," Jane said.

Hailey gave a tight smile. "We bought it so you could have your own staple gun."

"If you don't want the staples," Dev told her, "I'll take them back. I kept the receipt."

"You have to use these," Kerry said. "*You do.*"

ON LUCINDA'S NIGHT to cook, she planned to prepare gnocchi with pesto. Hand-making the gnocchi seemed too ambitious, not to mention time-consuming. Such an endeavor also struck Lucinda as a stab at overachievement, alluring only to the deeply insecure, so she'd purchased ready-made gnocchi, and Leah offered to contribute the fresh basil she had left over from a previous meal. Lucinda had only to grind this in the food-processor with olive oil (contributed by Kerry) and the grated parmesan and pine-nuts she'd bought at the supermarket. The whole thing should take no more than thirty minutes, even with a salad.

Really, the women at the retreat were too obsessed with food, and Jane—when Lucinda broached the subject with her on an afternoon walk—concurred with this.

"At any given moment," Lucinda had said, "there are no fewer than six heads of garlic in that basket on the counter."

"Along with eight overripe tomatoes, when I last counted them, and at least five dozen eggs in the fridge." Jane then performed an impromptu bit about some spinach whose ownership had confounded Leah, a mystery she was weirdly driven to solve. "*Whose spinach is this?*" She mimicked Leah's high-pitched, saccharine voice tightening with stress. "*Is it yours? Is it Dev's? Is it Hailey's? This spinach didn't get here by itself.* Jane had held aloft an imaginary plastic bag. "*Is it Kerry's? Jane, did you buy this? How about you, Lucinda? Come on, now, fess up! Who the heck's spinach is this?*"

Lucinda was a capable, if plain, cook, unconcerned with the provenance of produce that had nothing to do with her. She focused instead on simplicity in selecting dishes to prepare. Not only was the meal Lucinda planned easy to put together, best of all, it could be served at room temperature. At midday she launched a quick email message to the others at the retreat: *I know we are all growing busier and busier with our work, so tonight there will be no sit-down dinner.*

Pick up a plate and eat when and wherever you like. A volley of emails flew back: *Thank you! Great idea! Yay! Should have thought of this sooner—those dinners are torture to me, a real torture.* Everyone, but Leah, expressed glad relief, and Lucinda dared to hope that the sit-down dinner, otherwise known as *The Leah Show*—a sixty-minute program of mind-numbing trivia, unappetizing medical disclosures, and scattershot interrogation that was already into repeated episodes—might at last be cancelled for good.

Near dusk, after Lucinda put a large pot of water on the stove to boil and commenced setting out ingredients for her dish, she found Leah's basil not only wilted, but inky with sludge. Even the greener leaves were furred with gray mold. "Shit," she said, "shit, shit, *shit*." When Lucinda asked Leah if the basil was still good, Leah had assured her, had sworn on the Matthew McConaughey eyes of her injured husband that the basil was perfectly fresh, really a shame to waste, and Lucinda, let's face it, was not someone to spend money when she could save it. Of all the women at the retreat, she was the only one squirreling away a good portion of her stipend check. So, okay, she'd been overly parsimonious and had not checked the basil for herself. As such, Lucinda easily could have borne the blame for this *fucked-up bullshit,* instead of cursing Leah through clenched teeth, while she stuffed the gooey leaves into the garbage disposal.

The pot on the stove boiling, Lucinda swiftly embarked on Plan B: She would make an alfredo sauce, something that should be eaten with immediacy, but the hell with that—like the philosophers of old, she would not recant. Nothing could compel her to email a retraction. Since the sauce took only minutes, she would prepare that last. So the salad would be the next item on her to-do list. Lucinda flung open the refrigerator door and yanked wide the vegetable bin, where bags containing the lettuce and cucumber she'd bought, Kerry's bell pepper, Jane's scallions, Dev's carrots, and Hailey's mushrooms were submerged in a yellow-tinged swamp sloshing at the bottom of the drawer. "*What the . . ., what the . . .*" Lucinda glimpsed a sideways leaning plastic container of some citrus power-drink on the shelf just above the crisper. The bottle, improperly capped and haphazardly tossed inside the fridge, had drained into the vegetable bin.

Leah!

This was her doing. When half-filled cups of mold-splotched coffee were discovered all over the house, browning banana peels and apple cores left to stain the wooden bench near the fireplace, moist and clotted tissues strewn on the dining table, it was Leah, always Leah, the slovenly Leah, who was *so, so, so* sorry when claiming responsibility for such messes. No time now for a satisfyingly thorough cursing-out, Lucinda pulled out the produce drawer. It dripped on the floor as she carried it to the sink to fish vegetables out of the sticky, sour-smelling fluid. She rinsed the vegetables and arranged these for drip-drying on the dishrack. While Lucinda sponged the bin with hot soapy water, Dev popped into the kitchen.

"What's with the vegetables in the dishrack?" she asked.

"Someone shoved a bottle of some lemony drink sideways into the fridge. It spilled into the crisper. Someone sloppy and stupid and—"

"Leah?" Dev approached the refrigerator to see for herself. "Looks like you got most of the mess, but the floor's sticky," she said. "I'll give it a quick mop."

"I'm about to lose it." Lucinda flushed suds out of the bin, an everlasting chore, given the sliminess of the over-treated tap water. "If she sets foot in here, I swear—"

"I can take over," Dev said. "If you want to sweep the dining room or straighten up your room to relax . . ."

Lucinda shook her head. "I'm just going to toss a salad while the gnocchi's boiling and then make a quick white sauce. Guess whose basil was bad after she swore it wasn't."

"I heard her. She swore on her husband's eyes."

"I hope he goes fucking blind."

Dev drew a sharp breath. "I haven't yet dusted upstairs, if you want to grab the Pledge and let off some steam. I'll make the dinner, no problem, but don't start up with Leah."

"I can at least confront her about this."

"I wouldn't," Dev said. "I mean, she's pissed me off plenty of times. She will not let it go that I sent back that seafood Caesar salad, and have you heard how she talks to me? Plus, she can't keep her germy hands off my food. But no way do I want to be known as that angry black bitch who went off on some sick white lady. And I don't think you want to be that tempestuous Latina who lives up to the negative stereotypes. Besides, I don't know about you, but I really, really need this job. I'm not about to mess things up."

Lucinda looked up from the steamy water gushing into the bin. At thirty, Dev was the youngest at the retreat, and now—her eyes round in alarm and her hair scraped back into a tight bun—she looked more like an anxious student than an English professor. "Just don't let her get to you. Think of her like a mosquito buzzing nearby, and tune it out."

Lucinda wondered if Dev knew that mosquitos carry malaria, a disease that—much like Leah—sapped energy, depleted resolve. "Okay, no promises here, but I'll try."

"I can help with the salad, and after dinner, I'll mop the floor."

While Dev tore lettuce into a salad bowl and Lucinda whisked parmesan into melted butter and hot milk, Leah barged into the kitchen. "Lucinda, how're you doing today? Time," she said, "time heals. Dev, hey, girlfriend, how you been?"

"We're good," Dev told her without looking up.

"That face!" Leah said. "I still can't get over that face you made. It was like, you calling this a Caesar salad with shrimp? Nah-*uh*, they is no way, baby." Leah's congested chuckling bloomed into a smoker's hack. She coughed her way to the end of the counter to grab a tumbler for her first vodka and tonic of the day. "*Ugh*," she said as ice clattered into the glass. "The floor's all gummy."

"Someone," said Lucinda, unable to resist, "some idiotic person left a citrus power drink sideways and uncapped. It flooded into the vegetable bin."

Dev shot her a warning look.

"Really?" Leah poured vodka into her glass. "Whose was it?"

Lucinda produced the empty bottle, which she had on hand for such a moment as this. "You tell me."

"Oh, gosh! That's mine. I'm *so, so, so* sorry. My bad! Gee, I feel terrible, just terrible. Those meds! I am seriously going to talk to my doctors when I get back. Is there anything I can do to make this right? Do you want me to set the table?"

"There is *no sit-down dinner tonight*," Lucinda said. "Remember?"

"Listen, Leah." Dev turned to her, wiping her hands on a dishcloth. "It's so warm out, why don't you have your cocktail on the patio? The weather right now is perfect for that."

"I want to help. Can I make an appetizer or just keep you all company while you cook?"

"Take. Your. Drink." Lucinda pointed the whisk at the sliding glass door. "*Outside.*"

"Really," Dev said. "Enjoy the sunset."

"Oh, okay. Gotcha." That wink.

Lucinda set the pot of gnocchi on the still-warm burner. Through the picture window, she caught sight of Leah on the patio. She was seated at the wrought-iron table, her dewy drink before her and her head inclined toward it as if she were about to receive sentencing for a crime she couldn't recall committing, punishment that surely exceeded any harm she'd done.

"Thanks for not going off on Leah," Dev told Lucinda. "I know that wasn't easy."

During the time they prepared the meal, Dev steered clear of Lucinda, while sending a few covert glances her way. She jumped when Lucinda made sudden movements and gasped when Lucinda called the stuck garlic press a "dumb bastard." Anger intimidated Dev, and this knowledge filled Lucinda with a surge of power that soon mutated into regret and then impatience. Yes, there were stereotypes that shouldn't be validated, but apart from avoiding reinforcement of these and jeopardizing her new position, Dev deeply feared conflict. She, like the other women at the retreat, shrank from that unspeakable temptation not to be nice.

Just before the inaugural no-sit-down dinner, Jane slunk into the kitchen to grab a bottle of Chardonnay from the fridge, the corkscrew, and a trio of wine glasses, and then Kerry appeared to snatch three sets of silverware and napkins, while Lucinda served salad and gnocchi on three plates that she balanced waitress-style on a large tray to keep one hand free for opening and closing doors. She scurried out after Kerry and Jane, heading for the building that housed the artists' studios. Right after sending the email cancelling the sit-down dinner, Jane had invited Kerry and Lucinda to eat with her in the kitchenette/common area next to the visual artists' work spaces. Lucinda and Kerry accepted and they commenced planning a private meal together.

Once she reached the kitchenette and set down the plates, Lucinda yearned to whoop or cut a swift jig to celebrate their escape. Jane poured wine into their glasses and they toasted the meal—the uninterrupted conversation!—they looked forward to enjoying.

"Here's to us," Jane said.

"To us," echoed Lucinda and Kerry, and they chinked their glasses together.

"Um." Kerry squinted in the direction of the shadowy hallway leading to the studios. "Does anyone know where she is?"

"Dev banished her to the patio," Lucinda said, before telling them about the basil and the citrus drink. "She'll probably return to the kitchen for another drink soon, and then she'll likely load up a plate to eat at the dining table."

Kerry stretched her neck, rolled her shoulders a few times. "Even though I know she's in the house, I keep expecting her to burst in and pull up a seat. We're really not doing anything wrong, but I feel like we're about to be caught."

"Relax," Jane told her. "Let's enjoy this while we can."

Lucinda sipped her wine, savoring its sharp flavor, and the women smiled at one another, before lifting a few tentative forkfuls to their mouths.

"This is delicious," Kerry said, and Jane nodded.

But the sauce had congealed, coating the gnocchi like paste. "It could've been worse, I suppose." Lucinda turned to Kerry. "I forgot about your issues with gluten! The pasta's potato-based, but there might be some flour involved."

"That's fine," Kerry said. "I don't actually have celiac disorder. My parents do, so I keep my kitchen gluten-free and avoid eating wheat in case of genetic predisposition. And I love the parmesan sauce. I love any kind of cheese."

"Me, too," Lucinda told them. "Why, if you covered an old gym shoe with Cheez Whiz, I'd eat the whole thing and clamor for more."

Eyebrows raised, Jane drew back.

"We could never have cheese when I was married," Kerry told them. "1976 through 1996, the cheese-less years."

"That's a long time," Jane said, "to go without cheese."

"It's a long time to go without a lot of things." Kerry probed the salad with her fork. "Takashi is lactose intolerant. We couldn't have milk, cheese, butter, ice cream. Can you imagine raising kids without ice cream?"

Jane and Lucinda shook their heads.

"Twenty years." Kerry gazed off toward a focal point in the middle distance. "Now, Takashi won't have anything to do with us. He's remarried, and it's the new wife's influence—I know it—but still, he won't talk to our children. He didn't even go to our daughter's wedding."

"What did he say?" Jane asked. "What excuse did he give?"

"That's just it," Kerry told her. "He doesn't *say* anything. He won't talk. To any of us."

"*Ever?*" Before considering the grief this would cause her daughter, Lucinda would lull herself to sleep at night serenely imagining the ways in which her ex-husband might incur a mortal wound while playing around with the many guns he collected. These days she modified her fantasies, picturing a button she could press that would send him to live out the remainder of his days in Antarctica. He could mail their daughter postcards from there, if he liked, but the harm he caused would be contained at the South Pole. If only she'd had the foresight to marry someone like Takashi . . .

Kerry shook her head. "He doesn't return phone calls, answer email, letters, nothing. Not ever."

"How hurtful that must be to you," Jane said, "and to your children."

"It is. It really is, especially for them. It's like he died. He's dead to us. I can never tell my children what I know. It just wouldn't comfort them the way it comforts me."

"What's that?" asked Lucinda.

"All love ends tragically. The stronger the love, the more tragically it ends."

"But what about when things work out," Jane said, "I know I was too young when I got married, too immature and dependent, but what if I was more who I am now back then. The marriage might have lasted. We could have had a trusting and respectful relationship."

Kerry shook her head. "Those end worst of all. When one partner or the other dies, I imagine the sorrow felt by the survivor can be unendurable."

Lucinda swabbed the cheesy residue on her plate with a last forkful of gnocchi. "Well, I, for one, would much rather be sad than dead."

"I suppose." Kerry's pale face lengthened, her eyes pink rimmed and glistening. "Let's change the subject, shall we?"

"I read somewhere," Jane said, stabbing the air with her fork, "that the average person lies about fourteen times a day."

"*Only* fourteen times?" Lucinda's voice rose in astonishment. "I would have thought twice as many times as that."

"I don't think I lie much," Kerry said. "I have no aptitude for it, so I try not to lie at all."

"That's a lie, right there," Jane told her. "You *do* try to lie. We all do. We work hard at this to keep peace here."

"You lie each time Leah walks in a room and you don't tell her that you're irritated by the sight of her," Lucinda said.

Kerry shrugged. "Oh, well, lies of omission . . ."

"Lies of *o*mission," Jane said, "and lies of *com*mission. For instance, what do you tell Leah when she bursts into your studio, saying that she hopes she's not bothering you? And remember that I'm right next door. I can hear everything."

"Okay, I do lie." Kerry flushed. "I tell her it's no bother at all."

"Why?" Lucinda asked. "Why don't you tell her the truth?"

Kerry sighed. "Then I'd have to deal with her for an hour instead of fifteen minutes."

"She'd wink," said Jane. "She'd wink and say *gotcha*, before backing out of the studio like she understood completely, and then after a few minutes, she'd be knocking again."

"To apologize," Kerry continued. "She'd insist on coming back to say how sorry she is for interrupting. Then she'd go on and on about it, and all the while, I'd be telling her not to worry, that it's okay, it's fine, fine, *fine*—meaning: please, just go."

"But you can't rush things," Jane said. "Oh, no, you have to make it seem like you have all the time in the world to assure her she hasn't bothered you, or she'll never leave."

"Why put up with this?"

"Honestly, you'd put up with it, too," Jane said. "You don't know what it's like here when we're trying to work. If you had to share this space with her, you would do whatever it takes to have some peace, to steal a few solid hours to—"

The front door shot open, and Leah loomed in the doorway to the bright kitchenette. Lucinda, Jane, and Kerry froze as she looked from one face to the next and the next. Then her gaze fell to the tabletop, the empty plates and wine glasses. Heat crept up Lucinda's neck. But Leah said nothing. Her jowly face locked in an expression of suspicions confirmed, she nodded. Unsmiling and silent, she headed to her studio. Once inside, she shut the door with more force than needed.

"WELL, I GOT a letter, too," Jane told Lucinda as they hiked the cow path through the acreage behind the residency, a sludgy gash in the grassy terrain, splotched with many cow pies. Lucinda wielded a stick in case rattlers appeared on this warmer afternoon. On the lookout for snakes and worried about the potential for aggressiveness in the cattle grazing nearby, Lucinda asked what the letter was about.

"It was an apology."

"For what?"

"For being *too eager* about our friendship."

"Oh no, what did you do this time?"

"I snapped at her when she knocked on my door as I was painting a nude self-portrait."

"For the *exhibit* in August?"

"Not for that, for myself. I was inspired, I guess, by Alice Neel and Maria Lassnig. Have you ever seen Lassnig's *Self-Portrait with Pickle Jar*? Anyway, I thought I was safe because she'd already intruded three times that morning. Once to see if I could spare some gesso, again to return it, and then to apologize for bothering me about the gesso, so I thought I had at least an hour."

Lucinda pictured Leah after shopping day next week, gathering a trio of gesso containers to her bosom and sputtering tearful gratitude. "You're never safe," she told Jane.

"I forgot that. Inspiration, enthusiasm for the project, and . . . *hope*. Hope must have clouded my thinking. It's one thing to wipe paint off my hands, another to have to clean up *and* get dressed before opening the door for her."

"So what did you say when you snapped?"

"I said I was trying to get some work done. Nothing too bad, but my tone was sharp. So ten minutes later, this envelope slides under my door and right after that—*knock-knock-knock*—she wanted to know if I got her note."

Lucinda laughed.

"And wait, that's not all. After another pause, she knocks again, this time to apologize for bothering me with her note. So here I am again wading through bullshit. Only it's much nicer to do this here with you than back in the studio with her."

"Thanks, I guess, but that's kind of like saying it's better to stub a toe than to be pierced with a fork."

"I've heard that what we resent about others often relates to what's lacking in our own lives," Jane said. "Maybe I'm jealous that she's got this great marriage with Richard Gere—"

Lucinda shook her head. "Matthew McConaughey, not Richard Gere. Now she says her husband looks just like Matthew McConaughey."

"But that makes no sense."

"Correct."

"So maybe I'm jealous because it's been almost twenty years since my divorce. I would like to get married again, wouldn't you?"

"I didn't have such a great time of it, remember?" Lucinda had confided in Jane about the trips to emergency rooms, the arrests and restraining orders.

"Marriage doesn't have to be dreadful," Jane said. "I mean, if Leah can find someone who loves her, why can't we? I guess I *do* want what she has."

"Okay." Lucinda stopped short to look into Jane's wistful face. "But would you be willing to *be* her?"

"Ooh, would I get to sleep with Matthew McConaughey?"

"Every night, you could sleep with him or with Richard Gere—or both."

Jane exhaled loudly. "Even if you threw Johnny Depp into the rotation, I wouldn't want to be her, not even for a minute."

"So there it is," Lucinda said. "You're not jealous. You're irritated. We all are—irritated and distracted. I came here to work. I've never had a chance like this to be just a writer, and nothing else. For me, this is a dream I didn't even *dare* to dream."

Jane nodded. "It *is* an amazing gift—this time, this place—but instead of taking full advantage of it, we have to deal with Leah. She's like some composite creature made up of all the people in my life—ex-husband, boyfriends, parents, colleagues, bosses, even my sons—who demand my attention, diverting me from my art."

"Except, unlike lovers, family, friends, even coworkers, she's not at all likable," Lucinda said. "It's like she's lodged herself in my brain like some obnoxious squatter who doesn't pay a penny of rent." Here, she imagined the black-garbed Leah, smoking while sprawled like a stain in a white-walled and empty room. Though envisioning her mind as barren as this troubled Lucinda, she focused on her outrage at Leah's presence in it.

"Why don't you talk to her?" Jane said. "You're safe in that writing studio office. Even if she dared to barge in on you, there's that lock on the door to the entry way."

"There is?"

"A deadbolt. Lock it and wear headphones—you wouldn't even hear her knocking."

"If I did talk to her, what would I say?"

"You could tell her how you feel, how we all feel. You could ask her to leave us alone."

Lucinda considered this. "I suppose I could tell her that for me there is absolutely no payoff for her claims on my attention and time. I could tell her she's like a vacuum sucking up the psychic energy of others. I could say that though I'm not a violent person, I can't count the times I've been tempted to—"

"Well, give it some thought."

As they hiked over a rise, a herd of cattle appeared to form a densely muscled wall of dark umber hide, flinty hooves, and oversized heads in which limpid eyes stared out in mute accusation. Lucinda drew a sharp breath, the odor of dung filling her nostrils. She had little experience with cows. Just last week, she'd made a fool of herself in the saddle museum by wondering aloud where the leather straps cinched so as not to interfere with udders. Now, facing the monstrous creatures, Lucinda's limited knowledge of livestock shrank as her imagination with regard to vengefulness in cattle expanded wildly. What was to keep this herd from trampling her and Jane for invading their grazing area? One released a plosive snort, and Lucinda whispered, "Um, maybe we should go back."

"Why? They're just cows."

"They don't look too friendly." Lucinda kept her voice low, so her words would not be overheard by the cattle. "They look kind of angry, like they don't want to be bothered."

But Jane singled out a particular cow, not the big one in front, but another a few yards behind it, in the middle of the herd. She strode toward it, raising and lowering outstretched arms, and shouting, "*Yah! Yah! Yah!*"

And damned if the entire herd didn't turn tail (literally) and stampede away from the women. Their hooves drummed the hard-packed earth as they fled, churning up a gingery cloud of dust in their wake.

"How on earth . . . How did you do that?"

"Linchpin," Jane said. "Merle once told me that the key to moving cattle is to pick out a linchpin—a cow in the middle of the herd. If you make an impact on the linchpin, the others follow along. It's basic group dynamics, really."

The cows wended up a steep bluff to regard the women from a safe distance.

IN THE THIRD week, the women had an Open Studio exhibit, where the visual artists mounted work in their studios for the others to tour—individual gallery shows—before a reading by the writers in the retreat house. The first stop in the tour: Jane's studio. Nearly every foot of wall space held vivid landscapes in oil and watercolors, pen and gouache renderings of birds' nests she'd found, matchbook paintings, and the stunningly frank nude self-portrait that she'd titled *Gravitational Pull*. The others were awed and congratulatory, but Leah, clearly struggling to relinquish the spotlight to Jane, blurted, "This is great, Jane, through I'm afraid it's all downhill from here."

Lucinda glanced at Hailey and Kerry, both of whom seemed puzzled rather than offended by the self-deprecating remark that also impugned their work.

"I'm talking about me, obviously," Leah said, "and my stuff."

They moved on to Kerry's studio where the artwork appeared as meticulous and thoughtful as she. Tables and walls displayed miniature pointillist renderings on vellum of human brains and hearts pulling apart and oozing viscous threads between them; acrylic paintings of sky-scapes in black and white; detailed sketches of lichen superimposed on aerial views of islands, some real and others imagined; and one portrait that perhaps only Lucinda recognized as a portrait. The charcoal-and-chalk drawing resembled an x-ray or photo-negative, a shadowy background featuring a lucent image: a small bright wedge like a sharp tooth hooked near a ribcage. It was Leah, of course, that *thorn* in Kerry's side.

Vibrant textiles brightened Hailey's studio. On its walls hung quilts she had fringed, frayed, and then whitewashed to create canvases before splashing these with orange and yellow hues; fabrics whose threads she'd pulled for a waffling effect; and various kerchiefs she'd seared with a cattle brand. Atop a table in the center, a computer screen displayed a slideshow of her work photographed in the landscapes that inspired it. After guiding the women from piece to piece, Hailey presented each with a branded kerchief, just as Kerry had given them postcard-sized drawings and Jane provided matchbook watercolor paintings to all.

They viewed Leah's work last. The same small unfinished canvases that she presented in town comprised the highlight of this, though she also strung up three long panels that likewise struck Lucinda as unremarkable. These vertical banners looked to have been striped by someone with hand tremors wielding a paint roller. Despite the paucity of effort evident in this work, Leah claimed to be preparing for an upcoming show in Austin. Austin, Austin, Austin. When not peppering the others with questions or flattering Lucinda, Leah boasted about showing her work in Austin. But Lucinda had visited Austin and encountered many seeing-eyed people there. They would not be impressed with such an exhibit as this. After showing the banners, with their alternating bands of sputum yellow and bile green, Leah offered to cut one of these into pieces for the others as gifts.

"Oh, no," Kerry told her. "Don't cut up your work. You shouldn't do *that*."

"I'm fine without a gift," said Dev. "I'm not giving anybody anything."

"Neither am I." Lucinda, wracking her brain, couldn't come up with anyone she disliked enough to pass a gift of this kind onto—apart from Leah herself. While temptingly cruel, that would make no sense at all.

Hailey raised her hands as if to fend off such an offering. "I'm good."

"So it's unanimous," Jane said. "No need to take scissors to your panel."

Since the gnocchi alfredo, the sit-down dinner had been abolished, and Lucinda, with her graduate degrees, her few published stories in small journals, and now this teaching position at Birnbrau, counted putting an end to the sit-down dinners at the retreat as one of her greatest accomplishments. But at the reception in the kitchenette after Open Studio—a tableful of hors d'oeuvres obsessively photographed earlier by Dev—they all sat together again to eat, and seizing the opportunity, Leah commenced holding court. She opened by gushing over the food, rambling about how they spoiled one another with all the great meals they've enjoyed. "Why, imagine," Leah said, "if we had a man here with us, how we'd fuss over him." She laughed. "We'd never get anything done!"

Jane raised an eyebrow and shot Lucinda a look.

"As it is," Lucinda said, "some of us didn't get as much work done here as we hoped."

"Oh, I *know*." Leah sighed before saying that this was the first time she'd been on an artists' retreat, as if to explain why she hadn't been more productive.

Severe—if indirect—rebuke bubbled pleasurably in Lucinda's chest. "It's my first time, too," she said. "And I expected to focus on my work, so forgive me if I've been brusque. But I'm not inclined to tolerate distractions due to constant demands on my time and attention."

She swept the group with her gaze to make her pointed words to Leah seem less specific in their accusation. No, the time was not right for this yet, so Lucinda mentioned being raised in a large family and how that makes one mindful about giving others space and respecting boundaries. "In my family," she said, "the worst insult we could levy was to accuse one another of just wanting attention, meaning there is nothing of value offered in exchange for that."

"I find it appalling," Lucinda continued, "to have conversations interrupted, dominated, and directed. Discussions do not need to be orchestrated. Everything doesn't have to be commented on by one person." Here, Lucinda looked straight at Leah; the time for this had come. "It's really okay to be silent and just listen to what others have to say."

"Gotcha." Leah winked. Then she apologized for expecting a sorority experience. "I'm sorry," she said, "for wanting all of us to be friends."

Lucinda and Jane traded a glance—yet another mea culpa lauding Leah's goodwill.

"I often have to work alone." Leah's voice quavered. "I was looking forward to camaraderie here and—"

Jane shook her head. "This is *not* what we are here for, not at all."

"I thought we were here to work," Kerry said. "That's what I thought."

Dev and Hailey gazed down at the forlorn crudités—dried and curling carrot and celery sticks—alongside desolate mounds of hummus remaining in their plates.

For the rest of the reception, Leah struggled to keep quiet so others could speak, but by the time the writers gave their reading back at the house, Leah nursed her second tumbler of red wine on ice, and a look of barely contained garrulousness bloomed on her ruddy face. First Dev read a series of poems that she introduced by explaining that these were new pieces, composed at the retreat, and they were all written in homage to the natural environment that had captured her imagination while in Wyoming. Leah interrupted her reading a few times to ask questions about where the poems were set, when they were written, and what inspired the work.

After Dev finished and all had applauded, Leah stood in the center of the room. "If no one minds mind," she said, "I have a short poem to recite. It's 'The Second Coming' by William Butler Yeats." Though she swayed tipsily, her voice was crisp. Leah closed her eyes, clasped hands together as if in prayer, and began: "Turning and turning in the widening gyre . . ."

The room remained silent for several seconds after Leah's impeccable and deeply moving recitation of the entire poem. Lucinda, who'd written a paper on "The Second Coming" in graduate school, felt as if she were experiencing it for the first time; its resonances newly evocative. The falcon and falconer, the blood-dimmed tide, those indignant desert birds, and that griffin with its slow-moving thighs. Devorah was the first to speak. "That's amazing. How do you know that poem? I mean, how did you learn it?"

Leah gave a rueful smile. "After my mother left, my grandmother raised me. She was old school, believed in learning through memorizing. If I wanted anything—new shoes, money for a school trip, even dessert—I had to learn a poem. Then when she'd have her friends over for bridge, she'd trot me out like a little poodle to perform." She laughed. "The good old days!"

Lucinda knew only one poem by heart, "The Love Song of J. Alfred Prufrock," admittedly a long poem, one she'd struggled to learn in college, despite the song-like meter and rhyme. She now pictured Leah as a child, repeating and repeating lines until they stuck in her brain, somehow without poetic perceptions and insights ever attaching to her long-term memory. Still, Lucinda winced inwardly for the young girl stammering poetry at a gaggle of oldsters, eager to play cards.

"Gone," Leah said now. "All those poems are gone for me now, except that one. And these days it's hard for me to speak in front of an audience, believe it or not."

After the presentation in Sheridan, Lucinda had no trouble believing that.

"It was beautiful," Kerry told her. "Just beautiful."

Hailey nodded. "Pretty great, yeah."

"Well, Leah," Jane said, "thanks for that, but isn't it Lucinda's turn to read? I want to hear what she's been working on."

Straightening the pages in her lap, Lucinda told the others to save comments until she was done reading. "Interruptions are very distracting to me," she said, again piercing Leah with her gaze. She then read a just-drafted scene featuring a group of women annoyed by a male character—for this reading, Lucinda had disguised Leah's avatar through gender reassignment—given to obsequious flattery, obsessive winking, and persistent questioning of others. When she finished,, Leah prevented anyone from commenting, beyond brief congratulations, by launching a flotilla of insincere praise and then upshifting into interrogation mode. Lucinda longed to know what Jane, Hailey, Kerry, and especially Dev thought of her new work, but she had no way to keep them from hurrying out of the library. She would have found such haste unseemly had she not realized that they were intent on escaping Leah, who remained behind, wheezing fermented fumes in Lucinda's face as she asked about the scene.

"How on earth do you manage to juggle so many characters?" she asked. "I bet you come from a large family, right?"

"What did I say earlier?" One could speak quite clearly, Lucinda had discovered, without parting teeth. "Can't you at all remember what I said at the reception?"

"Oh, okay. Gotcha," Leah said, and she winked.

LONG AFTER LUCINDA drifted off to sleep that night, she was awakened by a pecking sound that she at first wove into a dream of being encased egg-like in a shell chipped at by some external force. Groggily, she lifted her head from her pillow. The digital clock on the nightstand read 4:46 A.M. Someone was rapping on the door to her bedroom. She flung off the quilt and staggered to the threshold to yank the door wide. There stood Leah, an eager look on her face.

Lucinda yawned, rubbed her eyes. "Why'd you wake me up?"

"You have a phone call," Leah said. "Your sister."

Adrenaline coursing, Lucinda pushed passed Leah and flew to the kitchen to grab the receiver. "Bertha? What is it? Is Anita okay?"

"First, relax," Lucinda's sister said, "It's probably nothing."

"What's probably nothing? What's going on?" Lucinda shot a look at Leah who had trailed her to the kitchen and now stood before her, wringing her hands like the heroine in a silent film, a melodrama. "Let me talk to Anita."

"See, that's the thing," Bertha said. "She's not here."

"What do you mean? Where is she?"

Bertha emitted something between a groan and a giggle. *A griggle?* "You know kids," she said. "Remember how we used to sneak out.

And she's nineteen. She can come and go as she likes, I mean, legally, so it was sort of silly for her to pretend to go to bed and then climb out the window, right?"

"Wait, wait, wait," Lucinda said. "What happened? Was she upset? Did you fight?" Sometimes, after an argument, Anita would storm off, but she'd return within an hour or so, calm and ready to talk through whatever conflict they'd had.

"Nothing happened, I swear. Everything was fine. She said she had a headache and went to bed kind of early."

A brain tumor? These things could just crop up, a sudden headache clouding all sense and reason. Perhaps Anita was wandering the streets of Los Angeles in her nightgown, dazed and disoriented. How would Lucinda ever find her? Leah now drew near, straining to overhear Bertha's words. Lucinda swatted her away and pivoted, turning her back on the snoopy woman.

"It's probably nothing," Bertha continued. "I bet she just wanted some air and didn't want to disturb me."

"At this hour?" It wasn't yet dawn in LA. Lucinda rolled her eyes at the unlikeliness of this. "How long has she been gone?"

"I have no idea. I wouldn't even have known she was gone if not for the smoke alarm in her room. Damn thing beeps when the battery is low. It woke me up. I went to shut it off and saw she wasn't there. She'd put a pillow under the covers like we used to do to fool Mom, remember?" Bertha chuckled. "So wherever she is, she probably went, like, intentionally."

Lucinda remembered signs for a Greyhound station in Sheridan. There might be a timetable on the rack with sightseeing information in the mudroom. "I'm coming," she said.

"I really don't think you have to—"

"I'll get the next bus to LA and be there as soon as I can." Before hanging up the phone, Lucinda made Bertha promise to call her cell phone if she heard anything from Anita. She then whipped around, ready to blast Leah for nosiness, but she had left the kitchen. Now Leah reappeared from the entry to the mudroom, proffering the

Greyhound schedule to Lucinda. "I'll drive you," she said. "That way I can bring the van back."

Lucinda gave a curt nod, and hurried back to her room to pack.

OF COURSE, LUCINDA did not trust Leah to drive, so she grabbed the keys and shot into the seat behind the steering wheel before the woman emerged from the retreat house in her usual mourning garb. Leah boarded the van with a somber silence that lasted to the main road.

"I bet she's perfectly fine," Leah said as Lucinda turned west onto Highway 14.

"Hope so," Lucinda murmured.

"Kids are always running away."

"Mm," said Lucinda, who didn't think her daughter had run away. She'd probably just snuck out for the evening, though at nineteen, Anita could have simply sauntered through the front door. Lucinda's ex-husband lived near Los Angeles, but he had a full household of youngsters with his second wife—the reason Anita stayed with Bertha, instead of with him, when she visited California. Despite being contemptuous, even cruel toward Lucinda, he would have no reason, desire, or energy to lure their daughter away in the middle of the night.

Leah gave a self-deprecating laugh. "Why, I ran away from my grandmother's house in Marietta when I was fifteen. I hitched a ride to Atlanta to meet up with this boy I met at a concert . . ." From there, Leah's tale wended its way to a biker bar, then to a pool party in an apartment complex, where she stayed the first night. Leah spent the next few days cadging change downtown, the nights getting high and sleeping in an abandoned building with a group of runaway teenagers. Leah never did reconnect with the guy she'd set out to find, and after nearly a week of this, she called her grandmother from a payphone. Within an hour, Manuel, Me-maw's gardener, arrived in his pickup truck to collect Leah and drive her back to Marietta.

Lucinda wondered if any of it were true. Still she'd made sympathetic sounds at intervals while watching the sunrise flame the underbellies of clouds, creating a molten lava canopy. Fields and fence posts whipped past in the periphery, along with the occasional farmhouse and silo—all of this, even the mad woman's shack, her abandoned appliances, and the cinderblocks entombing the dead horse, suffused with peach-gold light.

With a glance at the speedometer, Lucinda eased up on the gas pedal. This was not the autobahn. What if a deer or rabbit shot across the highway? After retelling her adventures, Leah had grown silent. Panicked thoughts crowded into this void for Lucinda, who now pictured Anita passed out in a condemned property. She cleared her throat. "What happened?" she said. "What happened when you got back to your grandmother's?"

Leah laughed. "Oh, nothing."

"Nothing?"

"Me-maw was planning some reception. She was always so, so, so busy, but I remember she looked at me and said I might want to bathe and change for dinner."

"She didn't ask where you were? Why you'd left?"

"No," Leah said.

"Why did you run away?" Lucinda turned to glimpse Leah, who shrugged.

A tinkling tune sounded, and both women looked to the radio as if it had turned on by itself. She hadn't received a call on it for so long that Lucinda had forgotten her cell phone's ringtone. It took her a few seconds to recognize it. Then she reeled up her purse and scrabbled in it with her free hand to fish out the phone. She flipped it open to answer the call. "Bertha?" she said. "Is she back yet?"

"Mom?" a small voice penetrated the static crackling in Lucinda's ear like crumpled cellophane.

"*Anita*, my god. What happened? Are you okay?"

"I'm fine, really I am."

Thinking of Leah's incurious grandmother, Lucinda asked, "Where were you? Why did you leave like that?"

"I just went to Santa Monica. I wanted to sleep on the beach. That's all."

"By yourself? Are you insane? How did you get there?"

"It was just an impulse, a spur of the moment thing," Anita said. "I didn't go alone. I was with Diego."

"*Diego*?" Briefly bewildered, Lucinda then recalled that Diego was the name of Anita's supervisor at the fast-food restaurant. A married man whose wife had given birth not too long ago to a son, Diego Jr. "Diego from work?" she asked. "What's he doing in California?"

"He's in training out here," Anita said. "They're making him a manager. We went to the beach last night, and he brought me back before his first session."

Ah. Now Lucinda understood why Anita had not much resisted taking leave from her beloved fast-food job in order to travel to California. "I'm getting a bus to LA this morning," she told Anita. "We're flying home as soon as I arrive."

"*Mother*, don't even think about doing that," said Anita, who would levy the honorific like a curse word when furious at Lucinda. "If you come here now, *Mother*, I swear I really will run off. You'll never, ever see me again."

Lucinda's breath caught as if she'd been sucker-punched. She wanted to throw something hard and break it; she wanted to kick in a wall and then vomit. Instead, she waited, as if for a cup of tea to cool, ticking off seconds until her lungs filled, her stomach settled.

"Mother, are you there?" Anita said. "Mother? Mother?"

Lucinda swung the van in an arc, a wide U-turn, to retrace her route to the residency. After Lucinda assured her daughter she'd not take a bus to California and exacted Anita's promise not to disappear again and they'd ended the call, Leah made a clucking sound. "Boyfriend, huh?" she said. "I hope you've talked to her about protection."

"That's actually none of your business, but, of course, I have." Lucinda cast about in her memory for a time when she would have had such a talk with Anita and what exactly she might have said. She should have thought to give her daughter a box of condoms.

"I was late after I got back from Atlanta. I mean, really late. False alarm, but it scared me to death. I'd rather live on the streets forever than tell Me-maw she was going to be a great-grandmother. She'd

have flipped. As it was, she wasn't too thrilled to be a grandmother."
Leah gave a rueful chuckle. "But I bet you'd make a really good
grandmother."

"You don't know that," Lucinda said. Anita had returned, alive
and unharmed, and now Leah was planting a new worry in her head.
If only she'd thought to provide prophylactics . . .

"I can just tell." With this, Leah released an armada of flattery
interspersed with platitudes, a relentless flow that lasted all the way
back to the retreat house. Once they arrived, she commenced regaling
the others, gathered in the kitchen for breakfast, with the Story of
Anita's Disappearance, a tale in which she cast herself as the humble,
but supportive sidekick, a Sancho Panza of Highway 14. Wordlessly,
Lucinda slunk off to her room and shut the door.

IT WAS LEAH'S turn to prepare supper with Hailey, and Leah managed
to delay each step in the process, so the others grew ravenous long
before food was ready. Being hamburgers and French fries, the meal
had to be served hot. Another sit-down dinner loomed. At first, the
two women worked together quietly, but Lucinda, reading the
newspaper in the living room, soon overheard Hailey urging Leah to
wash her hands after handling raw meat.

Leah chuckled at this. "Stop bitching at me, bitch."

At this, Lucinda glanced up. Hailey stood before the sink, steamy
water gushing from the tap. "Seriously," she said. "The water's nice
and hot. At least *rinse* off your hands."

"Bitch, bitch, bitch—all you do is bitch!" Leah laughed again,
but made no move toward the sink. "I'm not your bitch, bitch."

Lucinda considered gathering up the paper to read it in her room
until supper was ready, but she disliked the way others (as in Leah)
removed the paper from the common area before everyone had a
chance to look at it. So she merely turned a page to read letters to the
advice columnist. *Dear Carolyn*, Lucinda imagined herself writing.
There is a certain woman I would like to plunge a blade into . . .

Before serving the food, Leah leaned against a counter by the
stove, idly running fingers through French fries on a baking sheet.

Dev, who'd appeared to set the table, beaconed a horrified look. Lucinda folded the paper and rose from her seat to enter the kitchen. She slipped on an oven mitt, and took the tray away from Leah. "Let's not handle the food, shall we?"

"I wasn't," Leah said.

"Yes, you were," Dev told her.

Lucinda placed the tray back in the oven and turned the heat up. "If they're cool enough to fondle, then they probably need to be warmed some."

"Oh, okay. Gotcha."

After several minutes, they all took their places at the table. By this time, Leah had gulped down a few vodkas, and now she was sipping from a tumbler of red wine on ice. She was in fine form, Lucinda noted. In very fine form for *her*, that is. "*Lucinda! Lucinda? Lucinda!*" Questions, this time, and not flattery, flew from Leah to Lucinda with lightning speed. When others attempted peripheral conversations, Leah called out their names to redirect their attention to what she had to say. The topic turned to games, and Leah launched an interrogation of Lucinda about strategy at Scrabble, a game at which Lucinda had been dominating the others—night after night—at the residency.

"There's no set strategy." Lucinda began. "You need to be perceptive of others and to act appropriately with that information. To play any game—or do anything intelligently—you must understand how to pay attention, instead of demanding others pay attention to you. It's not that complicated." Then, hoping to convey the unsaid so distinctly that it nearly snapped like a flag overhead, she added, "After all, I'm not *stupid*."

"I never said you were, did I?" Leah said.

"Well, no, but—"

"In fact, I think you're very wise. That's why you'll make such a wonderful, wonderful grandmother."

Dev, Jane, and Kerry looked up at Lucinda, who ignored the drumbeat of her pulse like a summons to war. Instead of succumbing to this provocation, she gave a stiff smile. "Thank you for that, Leah, though I'm not sure what such an observation has to do with anything."

Hailey suggested Lucinda repair to the library with her and Jane to play Scrabble, and though not her turn, Dev offered to clean up. Leah asked the Scrabble players if she could come upstairs to watch the game. Oh, how effusively Jane and Hailey thanked her for asking about this. But Jane admitted that it was difficult for her to concentrate with someone else looking on, and Hailey added that Scrabble is not really a spectator sport.

Kerry, poor Kerry, was abandoned, like a comrade fallen behind enemy lines. To go back for her presented a risk the others were unwilling to take, so she had to be sacrificed to Leah's insatiable appetite for attention. As Lucinda ascended the stairs to play Scrabble, Kerry shielded herself with a book, but Leah insisted that Kerry take a look at *her* book instead. As she had done to Lucinda with the eggplant at the supermarket, Leah was now thrusting a thin volume of poems in Kerry's pale face.

THAT NIGHT, DESPITE worry over Anita, Lucinda swiftly plunged into the untroubled sleep of the conscienceless. She usually did. But soon after opening her eyes the next morning, she trembled with anger over the previous night, and she made up her mind to speak to Leah about it first thing, while the woman was sober, likely hung over and subdued. Leah wasn't yet in the kitchen when Lucinda entered it for coffee, but Jane and Kerry were bustling about preparing their breakfasts, so she told them her plan. Kerry counseled against this, stressing, as Dev had, the necessity of being nice.

"But *why?*" Lucinda wanted to know. "Why do we have to be nice? Don't you see how she uses this against us? She holds us hostage in this cult of niceness. From the first time a doll is thrust into our arms, we, as females, are inculcated in nurturing and self-sacrifice. We're drilled in the practice of placing the feelings of others over our own. Men have taken advantage of this for centuries to secure privilege and power. Leah capitalizes on that compulsion to be kind, and she's exploited it every single day of this retreat. She harasses and harasses, drives us over the edge, and when we snap at her, she's all apologies and more apologies. All that *gotcha*, all those winks—because she has got us, right where she wants us, paralyzed by our own empathic impulses."

"You give her too much credit," Kerry told her. "I don't think she's that smart."

"Granted, she's not smart, but what she knows is this," Lucinda said, "when she irritates us, she has our attention. When she apologizes for this, she has our attention. When we apologize for snapping at her, she—as ever—has our attention. And the cycle goes on and on. Why do we have to be nice, when niceness is the straightjacket she's strapped us into, the gag that she's wadded in our mouths?" Lucinda drew a deep breath, astonished by her own eloquence. She thought of Kerry's one portrait, the x-rayed image of that thorn in her side. Truly, Leah inspired her, too.

"Well," Jane said, "when you put it like that . . ."

Hailey meandered in, and Lucinda told her the plan. Hailey pointed out that it probably wouldn't make any difference, but encouraged Lucinda to speak to Leah, if she thought it would make her feel better.

So, when Leah appeared—her sparse hair wetly plastered to her head, her face bloated and sallow from drinking, her eyes like raisins pressed into her doughy flesh—Lucinda seized her advantage.

"May I speak to you privately," she said.

Leah gave a magnanimous shrug. "Sure."

Together they made their way to the mudroom, where Lucinda said, "I'm sure you must be a decent person with some attributes, but you may have noticed that we're not getting along."

Leah nodded, a forgiving smile already teasing at the corners of her lips.

"I have to tell you honestly that I cannot stand you," Lucinda said. "As a matter of fact, you are aggravating to everyone, but I seem to be the only one who no longer feels any compulsion to be nice to you. Even so, I am asking you respectfully to leave me alone for the remainder of our time here."

Leah's tiny eyes widened. "I *have* been leaving you alone."

"Not last night."

"Can I tell you something?"

"Why not?" Lucinda retreated a step as Leah approached, her hands knotted into fists.

"What you've just told me is the final cruel slap in my face."

At this, Lucinda's right palm buzzed, her fingers tingled. Never before had she felt such temptation to strike another person. *I'll show you what a slap really is.* She imagined her skin zinging, the satisfying smack as it connected with Leah's pallid flesh. With a gasp, she stepped back again.

For a full decade, Lucinda had been in deep and dark, dancing with the devil, as she thought of it now: broken nose; cracked rib; split lip; bruises mottling her face, throat, arms and thighs—ruddy patches that bloomed blackish-blue as thunderheads crowding the Wyoming sky, and she had never once raised a fist. To anyone. More than any of the others, she *knew* what striking a woman meant. As Leah turned away, shame flooded Lucinda's face and neck with thumping heat. In the wake of Leah's solemn limp-step, her rounded back, and bowed head, Lucinda fought the impulse to trail after the woman, to call back her words and ask forgiveness.

She shook her head as if to dislodge insects in it. Clemency proved a perilous enterprise for Lucinda, who'd squandered a full decade of her life, forgiving and forgiving. An apology was exactly what Leah calculated she'd receive, and it would undo the hard struggle Lucinda endured to arrive at this confrontation. Not usually an optimist, she nonetheless recalled Leah's claim that she'd been dealt a *final cruel slap*, and savoring the word *final*, Lucinda strode out of the mudroom, elation filling her with a deep intake of breath. Shoulders back and head level enough to balance a book, Lucinda glanced through the doorway to the kitchen as if this were a full-length mirror in which she might glimpse her own triumphant image. Instead, she caught sight of Jane, approaching the dining table with sure and measured steps. Her coffee cup held in one hand like a scepter, *she* appeared quite regal without being the least bit remiss.

THE LAST REMAINING days of the retreat, the visual artists packed portfolio pieces between foam boards for shipping. They engaged shippers that charged hundreds of dollars to transport their materials and work. Then they cleaned out their studios, filling holes they had made in the walls to hang their art, whitewashing these, then sweeping and scrubbing paint from floors. Again, Lucinda and Dev traded self-congratulatory glances as if it had been with tremendous foresight that they'd opted to become writers who needed only to disconnect and encase laptops and mail home books at the discounted media rate.

On an afternoon walk in the last week, Hailey reported hearing a series of sighs from Leah's studio. "The broom rasps over the floor," she told Lucinda, "and a loud breath whooshes out, this big dramatic sigh, then another whisk of the broom followed by more sighing. Whisk-*sigh*, whisk-*sigh*, whisk-*sigh*. I finally went over there to ask if she needed help. She just gave me this hopeless look and shook her head."

Since Lucinda had confronted her, Leah not only left Lucinda alone, but she'd grown quiet, even self-conscious and abashed with the others, the way she'd been the night they'd presented their work in town. Her relentless chatter had been replaced with mournful somberness by which she attempted—with the sighing—to draw vestigial concern. But the others easily tuned this out to enjoy uninter-rupted thoughts and even full conversations among themselves. Jane, Kerry, Hailey and Dev sent Lucinda many grateful glances, and she insisted to herself she should feel proud of this accomplishment, but remembering how her palm had tingled still caused her ears to burn.

The women took one last trip into Sheridan at the end of the week, so they could mail postcards, gifts, and books at the post office, haul off recycling, and purchase last-minute souvenirs. Before shutting down, Leah had been quite vocal about returning to the saddle museum, so Lucinda determined to avoid the place. After mailing her books home, she planned to buy a few more postcards and to find the boutique where she'd spotted a butterfly-etched pot that she planned to purchase—a gift for her boyfriend.

On the drive into town, Dora, at the wheel, allowed Leah to sit up front with her. Lucinda took her favorite seat in the far back, Jane climbed in beside her, and the other women sat in the middle seat. With Leah newly subdued, Kerry, Hailey, and Dev started a lively conversation while Jane and Lucinda discussed plans for when they returned home, both committing to continue hiking and preserving much of the day for their creative work. Once the van barreled along the highway, Hailey turned to face the back seat. "We were just talking about *The Wizard of Oz*," she said. "Everyone's seen the movie, right?"

Lucinda and Jane nodded.

"Okay, so, I'm curious—which character in the film is most like you and why?"

"The Wizard." Lucinda glanced at the back of Leah's now humbly inclined head. "Definitely Oz."

"I can see that," Kerry said. "I really can."

"Who would you be?" Lucinda asked Hailey.

"Toto. I sort of identify with Toto." Hailey smiled.

Though Hailey was blond and fair-skinned, there was something playful and puppyish about her. Like Toto, she inspired affection in others. *Who could resist Toto*, thought Lucinda, experiencing a pinprick of envy.

"I'd be Dorothy," said Kerry.

"Why?" Lucinda thought that Kerry, with her disappointment in marriage and doubts about love—not to mention her stiff-legged gait—was more like the Tin Man than Dorothy.

"Everyone can relate to Dorothy, right? I mean, she's the main character, and I like to think I'm the main character in my life."

"I'd want to be one of those Lollipop Guild singers," said Dev. "*I represent the Lollipop Guild, the Lollipop Guild, and I'd like to welcome you to Munchkin Land,*" she sang in a melodic falsetto. "I'd actually like to live there or in the Emerald City. Both are much nicer than Atlanta." More than a few times, Dev had told the others of her desire to move to Sheridan. She admired the austere beauty of the landscape and the clean streets downtown, and Dev didn't seem to mind the gawking she elicited from the elderly and from children. Babies and toddlers, in particular, appeared mesmerized by her skin color. One codger even approached her after their presentation to say, "We don't get to see many people like you around here."

"Who would you be?" Hailey asked Jane.

"Glinda, the Good Witch."

"Of course," Lucinda said. Who else but Glinda could Jane be? She was kind and wise, a well-loved and powerful—

"All that fluffy hair, that sparkly headgear." Jane raised a hand to her head.

"Glinda's always hovering, isn't she?" Hailey said.

Jane cocked her head. "Is she?"

"Yeah, you never see her, like, just standing level with others."

Leah cleared her throat, and Lucinda's shoulders stiffened. But instead of barging into the conversation to tell how she was a direct descendant of L. Frank Baum or how Judy Garland once had dinner at her grandparents' house, Leah merely followed this with a wet cough.

On Main Street in Sheridan, Lucinda and the others gave wide berth to the saddle museum, into which Leah had vanished to explore her eleventh-hour inspiration. Lucinda, Jane, Kerry, and Hailey revisited various shops and galleries, while Dev scurried about, as if on a photographic scavenger hunt, snapping pictures of the many bronze sculptures—cowboy, horsehead, rhino, mountain lion, and so forth—for posting to her website. Just before entering an art gallery with the others, Lucinda said, "I need to make a quick call. I'll catch up with you in a bit." Outside the gallery, she phoned her boyfriend at work. He was taking a short break, so she had time to tell him, as in to brag about confronting Leah.

He laughed. "So another one bites the dust."

"What do you mean?"

Lucinda's boyfriend reminded her of the conflict with her friend from graduate school, the woman who'd been diagnosed with lupus, recalling that Lucinda had broken off the friendship the day before that friend was moving to Savannah for a teaching job. "Congratulations, cowboy," he then said. "You worked yourself up for the showdown *two whole days* before leaving the residency."

"That is not helpful. You are *not* being helpful."

He laughed again and told her where to meet him at the airport. She half-listened to this, glad that she'd called before finding the shop where she'd seen the butterfly pot. She snapped her phone shut as Jane, Kerry, and Hailey emerged from the gallery.

"Remember that 3-D pancake poster we saw in the saddle museum?" said Jane.

Lucinda nodded. The Best-Out-West pancake mix ad displayed a stack of hotcakes dripping with syrup that shifted when viewed from a different angle, the pancakes transforming into the image Lady Godiva on horseback, wearing just a cowboy hat. The rhyming caption below read: *If Lady Godiva rode with nothing to hide her/would that make her a bareback rider?* She and Jane had wondered what a naked woman had to do with pancakes before deciding that—for many men—shapely nude women had much to do with just about anything.

Jane jerked a thumb at the gallery. "We just saw it on display."

"In an *art* gallery," Kerry said.

Hailey grinned. "It's actually one of the better pieces."

"Can you believe that?" Kerry shook her head. "In an *art* gallery?"

Compressing her lips, Lucinda nodded.

Jane drew near, touched Lucinda's forearm. "Are you okay?"

"I'm fine."

They passed the JCPenney before entering another gift shop. Lucinda perused the postcards while Jane examined turquoise pieces encased at the front counter. Hailey and Kerry disappeared into the recesses of the store. Lucinda picked out a few more cards, though she had nearly run out of people to send these to. The last batch she'd mailed included one for her great-aunt in a nursing home who would no doubt be baffled by the image of a snow-covered buffalo sent to her from a relative she might not even remember.

Hailey approached Lucinda, holding aloft a white T-shirt. "Look." She pointed at its appliqued image: a black Scottie dog on a glittery yellow pathway.

"It's Toto," Hailey said. "I *have* to buy this. A bit big, but it'll shrink in the wash." Hailey gathered up the T-shirt to slip it on over her shirt.

"Nice," Lucinda said. Toto had been the one to provoke the apple-throwing trees and even the Cowardly Lion, hadn't he? The dog had also scampered behind the curtain, ultimately exposing the wizard. Toto's something of an instigator, thought Lucinda, as Hailey's head popped through the neckhole.

"Where'd you find that?" Jane asked, and Hailey pointed at the rear of the store.

Perhaps Jane hoped to find Glinda's headgear where Hailey had discovered the T-shirt. That towering sparkly thing atop Glinda's head was undeniably a crown. Everyone—from the adoring Munchkins, to Dorothy and her cohorts who eliminated the remaining wicked witch, to the Wizard himself, who set them on that quest in the first place—*everyone* worked for Glinda. Lucinda set her postcards on the counter and pulled out her wallet.

"Where to next?" Lucinda asked Jane, when she returned to the register to pay for a squash-blossom necklace.

"Didn't you want to find that place with the butterfly pot?"

"Not really."

"Let's get coffee then."

"We should get something to eat." Kerry ambled toward the counter with cowboy-decorated placemats. "We really should eat."

After the first shopping day, when they'd sat in the van, famished and foul-tempered, while waiting for Leah, they had learned to eat while in town. Now they continued up the street to Java Moon, the café where they'd arranged to meet Dora. The previous week, Jane and Lucinda had shared an avocado, turkey, and bacon sandwich there that had been quite tasty. Lucinda had saved the bacon from her half of the sandwich to give to Elvis, Merle's little terrier who greeted them with acrobatic leaps of ecstasy when they returned on shopping days.

They were headed for the café when Jane remembered she had to buy a gift for the friend who would be picking her up from the airport. She hurried back to the souvenir shop, and Lucinda split a sandwich, on gluten-free bread, with Kerry. Hailey, after making sure no apples were involved, asked for a smoothie, and Dev turned up to order a full sandwich for herself. Leah, then, appeared, eyeing the other women at their table before heading for the restroom. When she emerged, Leah purchased a cup of coffee, which she drank standing before a bulletin board in back, as if too absorbed in what was posted there to sit down with her drink. Jane arrived after a bit, a coiled rope looped over one shoulder, and she, too, bought a full sandwich, planning, she said, to save half for her flight back early the next day.

"A lasso?" Kerry pointed to the rope Jane hung over a chair post.

"I got it for my friend, the one who's picking me up at the airport."

"I thought he wanted a sweatshirt," Lucinda said.

"Sweatshirts are so unmemorable. But who can forget a lasso? This way, he'll look at it and think . . .well, he'll *remember* that I gave him an authentic lasso."

"What a unique idea." Kerry nodded. "Really, it is."

"No one has ever given me a lasso," Hailey said, "or even as much as a spur."

Dev fingered the braided hemp and wiped her hands on a napkin. "What will he do with it? I mean, where would he keep it?"

Jane's forehead creased with doubt.

"He'd hang it up, right? On a wall somewhere, maybe the garage," Lucinda said. "Men like things like that. I bet my boyfriend would be thrilled to get a rope." In truth, he would more likely be confused, even alarmed by such a gift.

"What did you end up getting for him?" Dev asked Lucinda.

"An ornament."

Kerry gave Lucinda a puzzled look. "Like for a Christmas tree?"

Lucinda shrugged and took a bite of her sandwich, too salty even after she'd removed the bacon. She washed this down with a sip of water.

Dev squinted at her. "But didn't you say he's Jewish?"

"He doesn't have to put it on a Christmas tree," Jane said. "He could put it . . . oh, just about anywhere."

"I've also got postcards." Lucinda patted the flat shopping bag atop the table. "I can give him a few of those, too." Hailey drew on the straw in her smoothie, air rattling noisily in it, since she had finished the drink, and the plastic cup was empty.

LATE AFTERNOON, MERLE arrived to prepare the last dinner and to dine with the women. She roasted two chickens with fingerling potatoes, steamed green beans, and tossed a salad. The appearance of a new face at the table enlivened Leah, as Lucinda feared it might, likely wiping from her memory the fact that the others found her annoying. Plus, she again polished off at least two vodka cocktails before starting in on a tumbler of wine. By suppertime, Leah's face was flushed and shiny, her jowls full as if to burst with the blather she'd soon release. Since Merle planned to join them for the meal, a sit-down dinner loomed, and Lucinda steeled herself for another excruciating episode of *The Leah Show*.

After they were seated, Merle, oddly, said grace. The others—agnostics all—bowed their heads in awkward silence, and when Merle finished giving thanks to the Lord for the food, Leah sang out, "*A-men!*"

"Ooh, this looks good!" Leah flapped her napkin open on her lap. "Fingerling potatoes! Oh, I just love fingerling potatoes! Aren't they great! Fingerlings are so wonderful! They always remind me of—"

"Anyway," Merle said, "I want to thank you all for being mighty fine guests here at the retreat. We've had all kinds of people here, and you folks, hands down, are the tidiest we've ever seen. Why, this place is cleaner than when you got here."

Lucinda and the others snuck glances at Dev, who lowered her eyes in modesty.

"Oh, we're all neat-freaks here. Obsessive compulsives, the lot of us," said Leah, the slattern. "We are just so—"

"Listen, here," Merle told her. "You listen here now because you talk too much, and that interferes with my thinking. So stop it. You got that. Just stop."

Wide-eyed, Leah nodded.

Lucinda regarded Merle's wind-seamed face with awe.

"So, okay," she continued. "Ariadne asked me to say a few things. She's glad you all came to work here and that you kept the place real clean. She appreciates it and wishes you success as artists." Then Merle led a quick round of applause, after which the women began eating and chatting about their experiences in Wyoming, before asking Merle how she came to work for the artist/heiress. Merle explained she had a job at a bank in Florida before traveling out west on a vacation. She told how she met Ariadne who offered her a position and a place to live, and she described her experiences managing the heiress's cattle ranches when not overseeing the residency. "I'll be sorry to give up the ranching," she said.

"Why are you giving it up?" Hailey asked.

"Now that we're launching the residency as a national arts colony, I need to be more hands-on here."

"Is the rumor true," Kerry blurted out. "Is it true that enrollment is low at Birnbrau for studio arts courses?"

Merle shot a look at Jane, who fixed her gaze on her plate. "I'm not supposed to be telling you this, so you didn't hear it from me, okay? But since you asked me flat out, I won't lie. It's under what they expected, way under. You writers," she said, jerking her chin at Dev and Lucinda, "you're fine. They've got composition classes galore for you all."

Dev sat frozen, relief evident only in her shining eyes. Jane's expression of concern did not seem especially concerned, while fear blanched Kerry and Hailey's faces. Leah—as usual—was not listening. Instead, she mashed her fingerlings with a fork. While Merle spoke, Lucinda recalled Jane mentioning that whenever business brought Merle to Atlanta, she would call Jane to meet her for dinner and sometimes stay overnight at her house.

"Again, you didn't hear this from me," Merle said, "but they've crunched numbers again and again, and it's just not going to work for all four of you. One position will have to be cut, but that's a decision the board will make after evaluating portfolios of work produced here."

That seemed to penetrate Leah's potato-pulverizing haze. Her mouth fell open.

"Now, let's talk about tomorrow," Merle said. "I'm driving Jane to the airport before six, but I need to know when the rest of you are headed out, so Dora can make transportation plans."

It turned out that Lucinda, heading for Los Angeles to pick up her daughter, had the latest flight out, but she agreed to go to the airport with Kerry, Hailey, Dev, and Leah, and to wait there a few hours to save Dora an extra trip. They finished the meal while discussing travel plans, and Leah—perhaps feeling doomed and having nothing to lose because of this—tried in halfhearted ways to commandeer attention, once by asking Merle how old her house was and receiving squint-eyed silence in response from the ranch manager.

After dinner, the early evening remained sunny, so the women stepped out onto the patio. Merle produced hula hoops from a storage closet in the mudroom, and she encouraged the women to try these out. Everyone but Leah grabbed a hoop. Of course, they made a contest of it, counting revolutions to see who got the most. Lucinda, competitive in all things, was the winner. Merle stowed the hoops and then tossed a deflated soccer ball for Elvis to fetch. When the ball rolled to Lucinda she chucked it across the yard, joining Merle to play with the little dog.

"Does Elvis ever bite you when you stop throwing the ball?" Lucinda told Merle about a dog she'd had that snapped at her when she ended their games of fetch.

"Oh, no," said Merle. "I can't stand bad behavior, so I don't tolerate it one whit."

"I guess I must not mind it too much because I tolerate it way too long."

Merle laughed. "Then that's *your* bad behavior." She tossed the ball one last time, and then she said, "Enough!" Elvis wagged his stubby tail and settled at her feet.

JANE ROLLED HER suitcase down the hallway before the first light of day. Its wheels creaked, rumbling over the wood floor outside Lucinda's door, but she didn't get up to say goodbye. They'd issued farewells and embraced the previous evening, promising to be in touch before the semester started. Though Lucinda was alert and unable to get back to sleep, she remained in bed, not wanting to distract Jane from last-minute preparations for her departure.

Midmorning, Lucinda, Kerry, Dev, and Hailey took one final five-kilometer hike to the highway and back, a last chance to exercise and chat before leaving for the airport. While they marched along the dusty road, they discussed their first impressions of one another, just as they had shared their early thoughts about Leah in the Silver Spur over breakfast weeks ago.

"You struck me as thoughtful and sensitive," Lucinda told Kerry. "Really?"

"Yeah," Hailey said. "I picked up on the sensitivity, too, and I also thought you were really meticulous and thorough."

Lucinda and Dev nodded.

"I am," Kerry said. "At least, I try to be."

They all agreed that Dev seemed highly organized and focused, and that Hailey appeared open, warm, and funny.

Dev turned to Lucinda. "I thought you were kind of intense, a little angry."

"Angry?" Lucinda was stunned. "I looked angry?"

"Maybe not *angry*," Kerry said, "but you did seem very aloof."

"You scared me at first," Hailey admitted.

"Do I still scare you?"

Hailey shrugged, and Dev said, "You *can* be kind of punishing."

Lucinda missed a step, stumbled over her own boot, but caught herself before falling.

"Are you okay?" said Kerry.

Punishing. Lucinda thought of her ex-husband that way. She even called him "The Punisher" when she spoke of him to her sister. If Lucinda didn't behave the way he wanted, he would muscle her into their bedroom, shut the door, and pull down the shades, his face a hard mask of righteousness and regret.

Hailey cast Lucinda a sidelong glance, a sympathetic smile.

"I wonder where that dog is." Kerry shielded her eyes, peering into the distance.

Dev gave her a puzzled look. "What dog?"

"The barker," Lucinda said, realizing she'd never before hiked with Dev and that Dev might not have encountered the hellhound on her solitary walks. "There's this dog that always barks insanely from a truck that passes us on the county road. The same dog in the pickup near the supermarket, remember?"

"Oh, *that* dog. I've seen it out here a few times." Dev, too, cupped her eyes to scan the highway, but the rusted pickup never appeared that last morning.

When they returned to the residency house, Leah greeted them with the breathless news that she had seen *her*. She'd roamed past the cattle guards, trying to get a cell phone signal to call her husband, when Ariadne Warwick Murdoch drove by in a black Cadillac.

"I waved and waved," Leah told them. "I was right in the middle of the road, but she must have been in a rush. She just sort of swerved around me. But she tooted her horn. She honked at me, as if to say, *goodbye and good luck.*"

"Or get out of the road," Hailey said. "Maybe she was afraid she might hit you."

"I really wanted her to stop. I wanted to tell her about the show in Austin. I didn't get as much done here as I'd hoped, but she doesn't know about the show in Austin . . ."

Without a word, Lucinda bypassed Leah for her bedroom. Her belongings had been packed and the room—apart from the stripped bed—restored to the order in which she'd found it. Now she slipped the postcards in the compartment of her luggage that held the ornament Leah had given her, but as Lucinda inserted the shopping bag, she heard a crackling sound. She pulled out the ceramic cow to find a booted foot had broken off. Ridiculous thing—a skirt-wearing cow gotten up like a cowgirl, raising a lasso over its head. What was it supposed to be roping? Humans? Still, Lucinda replaced it in her suitcase. She would mend it at home with glue.

At the airport, Dora dropped the women off at the curb. Hailey, Kerry, and Leah headed inside for the check-in counter, and Lucinda rolled her luggage to a waiting area outside the airport. She leaned her bags against a bench, settled herself on its sun-warmed lap, and opened a novel she'd brought. A soft gust buffeted her, rattling leaves in the trees nearby. One by one, the others—first Dev, then Hailey, and last of all Kerry—emerged from the airport to embrace her and say goodbye. Kerry urged Lucinda to come inside and sit with them before their flight, but Lucinda shook her head. "I'll say goodbye out here. I don't want to go in and have to . . ., well, hug her."

"Oh, dear." Kerry's face clouded. "She'll expect that, won't she?"

"Say you have a cold or even strep."

"I can't lie," Kerry said. "Well, I can and do lie, but I can't plan to, I suppose."

"Are you worried? About what Merle said?"

"Not too much anymore. Jane planned to have a long talk with Merle this morning, and she told me Merle lives with *her*."

"Lives with whom?"

"She lives with Ariadne Murdoch Warwick, our benefactress—like Gertrude Stein and Alice B. Toklas," Kerry said.

"Jane just knows everything."

"Oh, she does. She really does. Jane knew about enrollment back in March. That's when registration opened for the college. Merle told her before we even got here."

Lucinda's stomach flipped as if she were already airborne, the plane hitting a pocket of turbulence. "That makes me feel . . . a little weird."

"She knew you were safe. Jane always knew that."

"Still."

"We do what we can, and somehow we also find ways to do what we can't. We lie fourteen times a day, even if we don't plan to, and especially if we *do* plan to."

"So Leah never had a chance, did she?"

"Leah being Leah," Kerry said, "made things easier for Jane, for the rest of us."

"I suppose."

Kerry gave Lucinda a shy smile. "I know I'll see you in a few months, but it won't be the same. *We* won't be the same as we were here. I'll miss that."

They embraced again, and though they would be working together in the fall, uncertainty knotted in Lucinda's chest, and she experienced a premonition—a shadow thought that caused her to cling for a few extra seconds before releasing Kerry to head back to the airport.

"Happy trails," Lucinda called after her, and Kerry waved before disappearing through the glass doors.

Nearly an hour later, Lucinda glanced up from her book as the plane the others had boarded—the only midday flight out of Sheridan—ascended into the shredded veil of clouds. She cupped her eyes against the sun and bid silent farewell to Kerry, Dev, Hailey, and to Leah, especially to Leah, whom she expected never to encounter again. Thinking of her, Lucinda remembered the Talmud, the passages she'd read when she flirted with the idea of converting to Judaism, a time when she thought there was a chance she might marry again. A quotation from it floated to the surface of her thoughts: *We see things not as they are, but as we are.* Leah's appalling behavior bounced back an image of Lucinda's own domineering willfulness as if in a funhouse mirror, the sight of it grotesque and startling, but urgent to behold.

Even so, she wished she had not wasted so much time and trouble on the woman. Lucinda stowed her book, and then she glanced about, taking a few last mental snapshots before entering the airport to buy a cup of coffee. Beyond the clustered trees and concrete bench, four shades of blue layered the sky. Beneath this, camel-colored fields, pocked and grumous as the moon's sallow face, unfurled toward the snow-traced range, but just before the indigo mountains, the terrain flattened out, becoming uninflected and treeless. With a panorama as distinct and visible as this, Lucinda had—if briefly—succumbed to the illusion that she knew exactly where she stood, and even who she was, while here in the gerund state.

Acknowledgments

In addition to *las tres comadres* to whom this book is dedicated, I must thank my trusty peer readers and long-suffering, but encouraging friends and colleagues: Beth Bachmann, Joy Castro, Lee Conell, Debra Dobkins, Tony Earley, Meredith Gray Grener, Mark Jarman, Claire Jimenez, Marysa LaRowe, Miriam Mimms, Lorrie Moore, Rafael Ocasio, Justin Quarry, Nancy Reisman, Anna Silverstein, and Janet Thielke. Further, this book would never have come about without inspiration from Jennifer Baker, Joyce Ely-Walker, Karen McAlister Shimoda, and Rachel Meginnes. Nothing much—literary or otherwise—happens in my household without the considerable efforts of Louis Siegel, my husband who reads, with thoroughness and care, everything I write. Further, I am deeply indebted to Ben Furnish, whose belief in this project brought it to the page. In my convoluted writing life, I have worked with many publishers and editors, but none as conscientious, patient, and generous as Ben. It has been my privilege to work with him, Cynthia, Max, and all the talented and dedicated people at BkMk Press.

I am also grateful for generous support from the Vanderbilt University Research Scholar Grant, Humanities Tennessee, Macondo Writers Workshop, and the Jentel Artists Residency Program—all four provided resources that enabled me to complete this collection.

Finally, "Passionate Delicacy" was published as "Women Speak" in *Homicide Survivors Picnic and Other Stories*, and "Careful Interventions" appears in *South Atlantic Review: Volume 85/Summer 2019*. Excerpted lines from *String of Beads: Complete Poems of Princess Shikishi* are presented here with permission obtained from University of Hawai'i Press.

Lorraine M. López is the Gertrude Conaway professor of English at Vanderbilt University, where she teaches in the MFA program. She is a cofounder of the Latino and Latina Studies program at Vanderbilt and an associate editor of Afro-Hispanic Review. She is also the author of six previous volumes of fiction, including *Homicide Survivors Picnic* (BkMk Press), finalist for the PEN/Faulkner Award. Additionally, she has edited three essay collections. Her awards includes the inaugural Miguel Marmól Prize, the Paterson Prize for Young People's Literature, the Texas Writers League Award for Outstanding Fiction, International Latino Book Award, Independent Publisher Award, Foreword Award, and Borders/Las Comadres Selections. She lives in Nashville, Tennessee.

Also by Lorraine M. López